Life on Mars

life
on
mars

LORI McNULTY

Edited by Bethany Gibson.
Cover and page design by Kerry Lawlor and Julie Scriver.
Cover images: background image of Shanghai, Pexels.com; octopus, Shutterstock.com
Printed in Canada.
10 9 8 7 6 5 4 3 2 1

Library and Archives Canada Cataloguing in Publication

McNulty, Lori, author
    Life on Mars / Lori McNulty.

Short stories.
Issued in print and electronic formats.
ISBN 978-0-86492-888-7 (paperback).--ISBN 978-0-86492-928-0 (epub).--
ISBN 978-0-86492-929-7 (mobi)

    I. Title.

PS8625.N85L54 2017   C813'.6   C2016-907037-9
                                             C2016-907038-7

Goose Lane Editions acknowledges the generous support of the Government of Canada, the Canada Council for the Arts, and the Government of New Brunswick.

Goose Lane Editions
500 Beaverbrook Court, Suite 330
Fredericton, New Brunswick
CANADA E3B 5X4

For Kim

Contents

9   Evidence of Life on Mars

31   Battle of the Bow

55   Fingernecklace

75   If on a Winter's Night a Badger

105   Monsoon Season

133   WOOF

153   Last Down

177   Prey

205   Gindelle of the Abbey

229   Polymarpussle Takes a Chance

249   Two Bucks from Brooklyn

269   Ticker

Evidence of Life on Mars

Under my cement roof, at the top of the sloped underpass, I watch cars grow fins as they sail out along the flooding highway. Drivers lean on their horns in the heavy rain, as if the sound can open up a space I can soar through.

Blunt on my lips, I inhale a head full of stars.

Dust then darkness. I keep an eye on the intersection where my father's big rig will swing a wide arc off Albert Road. Ten tons of steel and rubber, its back end doglegging out onto the road. That huge silver grill grinning at me.

Chrome is tooth enamel for big rigs, my father said. As a kid, I used to polish the chrome-plated axle and hubs in the driveway. Got a buck a wheel.

My pocket buzzes. Il Duce again. *Mars. Get home. Now.*

Fascist. My sister Lizzie is a dead ringer for Mussolini, who was famous for bulging eyes and annexing Albania. She has perfect SATs to go along with Il Duce's unplucked unibrow and military-grade temper.

Coming home, I text back. Add two kiss symbols to drive her mental.

Floating downhill on my bike, I shred roots and rocks on the trails before kicking up asphalt alongside the same two-storey houses with double-lane driveways and identical lawns buzzed to three-inch pelts. I hop the sidewalk and swing around the huge pile of sawed two-by-fours growing mould beside the old man's shed.

If nothing changes tonight, I'll buy a one-way ticket. I'll buy two.

Carrying my sneakers in on shoehorn fists, I pad down the front hall in wet socks, scattering pebbles and dirt. On my knees, I moisten my fingertips, trying to pick up each fleck. The TV is blasting the news upstairs in my mother's bedroom. Homicides at six. Natural disasters at eleven. Trauma piling up in my mother's lap because she's working overtime again, writing legal briefs to help the corporate drones baffle the court of justice. Plus a pitcher of something bloody to wash her sins down.

Me, I try to stay high all the time. Show up late to advanced physics, cough up all the impossible answers, and bolt whenever someone catches my glassy vibe. Right and wrong are handcuffs, my father told me. Give up on being so good and the whole world opens up for you.

Toe inched inside the kitchen, I peek around the corner to see Lizzie gather up two toppled plastic grocery bags off the floor. A pound of fresh ground beef is flopped upside down, still wrapped in cellophane. She tears at the wrapper with her pinky fingernail, gives the meat a long sniff.

"Hey, Lezzie," I say, slow-shuffling in.

"You were supposed to be here two hours ago," she says, and the fleshy pockets below her eyes sag, blown out by too many late nights studying the metaphysics of ancient Greece.

Squinty-eyed smiling, I notice the whites of her eyes look firm, like hard-boiled eggs, as if she's been trapped in an existential windstorm.

Lizzie turns her back on me. Setting the slopped meat on the counter, she opens the cupboard, grabs a can of chunky tomatoes, turns, and tosses it at me.

I pitch it back like it's a live grenade. "Chill out, dinner Nazi."

"And you're a gassy planet with an asshole for an orbit," she says and slams the can on the counter. More thrashing as she pulls out a lidded pot and fills it with tap water.

Slamming the pot on the stove, she turns and drops the can back into my hands. "Open it."

Lizzie dials up the stove heat. She rips the pasta box apart, spilling strands across the counter, still furious.

My shiny head is sitting on my body like a swollen lollipop. I stand and watch the pot lid sweat then quiver over the bubbling pot. Gripping the can opener with two hands, I can't get the metal teeth to sit right on the thin lip of the can. This I find incredibly funny.

"Shut up, Mars. Mom's going ballistic over her deadlines."

Ignoring my snorts, my sister slaps the quarter pound of ground beef into a large mixing bowl, adds some cereal, and rolls the meatballs in her oily palms. She pulls out a pan and sprays. Mesmerizing to watch those cornflake-encrusted brainlings strike a formation on the slippery pan.

"Look, Lezzie," I say, holding up a soggy, flopping tomato chunk from the can. "I found your heart."

She smacks me with a plastic spoon. "Weed is wasting you."

When I grab her wrist, she accidentally elbows the pot handle.

"Sorry, sis, sorry, sorry."

Holding her wrist, she shrieks, hops back as steaming water pours from the side of the stove. Then she grabs the serrated knife from the counter, turns the pointy part to my crotch, and grins.

"First I yank, then I slice," she says, taking a theatrical grab at my groin.

"You bullshitter."

Gripping the dishtowel, I slowly twist it and whip it out near her chest. Lizzie howls, dropping the knife.

When we lock arms, whipping each other around do-si-do style, still laughing, Lizzie stops with a sudden jerk. Our mother is standing over us, her cellphone pressed against her chest.

"I've got New York on the line," she hisses. "They think it's a goddamn home invasion."

I pick up the serrated knife and lay it back on the counter.

"Call you back," my mother says into her cell. "Gotta put my kids on lockdown." Her tone is light, but I can see her mouth twitching before she hangs up.

My sister jolts back, straightens out her rubber knees, touching her stinging jaw after my mother slaps Lizzie hard across the cheek.

"Get out," my mother orders me, eyeing my slow, sloppy face.

I step in front of my sister. Lizzie shoots me a look that says, It will be worse for me if you stay.

Kicking open the back door, I shove my feet into a pair of muddy boots and hotfoot it through wet woods like some scared, limp deer. What I think, as my face is branch-slapped, is that that I'm too fucked and stupid to stop the *shitstorm* that's raining down on my sister.

I follow the river marsh to where the scent of rotting leaves and old pine cones wafts through my decomposing palace. Using the light from my cell, I point a low beam toward the fetid ground I've trampled, slept on, set fire to. My usual stump is loaded with cigarette butts. Bending over, there's a whooshing wave in my ears, and for a second I'm ass-dumped. I straighten up. My hair is plastered to my skull like a crazy, wet wig. I grab a crushed beer can from the ground and clear away the curled leaves and candy wrappers.

The rain is spitting horizontal piss. Crouched over, I light up. A few deep inhales, *cough, cough*. Another few hits and the inchworms begin crawling across my skin. I lift my T-shirt, exposing my rib rack to the wind. Snapping open my father's penknife, I scrape skin across bone, dissecting the worms three ways. My skin splits so clean, the wound looks like a parted mouth. If the next cut sinks deep enough, it won't bleed, at least not right away.

The forest starts shuddering like a group of old men at a bus stop. From my guts an acid taste keeps building, backing up in my throat, as the night sky slackens over the bog. In my nostrils, I whiff the fungal stench of rock-bottom. I can picture my mother's face, her arm pressing

Lizzie's chest against the toilet rim, forcing her hand to pump up and down. My mother empties more spaghetti strands into the bowl. "This is dinner. Stir it."

Blue-lipped shivering, and my numb fingers are making it hard to get a tight seal over the blunt. Inhale and hold. My throat is thermal, like I'm a human incinerator, spilling sharp, dead flowers all the way to my lungs. Looking down, something spongy is growing between my toes. A floppy stump fungus I bash away with my heel. Bash, bash, and the leafy plants look up with their hungry mouths. The stub of my joint I toss. Chew away the bile backing up my throat with the pack of mint gum in my pocket. Then I tilt back and pitch my father's knife as far as I can into the ravine.

In the kitchen, the white countertops are blotched red. There's a sharp stench like fat dripping over hot barbecue coals. A jagged lemon wedge sits next to a glass pitcher drained of Bloody Mary mix, the fog of tomato juice and pepper still clinging to the sides. In the singed pan, the meatballs are tiny black orbs.

I grab my backpack and load up on fridge food, then follow the red droplets to my mother's room.

She's hunched over her binders when I crack the door. A celery stalk flowers between her teeth when she turns and looks at me. Her eyes seem as if they've been smudged with Vaseline.

"You have to stop it," I tell her, shaking my head.

She looks down at her papers, then takes a gulping sip from her tall glass that sets tears running.

"Where is your sister?" she asks, like she's been away for weeks and can't find her car keys.

I shake my head. "Lizzie doesn't deserve this."

My mother's body lies crooked on the bed. I don't remember a time when she ever sat up perfectly straight. Her spine twists, her hip sits too high. She wore a brace to straighten her back as a kid. Clamped in, seven days a week. Robot kid.

Her mouth opens and shuts like it's on a spring-clip. "Nothing good ever happens anymore."

I should have gone to Shiner's place and blazed one by the cracked window in his basement. Coaxed Lizzie to come. She barely tolerates Shiner. Hates his mangy beard and bad manners, plus the guy is about as subtle as an oil spill when it comes to girls, but she'll partake with us when the mood strikes.

"Your father left us," my mother cries.

Here it is. The story. Begins and ends with my father cruising down "God knows what interstate," leaving her high and dry. It all went downhill fast, she tells me, again, beginning with his first departure.

To me, the story made sense. All those months on the oil patch when he came home wrecked and sore. Decided to get his Class 1. Local jobs were scarce and all had shit pay, so he ended up steering north, hauling logs over gravel so rough it shook the teeth loose in his head. Came home with a bulging neck that forced him to shift gears, and persuaded my mother to take out a second mortgage to lease his own big rig. He had a plan. Go long-hauling across the US border as an independent, specializing in dangerous goods.

"It's a license to make money," he had told her, when he returned from his first run, eyes on high beam, fast-running mouth. He laid down a two-inch stack of photos on the kitchen table and spread them out for us. There was a classic chrome-and-vinyl roadside diner with an old couple dunking caramels into their sea of gravy. Mountain lakes full of fly fishermen. A white clapboard church with a blue neon Jesus and a huge red glowing crucifix that spelled out Jesus Saves. It was fucking beautiful.

I was transfixed by the heavy roar of the semis that tore past us on the Trans-Canada. How they kicked up dust and spit rocks as they sped by. I always got the trucker to pull the horn, and when I looked into the cab, his face seemed to belong to another age, like he'd be at home towing a wagon through open grasslands.

I remember the phone kept ringing. Fists were slamming. My mother was pulling the hair away from her face and wiping her nose with the back of her hand.

"You can't get views like this sitting behind some desk," my father insisted, pointing to his mountain scenes and highway sunsets.

"You can't raise two kids and run a law practice on your own," she shot back.

"Three weeks, then back here for two," he replied, tapping the table. "What else do you want?"

"Help with bills. School events."

"Give it time."

"We gave it five years. What about me?"

"Call it quits, then, Marcella," he told her, rising abruptly. "Do it."

I watched them grind each other down, until my father finally dropped a tissue box in front of her and headed toward the front door with his coat in his hands.

"Forget the desk drones. This is living. Right, son?" he said to me, winking on his way out.

Lizzie was away at some brain camp. I took my father's side as he loaded up his thermos with coffee and hugged me goodbye. Freedom is an instinct, right? You move toward it all your life. He was from people who could straighten a bent chassis in their driveway, using nothing but leather straps and a pair of scissor jacks. Third-generation truckers: part cowboys, part astronauts. Not order-takers. Not professional bullshitters. Couldn't she just let him be? He was making a living. Paying back the loans. No one was starving.

Lizzie was already golden. Her March on Rome would take her to the top of any kingdom, and everyone knew it. It was her graduating year anyway. School was an optional excursion for me, but I always managed to pull the grades, almost as good as my sister's unbroken row of As, despite being a year behind her. My mother told me we were touched by brilliance beyond our muddled class, that nothing was going to hold us back. I knew she meant our father. All his drifting and downshifting in eighth gear.

...

"Lizzie doesn't need this bullshit," I shout at my mother from the doorway. "She's better than any of us put together." In a family of disappointments, stoners, and crooks, Mussolini looks like a fluffy white kitten.

Surrounded by her binders and papers, lying on her back, my mother looks like a cargo ship run aground. More tears as she turns on her side and begins kneading the small of her back with her fist.

I close her door tight, leave her bulldozed by her Bloody Marys and grief.

After a few hits outside, I can picture the stretch of the Bitterroot River where rough waters bend like a soggy elbow, rippling up along the mountain base. In another snapshot, my father's wearing his favourite yellow-and-black Mack baseball cap with the bulldog on it, his curly hair flying out as he leans over the front end, mouth pressed to the rig like's he's about to make her a promise. Feel the fifteen hundred pounds of torque twisting up through my chest, the growing rage when my father has to pull the air horn to ward off some jerk ready to cut him off on the I-20.

"You have to do the miles, Mars. Nothing good happens until you do the miles."

He offered to take me along with him during summers, but it never happened. He still closes his annual email to me the same way: "It's such a lonely road when you're not on it, Mars."

After a few more hits outside, I go back inside the house and pound down the plywood steps to the basement with my backpack, clearing my throat so Lizzie knows it's me.

My sister is flopped on the split leather couch, reading. She draws an armful of cat to her chest, the pair either purring or quivering, I can't tell which.

She hasn't eaten. I can see her hair is tangled and wet from the shower. Absently, she looks over at me. Dropping my backpack on the cement floor, I approach with a stupid smile, my words too dammed up and demented to speak right away. I keep touching the place on my rib so it stings.

Lizzie scratches under the cat's chin. He purrs and begins kneading her shoulder and arm. She winces, then draws him around her face like a muffler.

"What's up, Lezzie?"

She examines my doughy face. "You're so fucking high, Mars," she says, shaking her head.

I pull out a can of Pringles from my pack and we sit in the dark, crunching for a long time.

"Wanna blaze?" I ask after a while, and show her my baggie full of primo weed.

Lizzie shakes her head.

"Come on," I say, lightly poking her ribs. "Unwind."

When Lizzie flinches, pulls away hugging the couch pillow tighter, I feel the familiar bile backing up my throat.

The cat stretches out, yawns, and drops to the floor.

We poke around the past, laughing at how many times we sat on this very couch together, trading punches and kicks over who got to choose the Saturday cartoons.

"Remember when Dad built us that fort up the Garry oak?" she says.

"Plywood and tin from the dump." I nod.

"Mom in her paisley pants, making curtains for the cut-outs," Lizzie says, but her words begin to drift.

"Then you kicked me out for farting."

Lizzie closes her eyes.

I sit up tall. "And that road trip to the Grand Canyon. We went camping and you brought along your best friend, Heather."

It was astonishing. We drove to where the earth was punched out, and the river running along the bottom was like some kind of ancient bloodline. South Rim running. My father made sure we were equipped for the trails, and we made it all the way to the bottom.

"The way Heather's curly hair bounced on that walk. My first big crush," I say.

"Making excuses to get into our tent. Bonehead move, Mars."

"My bone was moving," I say and finish it off with a wild whistle.

"Stoner."

"Ass-kisser."

"Masturbator."

"Chicks do it, too. I saw those hairy-chested freaks in the old posters from your locker."

For a while, we both sit back in our awkward sibling slump. It's like an energy transformation, the fields scattering between us. My brain is a live-wire act and I'm the drunken tightrope walker. Maybe if I watch Lizzie long enough, maybe if I can catch my mother on the edge one of her moods, maybe if I flick the knife edge just right, I can make room enough to set us all free. I'm so fucking high right now, my face feels like thumbed putty.

Lizzie looks up at me, droopy-eyed. I nudge her over so she tips her head onto the couch armrest.

All we need is a route, I think. On the road with my father and Lizzie, the mountain passes we'll climb, tunnels and bridge crossings all the way to the 101, and then up the coast to hear the sea lions bark in Monterey Bay. Three abreast in the front cab, we'll mock the monster RVs slowing traffic in that sticky southern heat.

"Be right back," I say, leaving her curled up on her side. The cat hops up into my space to keep her warm.

A few minutes later, I'm back with her suitcase. I drop it on the floor and zip it open in front of her. Inside I've gathered some of her sweaters. Her favourite novels. The heavy black lacquered box she protects with a puny padlock, as if I've never learned how to slip a lock with a paper clip.

She screws up her face. "You touched my stuff."

My mother's credit card is tucked inside my front pocket. I smile, show her the wad of cash I've put away from my weekend job, mostly selling pot for Shiner.

"Been saving," I say. "Dad's not far. Just across the US border. You always wanted to see Montana."

Lizzie shakes her head. "I'm almost eighteen, Mars," she replies, depositing the restless cat to the floor. "Full scholarship. Then I'm gone."

I pick at invisible curled leaves clinging to the elastic band of my socks. My mouth tastes ragged and sour, like some pissed-on paper bag.

Lizzie sits up again, so I unzip and set out my full stash of food. Doughnuts and pickles and cheddar wedges emerge like a magic show. Voila! A couch picnic. Like when we were kids and Mom would come home from work Friday nights to make our favourite bacon-wrapped wieners, then bake all weekend. Starting Saturday, me, Lizzie, and Mom would all be lying on two couches, devouring a slab of marble fudge right from the pan, no forks, waiting for the next batch to come out of the oven.

While I unwrap more carrots, Lizzie takes small, sour bites from a dill pickle. Tucked into a plastic container are two whipped-chocolate cupcakes. Lizzie picks one up, lifts the left corner of her lip, then drops the cupcake back into the plastic tray.

"She chose me," she says quietly.

Her whole body begins to quake. A whiff of rotting bog churns in the air between us. All I want to fucking do is pound my own throat.

"Come with me. Tonight." I tell her and slap the tent her blanket has made across her body.

She pulls at the frayed edges of the blanket and shakes her head. "We're all going to leave her, Mars."

The cat trots over to his food bowl and begins licking the tops of the dried food out of his green dish. I break up bits of cheese and drop them inside.

When we've finished off most of my stash, I pack up the leftovers. "You want anything else?" I ask Lizzie. "A chest like Heidi Klum?"

Lizzie tosses me the end of her stubby carrot. "Here's your butt plug, Mars. Found it in the cushions."

We laugh-snort. Lizzie removes one of her dirty socks and launches it in my face. I ball the sock up and toss it behind the furnace, next to our father's boxes marked "Goodwill" and "Dump."

When she waves her hand in front of my face, I notice the pads of her fingers are red and glossy. The flesh of her middle finger is peeling back, so the new skin underneath is shiny, almost liquid. She pulls her hand away and hides it under the blanket.

We watch in silence as the cat unwinds from his shrimp-in-a-plum-sauce pose. When he stretches and hops back on the couch between us, I hear thumping upstairs.

Lizzie draws the blanket up around her ears. She kicks me so I jump up to take a look.

At the top of the stairs, I slip down the hall, peek inside my mother's room, and notice her binders have dropped to the floor. She's snoring heavily. I slip back down again and shake my head.

"Nothing. Just your unibrow clippers recharging."

Lizzie starts to laugh. It's a thin one that catches the end of a sob, and she draws in a sharp breath. I grab her suitcase and agree to deposit it back in her room, will shove it into a dark corner, packed and ready for later.

The food remnants I bundle into my backpack. She lies back, slurs out a few aimless words about making her a promise to stay put. I tell her Shiner is picking me up in an hour so we can meet some fine ladies from the padded leather lounge that always let us in without ID. Tell her I'll be back before our mother makes her first coffee. Whisper, "I'll always be back."

I leave Lizzie tucked in beside the cat, which is kneading her belly.

...

Midnight is a flame tip in my skunky mouth, loitering near the Albert Street underpass, watching cars spit out of this shadow hole. Headlights glow bright then fade away behind me. Half-frozen in the drizzling rain, I imagine how long each driver has been travelling, what loads they're carrying, who will meet them at the end of the line.

The end of the line for me will be a ten-hour straight shot across the border, following my father's favourite route into the upper plains of Montana, easy as pie crossing from Alberta at Coutts-Sweetgrass. I'll track down the US trucking company from my father's last email. Call that dick dispatcher my father described. The phony bastard with the Texas drawl and sweaty JC Penny T-shirts, who started him on the worst routes, tearing down interstates with loads of diapers, telling him to suck back on more energy drinks and screw the logbook. Two years riding as an independent, trained for dangerous goods, yet he's still hounded by bottom-rung bastards. Or maybe now he's keeping the wheels turning for one of the bigger outfits. I'll stop in at one of those shiny truck stops with showers and 24/7 laundry. How hard will it be to find a Canadian trucker named Getsky with a son named Mars? Like the famous hockey player? they'll ask. Like the planet, I'll answer.

I yank my zipper up to my chin, pull on my blunt, until my head is so loose it's directing traffic. Back on the road, I hold my thumb out to hitch a ride. Save my stash to catch a paid lift across the border.

Just watch. My father and I will hit the road together, hauling cases of freeze-dried noodles, whole pallets of sealed Xboxes. On twelve-hour stretches through the Dakotas and down, I'll catch my father up on Mussolini. How Il Duce cozied up to Hitler and his Nazi pals at Munich, screwing over Chamberlain. The old Brit thought he'd negotiated peace with honour but ended up being frog-marched right into World War II. Concessions, appeasement; Christ, look what happens when you give in to a hard-liner? You're hopeless. Steer your own path, that's what my father followed. The old man could change his own oil when he was ten.

The rain is rattling hard against my backpack. Noxious fuel combusts in my lungs as I walk along the roadside, thumb out toward the trickle of cars motoring through the underpass. Mostly, I'm invisible, and the drivers keep their eyes steady on the road ahead. Then for a while, it's nothing but SUVs plus the odd out-of-towner looking lost on the road from the airport. They think we're all golden wheat fields and peeling grain elevators, not football-obsessed face painters with a fucked-up taste for pouring beer over Clamato juice.

The shaking starts in my shins. A tremor sent from the highway up my chest before I see it. A big rig, the size of Texas, roaring down Albert Street. I sprint further down the road so the trucker has enough time to see me under the street lamp. I try to look harmless, or at least not so stoned, even manage to smile. My thumb shoots out. The crystal-and-chrome headlamps flash at me. I can't believe it when the truck slows down and pulls up ahead onto the shoulder.

The massive engine idles, and I can make out a large man leaning over to open the passenger door as I run up to the rig. Climbing up the aluminum steps, I smile as he powers the window down.

"Where to?" he says. He's got a Midwestern accent, telling me he's going to drop two loads along the ring road off Highway 1, then head straight down Highway 39.

"Montana," I say, diesel fumes plugging my throat on the running board. I explain that my father is also a long-hauler, en route from Montana, and we're supposed to meet up just over the border.

The old guy looks me over and squints as the word long-hauler drops and swishes around in my skull. My tongue feels slack, weirdly thin. I keep smiling.

Finally, he says he can get me within spitting distance of Coutts-Sweetgrass and waves me inside.

Doors shut, we pull out. I thank him, then tip my head against the foggy passenger window, using my knapsack as a pillow for a while.

But the trucker's craving company, because as we drive on he curses the price of diesel, laughs about the polite Canadian prairie folk with their wide-open vowels.

When I point out that he's just missed the ring road turn-off, he leans over, promises to take me as far as I am willing to go, and strokes my wrist.

I pull my arm back, slowly, trying to keep things cool. He's just friendly, I think. Midwesterners are like that, my father said. Sunny, breadbasket folks, main street people, loaded up on so many carbs they've gone comatose. He reaches out toward me again. This time he grabs my knee and squeezes.

All right, I think, and pull the backpack from the window down to my lap. I fish inside. The penknife? Gone. All I've got is some boxers and a frosted cupcake.

Trucker shoots me an eager look. Door locks. Automatic. Can't even roll my own window down. He's got an antsy look, while I go through my knapsack mumbling about cookies. He releases one of his hands from the wheel and lets it crawl over his own lap.

So I tell him how Mussolini had a pet lion cub named Ras that he took everywhere. Mussolini's driver, a Hitler look-alike, would chauffer the dictator around town, his gloved hands tight on the wheel, glancing over in fear every once in a while at the front-seat passenger, because Il Duce always kept that restless lion on his lap.

"Il Duce loved to cradle that cub on long drives," I say, grinning, and then begin to pet the backpack on my own lap, wild-eyed and paranoid, an exaggerated stroke, my eyes popping.

"Oh yeah?" trucker says, his voice getting ragged and low. From the corner of my eye, I see him fishing under his shirt flap at the fly of his own jeans.

"Cub was a gift from the Minister of the Interior," I inform him, and my mouth is a desert, my whole body seizing, trying to keep things steady. "Il Duce rode up front in his bowler hat, flashing his bulging eyes at the cub, who had his one paw draped over his arm and the other around the man's neck, like some kind of house cat."

Jesus Fuck. Trucker looks like he's trying to one-hand juggle his own nuts.

He leans my way and reaches over with his right hand as if he's pointing to something out my window. He lets his arm drop between my belly and the backpack. I squirm in my seat. He's trying to grab hold of my cock. The trucker keeps smiling at the windshield.

"Crazy how fast that cub struck!" I shout.

The trucker howls, the rig pulls a hard right. "It was a fucking bloodbath," I say, and launch another fist at his throat.

He takes his foot off the gas, tries to cover his face, and we slow-crawl toward the red light. I unlock and kick open my door, the rain staining his custom butter-yellow leather seats.

Before he can grab a piece of my shirt, I jump out.

The rig stops. I notice all the placards in their metal frames on the side of the rig, the orange diamond with the flaming head that says "Dangerous Goods." Trucker is about to blast from his cab, come after me, but the light changes and a half-ton rolls up on his back end, honking. The old man curses at me out the window, holding his pulpy face as he rolls out.

I wave him off with a middle finger.

My knees give out. My mouth is a howl as I sink on the field and begin to bawl. And I can't stop. Snot. Shoulders heaving. Chest caving in. Like some whining coward.

It's so cold out. Trying to bust up this night in my brain, I light up. My fingers keep jumping when I set my blunt tip aflame.

...

I'm not in the middle of nowhere, but close. Drained of light, this far from the city core, it's like someone has dragged the constellations up to the end of my nose. The stars are so bright, hovering in this reckless void, I can almost smell hydrogen, like rotting eggs filling up my lungs. The stars will still be up there come daylight, but invisible, hidden by sunlight scattering across the atmosphere. Block out the sun, darken things up, and the whole damn sky would still be filled with stars. Like my father and me setting out on the road, looking out behind that curved windshield, breathing life into the eternal, starlit sky, nowhere to go but on.

In a week, I'll meet up with him on the road, and we'll be cruising together through Montana's pine-covered mountains on Route 93. My father in the upper bunk; me spread-eagled on the floor next to our growing laundry pile. We'll joke about traffic cops, Saskatchewan winters, and those damn trailer-swayers. One day I'll even tell him the one about the dumb-ass trucker and the killer cub.

If I hoof it over the railway tracks and across town, I can make it to the bus station before dawn. I'll join the mobs of students and drifters on the early bus heading out of town. All the way to the US border, my Greyhound seat will smell like flat Coke and old farts. Will cost me half of what I've got. The border guys will make a fuss, but I'll give them the signed consent letter that says I'm meeting my father at the other end. It will be a slow-grinding, six-miles-per-gallon crawl to the US crossing, and the fifty-five-seater coach isn't going to catch up to my father's big rig any time soon. But my trip is ten hours from empty prairie, and my dreams only travel one way.

Battle of the Bow

Two years after Marcus died, a man arrived in a blue sedan.

It was the Flood in reverse, Noah spilling out from his ark with his supporters, extending his peachy-pink flesh to the prairie faithful assembled on the church steps. They came in a blizzard. Five soft-jowled men in city suits stepped into the November chill. As snow gusted across banks three feet high, the reverend leaned into the wind, blinking frost from his lashes. The church committee encircled the men; their white fingers gripped around cups of powdery hot chocolate.

The idea had come to old pastor Sherman in a vision. Needing to bring his lagging congregation back to life, barely a trickle above twelve on a snowy Sunday, the pastor had sent his prayers south from Vermouth County along the latitude of the Lord.

On a stream of perdition and penance came the answer: the Reverend Evan Nack.

"Welcome to Vermouth," I hear Pastor Sherman say, holding out his hand, slipping his pocked skin into the young reverend's firm grip, then leading the men to the church basement.

Their buffed oxfords *clack, clack* along the polished floor I mop after Thursday bingo. The reverend can't be more than thirty-five, his tawny skin bright as a new penny.

I see the pastor's face pinched tight. Beneath the reverend's tan overcoat is a cotton shirt buttoned low, revealing an unwelcome wilderness. The old man averts his eyes, invites the city folk over to a folding table for tea and refreshments.

They say Pastor Sherman arrived in 1914 with a group of believers who came west along Alberta's Bible Belt, a straight shot from Highway 21 to heaven. They set up on the south bank of the Bow, where they built the church Gothic style, with a front-gabled roof, heaven-lit by one circular stained-glass window. When the droughts hit Vermouth soon after, few locals were interested in bearing witness. Then a later spiritual resurgence awakened weary hearts, and word spread like wildfire from Alberta to Saskatchewan of the coming glory days for lush fields and well-fatted cattle. By the time we arrived in 1962, the fierce summers had once again ravaged farms, leaving behind dry creeks, grasshopper infestations, and faith grown as parched as these prairie fields.

I listen to Pastor Sherman lead the young reverend through our town's dusty facts. A decade of drought. Farmers forced to sell their cattle or face a shortage of feed grain.

"No good, sir," he intones, his cracked lower lip trembling. Marcus always referred to the pastor as Bog Man, a repository of dead things.

Then the herd erupts. Mrs. Dodd and Joannie Peen with their "Praise the Lord" and "Pass the Judgment," just one everlasting wail from the Pentecostals.

"There's tuna and pickle here, Reverend, and cream cheese," Joannie chirps, pointing to her array of pinwheel sandwiches set out on the folding table.

"Fine, ladies. Just splendid. Thank you. We came straight through. Didn't stop to eat for a good five hundred miles," the reverend says as he smooths a dovetail of fine auburn hair along his nape, where a white stripe fringes his hairline, betraying the golden edge of a Utah tan. He drops two ham-and-cheese pinwheels on his paper plate.

"Always nice to see a caring Christian woman." The reverend turns, extending his smooth hand to me.

"I see you've met the Widow Thérèse." Miss Morris steps in between us. She hated Marcus. Blamed him, like all the rest. When Marcus died, she showed up at our house with a half-eaten casserole. Told me to repent, told me to pray. Told Zane that Marcus had met an early grave because his father would not summon the Lord's faith. Closed casket. And there she was yelling about the blessed Father. Not the one who came up bloated and raw.

"Blessed friends," the reverend turns from Miss Morris to address the crowd, "we hope you all come out to the Meeting tomorrow. And please bring your neighbours!"

Then he lays his hands on the pastor's sloped shoulders and, in his impassioned bass voice, promises the Meeting will change things.

...

They say change comes along when you give up fighting or are humming along, thinking you're doing just fine. Sometimes it comes towing an old utility trailer. Marcus cruised into my life in a rusted half-ton truck, his slate-blue eyes swallowing light. I was a seventeen-year-old mess of a girl pouring coffee in a highway truck stop outside of Calgary, owned by Edna Mildar whose famous bloody roast beef dinner attracted folks far and wide. Marcus ordered fried liver and bacon with fries, not once bothering to pick up his knife. I could tell by the state of his split, shorn heels, his leather boots were older than me. I winked, refilling his water glass for the third time. He kept his head down and tucked into his meat.

There are men who move mountains. Men who conquer the world, soil clinging to their heels. Marcus was a broken bridge over a spent creek. He held the hum of misery in his hands. In time, he told me terrible things. His father hauling him and his younger brother out into the woods with a length of chain. Each of them bent over a fallen tree, their bottoms parted to the wind to pay for some imagined mischief. Marcus remembered the dog barking at his father's heels. Without a penny in their pockets, the two young teens would pack up one morning and make their way to the foothills, carrying nothing but two hard-framed suitcases with brass fasteners. Marcus remembered his weeping mother had pitched in sweaters, dirty jeans, and all the folded money she kept hidden in the toe of her heavy wool socks. Two brass clicks, and off they went into the pitch-black. I knew wherever Marcus had begun in this world, there were surely fields of fire. Yet his heart song was rapture. So pure he kept it knotted in a burlap sack he had pitched to the river bottom. In his wind-bitten skin, his coarse, sun-flecked beauty, I hoped to find something of my own.

After a year of dating, Marcus agreed to move into my room, with its sagging double bed and metal desk set beneath a small window overlooking a downtown Calgary intersection. When we learned our Zane was on the way, I closed my eyes, pointed to a tiny dot on the map, some nowhere cow town where Marcus and I would endure eight years of small-town intrusion. He lasted longer than most who come to Vermouth. Haven't you heard? The sun here is vile and sharp as teeth. And the winters will cut a path clean through you.

Vermouth County was named after farmer Vern Clempt, whose people had settled the Bow region in 1897. Running south along the river, the land here is wide and flat, drawing farmers from the Ukraine, from England and France, cattle- and plow-born men, too root-bound to catch the oil fever that later gutted so many southern Alberta towns. Folks here put them together — Vern, the river mouth — and clapped their hands. That's when the river began rising.

Starting off as an icy-cold drip in the Wapta icefield, the Bow River begins its long journey high in the Rocky Mountains. Along the river's mid-section, the current cuts through rolling foothills and grain fields, stitched together by crisscrossing bridges. Marcus and I settled on the East Side, our tiny white clapboard house screened by scrub brush and old poplars. Vermouth was seventeen hundred strong, with neighbours close enough to know your business, tough enough to lend a hand with harvest. We told folks we had married in Saskatchewan where my parents owned a row-crop farm. We invented a wedding with a ribbon-wrapped carrot bouquet. When pale-faced Zane arrived that first year, we called him Cauliflower Boy, this new life hidden beneath a leafy cover of lies.

After Zane, and over time, I poured some of my own stories into Marcus.

In a faith-forged south Saskatchewan town, whispers of a girl gone wrong. A child born, long before Zane. Not without the young girl's hunger. Not by some wicked stranger. She acted on her lust for a man, not a mere boy. Don't you know? Desire in a girl leaves the world in a constantly agitated state. So that girl's got no choice. Give up what is stirring inside and face the future alone. Nothing left for her at home but the prison house they'll build her out of hatred and shame. So the baby is born six weeks premature, given another's name, and raised in another home. And that young girl makes her way to Alberta without the smudge of shame on her lips.

Listen. Hear me now. Secrets don't get their power because of something hidden away. They're things we treasure so dearly they're deep seductions. Maybe it's our righteous sense of truth, or the faith we cling to at night and keep polishing smooth as a river stone. The secret is a temptress walking and breathing in us. Hold her too tight, and she'll become your undoing.

After meeting Marcus, my past dissolved in me like the silt-bottomed Bow shedding its glacial sweep into the roaring South Saskatchewan. He did not speak to me of angels. Did not ask me to crawl on my knees before the crumbling Gates. Told me in his gruff tone, Don't surrender to His mighty hand. Sink your own hands into the minerals and mud. No sacrifice but the labour of soil and seed.

Marcus was my blood lamb, meant to wash me clean. They say the Lord only punishes those he welcomes as his children. But if God disciplines us on earth, doesn't that mean we're legitimate? Children of mercy? Children of vengeance? Listen deep and wide; maybe you'll hear the truth thundering in your ears. Are you the wicked repentant or remorseless sinner? Until Marcus passed, I didn't know.

Thirty-two of the faithful arrive for Meeting Day One. Most are curious, like Miss Morris who takes a whiff of the ammonia-slicked basement floor and topples back on her folding chair. We right her, she's fine, enough to send a bitter glance my way. The room holds over a hundred, so I pass the time counting the empty seats between me and salvation. Seventeen. Empty, then saint, saint, empty, sinner, saint, empty. Zane is wool-bound in his brown-checked suit. He's Marcus, right down to his brooding eyes. What would Marcus say, seeing his boy now? So eager to restore the promise of glory his father left behind.

A live microphone arcs out from an altar that stands

mid-room. You can hear the Grayson twins wheeze all the way to the back row; they tug on twisty blue-grey beards, making deep nests with their fingers. A billowing navy-blue velvet curtain hangs from three sturdy metal poles the city suits have set up and pushed forward a few feet from the back wall. The makeshift room, reserved for the lost-at-large, is a soft blue tide against the bleak prairie grey. We sit in silence, adrift on a ship of fools.

Soon gospel notes drown the room in cherry tones— sweet, lustrous sounds streaming from two walnut speakers positioned atop tall black pillars set on either side of the room. The sour, paper-faced congregation begins to clap tentatively as if suffering a singalong. I finger-count the pay-days in December. As the lights dim, the reverend strides down centre aisle, his copper face lit by a single spotlight. His smile nearly sacred.

He holds his arms out, ready to carry a great burden. "Bring me your sinners."

He glares at Zane, me, Miss Morris, Joanie Peen, the Graysons.

"Are you a sinner?" he shouts. His eyes stray across every damned face.

From the back comes a sound like a series of rumbling claps you hear before lightning. Windows rattle. A purse drops from a nervous lap. Zane squeezes my hand. We turn to look out the frosted basement window, expecting to spot a semi-trailer rumbling in off the highway. But the road is clear.

The reverend slips his right arm inside his charcoal-grey blazer.

"Dear God, the man's having a stroke," Miss Morris gasps, leaping to her feet.

The reverend's face turns the colour of blanched wheat. When he extracts his hand, an orange flame seems to burst from his palm.

"Fire!" We all point to Reverend Evan Nack's hand as he staggers forward and, with a swooping arc, pitches the flame out.

"Here," he says, clean palm facing outward, "is the Devil we cast out today."

Zane won't release my hand. I don't want him to. It's a conjurer's trick, I think, glaring at the man.

"What's an unbeliever, you ask." The reverend scans our harried faces, then turns away toward the blue-velvet prayer room. "An unbeliever is the Devil's possession."

Emerging from behind the curtains at the back of the room, a man shields his face from the spotlight. His eyes lift toward us. Facing him, we all lean forward in our seats. His name slips from our lips.

"Daryl? Is that Daryl Jane?" we whisper, as the poor man takes a few steps toward us, finally drops to his hands and knees in the front of the room.

"This decade has been your trial," the reverend says, gesturing at Daryl, whose farm was the first to fail. "The hard years have sewn despair into your hearts. Left you cursing your shrivelled crops and calling names." He pauses, places a hand on Daryl's head. "It's time to welcome the Holy Spirit back in."

The reverend's supporters take Daryl by the arms, gently guide him back behind the blue-velvet curtains into what they're calling a prayer room. The teary, bewildered crowd rises to their feet. Drowning in a resounding sea of amen, I pull Zane off his chair and dart out the church doors.

Adrift between sorrow and sleep that night, Marcus appears in a purple dawn. He leans next to me, whispering, "The Lord isn't here to heal you. He's a menace with a master plot. You've got to purge the enemy, or pay for his crimes."

Until I met Marcus, I was half done, like a foam cake bent on not rising, though you whip, you whip. Wild thoughts raced, wires snapped in my brain. Marcus was my power outage. *Poof.* He came in and all the noise went out of my head. Yet a current ran through his fingers where he held me. The man would vibrate just sitting there. He was handsome and grim and tender and over six feet tall. His refusal to get involved in local politics and gossip rankled some. But they needed him. He could fix anything with an engine: combines, hay balers, swathers, crop dryers, grain augers, manure spreaders. He could overhaul and fix them up without a bit of training. Farmers called on him day and night. Especially during harvest. Mostly he kept to himself, didn't much like when the work kept him indoors.

One day when I came home from my shift at the co-op grocery, I found Marcus alone at the table. His knuckles and the skin of his palm had been ripped raw. Torque wrench spattered with blood next to him. He was staring ahead when I drew near. Bolt blocked, he said, his hands shaking. Blood stippled the chair, trailed across the kitchen floor. His fingers were twitching, a terrible knee-jiggle. I tried to hold his leg still while I worked the wound, his eyes drifting so far away I couldn't call him back. Next day I learned he had been a foot away when a hired man's fingers were crushed by an auger blade. Marcus couldn't untangle the mess. It left something bleak and barren in his heart. That was the way it was with Marcus. Some days he just lost the thread.

Zane pitches a fit the next morning, until I agree to take him back to the Meeting. Redemption is luring him out to sea, I can smell it.

"Okay, okay," I say, finally, "but stay close to me." Damned if I let him stray, I think.

Sixty-one file into the church basement on Day Two. The reverend calls sinners to come forth. No body rises. No soul divides. Then Mavella hobbles forth with her walker, bony fingers curled around its sheepskin handles. She fancies herself as sin's sanitizer, one of the town's Sunday best. First in line for prayer, last to claim penance, her thoughts are calmed only by communion with her Lord.

She places one tentative hand on the reverend's waist. He kneels down, looks at her as if she's just appeared to him in a painted Sistine Chapel sky. Lightly, he touches her sleeve.

"You want to heal, but are you ready to hear? Are you ready to drive the Devil back?"

"My Spirit. My Saviour." She can't recite a recipe, yet here she is summoning the sacred in velvet tones.

The reverend wedges her face between his hands.

"My Lord. My Life." Mavella's lost in an incantatory

rhythm. She crouches, impossibly, joining the reverend on bended knee. It's only a bad hip, but still — "Praise Him! Save her!" the crowd chants.

Wake up! I want to say, as he pushes her head back. Look out. He's the lion tamer with his terrible whip.

The reverend turns his gaze toward us.

"The Spirit is in you," he says, then lets his head fall while Mavella whimpers.

"And the Devil is in you, too."

When Mavella returns to her unsteady feet, the reverend collapses.

Stranded in a sea of flailing arms, I hear the voice.

"Are you listening? Can you hear?" Marcus commands. "If the Lord is a fisherman, he's strictly a catch-and-release man. Soon as he grabs hold of you, he'll let go."

Was it ice on the roof, or tree branches moaning at dawn? The signs of a harsh winter are easy to spot. Bees build their hives higher in the trees, apple skins are tough, corn husks grow thicker than a large man's bicep. Folks say Marcus brought eternal desert to the town the way he died. Left us awash in sin.

None of this I tell the Reverend Evan Nack when I reluctantly agree to meet him in the lobby of the Travelodge. Double-cream coffees, matching plaid recliners, a frosted dish of pillow-shaped mints between us. The reverend presses my hand into his.

I pull it away. "I don't want you filling my boy's head with drivel, you hear me? No one brought you here to peddle false hope and promised lands. You should take that sack of Bibles and go home."

He pushes the tissue box toward me, folding his hands in his lap. "When a man dies without calling the faith to him…" the reverend begins quietly.

"You don't know anything about Marcus," I reply curtly.

He begins again. "Matthew says make a tree good, and its fruit will be good. Make a tree bad, and its fruit will be bad, for a tree is recognized by its fruit."

"Are you saying Zane is some kind of spoiled fruit? Marcus was some rotting tree? Had no right to seed?"

The reverend leans away from me like a boy shunned.

I explain to him how Mrs. Dodd showed up with her Bible and basket of bruised peaches when Marcus died. Miss Morris arrived with her blasphemy and half-eaten casserole. And me, left alone, my boy to raise, not enough money to make the mortgage.

"Don't lay your piety at my table, reverend. And don't go telling me these pilgrims in town are making progress."

The reverend rises to his feet, removes the jacket he proceeds to fold neatly across his lap. "You are absolutely right. You were left with your brave heart, your boy," he says, bending toward me. "Kindness. That's all you needed."

His eyes are flecked green, seem to bore breath from me. Hold the fear, his gaze seems to say, as my hand goes limp in his palm. Find the shore.

And I can see to the bottom of the Bow, river rock at my heels, a steady stream in my ears. Cool waters lashing my hips.

"Marcus was far away from his faith," the reverend says

in a quiet tone. "Separated from Him by his thoughts and deeds."

Separate, yes, but Marcus could see, I think. He is the Word.

Day Three. Zane wails and stomps and bargains with me, so I finally agree to return to church. Meeting news has spread through town. More than just farmers' wives now. Working men from the Keegster Dairy shuffle in, managers from the feed co-op over in the next town show up, stomping the cold from their feet. Zane and I settle in the third row. The Graysons shift over to make room.

Zane tugs on his earlobe when the reverend tells us the trumpet is beginning to sound. The reverend cups a hand to his ear for a long minute.

"Who among you has chosen to do the Devil's work? Examine yourselves now," the reverend implores.

An old rancher from Wellpley shouts back, "It's the Devil that done us wrong! You see any rain on the horizon, reverend? Got any hay we can harvest? Go ahead and look into your crystal ball. We'll wait."

Evan Nack walks up to the rancher, squares himself to the other man's barrel chest. Without a word, he lays a hand firmly on the back of the man's neck. The rancher shakes him off and jumps to his feet.

"Think you can see the horizon?" he asks the man. "Not with your fear. Not with your curses and complaints." The reverend begins to sway slightly on his heels. "What is seen is temporary," he says. "What is unseen, eternal. Fix your eyes on what is unseen," he pronounces, facing the crowd, raising his eyes high above our shoulders so our heads tilt up and back when he conjures moist fields, the soil rich between our fingers. Fine beef-cattle fences, and calves, their bellies heavy with feed, at the trough. Row crops doing their storm sashay before a flash afternoon shower.

He can see the storm coming. Just like Marcus, I think.

Marcus could dab his tongue into a palm full of earth to tell the exact measure of sand, silt, and clay. He predicted cracked soil and cloudless skies in Vermouth long before most. On my sad, listless nights, he wiped my tears before they hit the pillow.

Maybe it's the ancient church pipes or the reverend's sharp shiny heels, but I swear even the old ranchers can hear the drum-tap of rain. When the reverend finishes his sermon, the Graysons both rise, walk straight into the arms of the supporters who guide them to into the blue-velvet prayer room. No one sees them again that night.

In the grocery the next day, the Graysons tell me they're going to auction for more feeder cattle. Town's hearing a clatter on their rooftops, and shouting from them, too, they say. Talk has turned to expanding the herds with yearling and young red Angus.

"A terrible gamble," I say. "*Farmers' Almanac* has been calling for long-range dry spells," I remind them.

The taller Grayson gazes down at me, a wounded look crossing his face. "You can't always tell what's coming, Thérèse. Look at what happened to Marcus."

...

"Jesus is on the phone again, Ma!" Zane shouts, hopping from foot to foot, then slinging his arm around my waist.

Reverend Evan Nack tells me he wants to meet my boy if I'm willing. Says that he's got hand-pulled saltwater taffy that's been stretched from the Utah Valley to Vermouth. I tell him no. He replies that he only wants to offer comfort and promises to leave his Bible in the back seat of the sedan. Warily, I agree to have him join us for dinner.

My son leaps around the room like some band-winged grasshopper when the reverend shows up at our door that night. The man's buffed and pressed into a checked suit, holding a yellow carnation spray for me, a box of waxed paper-wrapped taffy for Zane.

He bends to the boy and offers the gift to him like he's conferring the king his crown.

"Did you know that this taffy is so special it only comes in chocolate, caramel, and cherry and is traded like money in New Jersey?"

Zane beams at him.

Sitting next to Evan Nack on the porch later that night, I tell him that he can't drive drought-stressed cattle with a swing of the good book. Faith may be faltering, but not good old-fashioned common sense.

"If it's hope you're peddling, we're still not looking to buy," I say.

Wearing a faint grin, loosening his tie, he assures me that faith isn't something you visit, like your aunt Alice after hip surgery.

"You've got to hold your faith loosely in your hands," he says, folding my hand in his.

My body bends forth like a young poplar to the wind, and soon my lips are grazing his ruddy cheeks. His skin smells of sugary coffee and baby powder.

"We cannot ask for answers," he whispers, "cannot count the reasons when there is so little time left to repent."

"I want in the room," I tell Evan Nack before Zane awakens the next morning, imagining the blue-velvet prayer room shrouding me in its quiet cape.

"You've not been abandoned," he tells me, his breath quickening in my ear. "You belong to Him. God's mercy will rescue you from the clutches of sin."

"You don't know," I say, thinking about all the love forsaken in me.

"You're not lost, Thérèse," he says again, "only lonely."

Endless the rooms, I think. Endless the false passageways through which we walk blind. Endless the nights when Marcus comes to me, tremulous and tired. Endless the perilous judgments, my brutal Fall, the anxious swim back to earth. Endless the savage dawn rising in me. Endless the disease that's spreading through these prairie souls like clubroot to cruciferous crop. Endless the hours in Evan Nack's hotel later, when he covers my sins in kisses, his hands exploring my body in His name. My earthly sins rock back and forth in these rooms. Lust and love, good and evil, my vexed spirit, my eternal salvation. In thy name, I'll pray. Praise will shake the rhythm of these rooms from me.

There are things no man can understand. How a woman can be a false prophet preying on the weak. How desire in her is seen as a damned river, while a man's fire can rage free. Why life after Marcus will never be the same for me in Vermouth.

Marcus hovers in my dreams, will defy anyone who tries to wash me clean. The holy waters are rising in me. Quench my spirit at God's fountain, the reverend insists. If she thirsts, God tells us, let her come.

"He's no local man, now is he?" Miss Morris complains later at the co-op while I run her order through, sliced bologna, whole milk, a two-pound bag of russet potatoes.

"That doesn't mean he isn't raised right," I offer. "Reverend's a heartbeat from his people no matter where he goes."

She leans forward, so her basket wedges against my waist. "Tell me, Thérèse, who leaves his heartland behind? Who drives all the way up from Utah in a blue sedan to some nowhere town like Vermouth? You telling me Utah is fresh out of sinners?"

Who wouldn't want to escape? I think but only bow my head.

Miss Morris raises her voice, slapping her hand on the conveyor. "He's got the Graysons building a new barn. My Charlie's talking about adding a heifer to a dying herd."

When I reach out to pull her basket from the conveyor and replace it on the pile, she takes hold of my wrist.

"And what's this I hear about the reverend helping you nightly?" she says, shaking her empty basket at me with the other hand. "People talk." She continues, before storming away, "This town is no place for private, Thérèse. Believe me."

Here's what I believe.

I believe that the gates of hell were forged by man, and guarded by him. That time will uproot truth, turn the soul's salvation to dust if you learn to read the signs. That inside my woman's soul, lies the Devil in dungarees.

On Saturday morning before the last Meeting Day, Marcus's mother calls me from her care home, invites me to come down for tea. Her husband long since passed, Marcus was her sweet summons, a reason to face the day. She serves me vegetable and barley soup on a TV tray in her room, with thick slices of homemade bread she butters on both sides. Since Marcus left, she confides, she can see stars in her soup.

"You mean twinkling in the night sky? Up there with Mars?"

"Absolutely not. What have they got you believing in Vermouth?" she snaps, with a vigorous head shake. "And not floating, star-shaped noodles either. Movie stars. Ernest Borgnine, Tallulah Bankhead, and such."

She sifts through the broth, spooning out faces. "Marcus watches the TV with me you know," she adds. "He sits right over there on the couch while I watch my shows."

"Yes," I confide, "I see him too." In Zane's smile, in the dented tool box we keep in the kitchen.

"Well, she had the double pneumonia you know," she replies.

"Who?" I ask, confused.

"Tallulah," she answers, indignant, "star of stage and screen!" She dunks her spoon into the broth, stirs up another celebrity constellation.

"Listen," she confides after a while, hovering so close to the steaming bowl her chin glistens. "Not everyone can commune with the famous."

"You must be blessed," I say, thinking the coarse and willing woman should never betray her real guide.

She only smiles back at me, holding her prayer hands together, rocking in her chair, imagining the winter will bring her more soup, more signs.

Roundup Sunday. Hundreds settle into steel chairs, more line the back wall, in dungarees, battered workboots. Farmers, shopkeepers, homemakers, knit-one-purl-two-ers, seed sellers, bankers, colluders and crooks, all streaming south off Highway 21.

Hope clings like frost to the branch when the reverend tells us today we will see what remains of those who sin.

"Let the droughts come," the reverend exhorts. "Let the wind blow and batter your houses down, still you will not fail if your foundation is rock."

Evan Nack's body, lit by a blue-tinged light, is beautiful, can hold all creation.

I watch the farmers' faces strain. Each one asks, how far

am I prepared to go? Where is redemption, if not here, if not now?

The reverend raises one hand, the look of anguish in his eyes. "Those who lose faith will harvest the consequences of decay. Those who call the Spirit can harvest everlasting life. Ask your fallen brother Daryl Jane."

Women cry, men tighten their faces.

Rooted, his body still, Evan's raised branch arms spread into every weary soul. As he stands and sways, the tall grasses of those prairie fields stretch out, each rolling hill a footstep, a fateful climb toward the blue-velvet sky.

"Let us strip off every weight, every sin that slows us down," he urges, removing his jacket, like a man intent on leaving no soul behind.

Men and women in the crowd rise.

One by one they come. They come to him.

"Only God can free man from the power and penalty of sin," he urges. "It's time to awaken the Holy Spirit within."

No one was awake the morning Daryl Jane set off to round up his cattle. Another Alberta freeze-up, three days running. Temperature dropped to a skin-biting minus thirty. Then the season's spell broke. Wet snow came drifting in on chinook winds, soft as steam, silent as sin. A thin layer of ice had formed across parts of the Bow, hidden by a thick coat of snow.

The radio announcer kept reminding cattlemen wintering their herds to check on them regularly, make sure they had enough water and feed. So when Daryl rose at dawn and pulled on his boots—his wife told me later—he braced for a hip-deep crawl in heavy snow to the dugout.

Daryl had built the dugout with a hand from Marcus a few years back. A wide, deep basin about the length of a full-size skating rink, the dugout collected runoff from the creek to keep the large herd watered in summer. When the waters froze over, Daryl would drill a hole to forge a water line. Most winters, the same ritual. He and Marcus would set up the sump pump, hook up the generator, and lay a water line fifty feet long to fill two bathtubs full of fresh water for the herd. Daryl would keep an eye out for leaks while Marcus filled the tubs. That winter, though, full of flu, crippled by a greasy bowel, Daryl had let the herd roam free a few extra days. Snowfall was clean enough to drink, he reasoned; the herd would be okay for a while.

Over the hill Daryl climbed that morning, headed for the dugout. When he reached the first clearing, Daryl told his wife afterward, he saw what looked like a cluster of shorn stumps off in the far distance. Must be the sun's glare, he thought, and pulled down his ball cap, as he crept on ahead toward the basin's edge.

It was after eight the morning Daryl's wife called our house in tears, saying she had the little ones crying, her husband had been out in the fields too long. Could Marcus come and see? Of course, I told her. Marcus picked up some tools from the shed, sped on his way in the truck.

As I heard Daryl tell it later, Marcus must have tried to trace Daryl's footsteps to the clearing, but the wind kicked up a fury behind him. Marcus wandered snowblind for a while before Daryl finally spotted him, then lost sight of Marcus again. The two called out to each other until Marcus found his way to the dugout edge.

When Marcus finally joined Daryl, he dropped to his knees, staring out at the calamitous scene. All two hundred and twenty head of cattle were dead.

Desperate for water, the herd had wandered out into the middle of the dugout and fallen through thin ice, Daryl told me, hardly finding the words. Marcus had wept seeing their torsos partially submerged, locked in, halfway between frozen and free. They must have struggled for hours, as the ice began to coat their shivering bodies, a filmy haze creeping over their eyes. Finally, too cold and confused, each dropped where they stood. Daryl described the scene as a frigid mass of death.

Marcus left a stunned Daryl back at the house, with the wife and baby at her breast, bawling, the whole house in shock, disbelieving. Daryl's wife said she saw Marcus jump into his truck and speed off like a man on fire. The heavy snows had finally lifted, but Marcus was already in too deep. Two clear lanes, no traffic. Where the road split, a fork at the edge of the Bow, four wheels pointed straight ahead. Truck went in clean, never came up.

Waist-deep in supplicants, Reverend Evan Nack drifts through the crowd toward me. They all part to make room. I wade through a field of clapping hands and waving arms when the supporters lift me up to the reverend, then lower me on bended knee at the altar.

You've got to love the lost only so far, I think, only as far as your own weakness.

My fingers tingle as the reverend pulls me forward.

"Do you hear the trumpet's call, Thérèse? Are you listening? Can you hear?"

I kneel before Evan, bury my head in his worthy hands. His whole body shakes as he invites me to take in the Word, his breath falling softly on my skin.

Look down, reverend, I think. Can't you see with me all the way to the bottom? See how the sky falls, the shadow walks? The truth is coming. Wait and see. Marcus may have never seen the light, but his eyes were always wide open. He knew the darkness would never lift from his heart, so maybe he took the plunge. Left me unwashed, monstrous, and free.

I look up at Evan, see the glory shining brightly in his eyes.

I'll stay with him. Cross my heart I'll pray for him, when my holy spirit drags him under.

Fingernecklace

Peppermint saliva lips. Two numb bums. Joe and Gus glance up from their work, exchange cutthroat looks across the salvaged oak dining table. First one to stuff and label one thousand envelopes gets an extra twenty bucks, plus his pick of the fresh cod Mrs. B. will serve tonight with garlicky roasted red peppers.

"All good, my jumblies?" Mrs. B. pokes her head in, scanning the mail metropolis forming at their elbows. "Break for fresh air?"

Joe stomps his feet. Gus pinches a threefold letter that he slides into a number ten envelope, keeping his head low. Tacky-tongued, the loose flesh beneath his chin feels itchy and two feet thick.

"Suit yourselves."

Mrs. B. has been group home supervisor since her husband accidentally shot himself eight years ago. Now she pitches lifebuoys in a sinking, four-storey heritage house in Greektown that Gus calls the HMS *Shitstorm.* If she had eyes in the back of her skull, she'd notice how closely Gus watches as she prepares dinner, manages intakes, soothes cries and tempers in the middle of the night. Tomorrow, when she's bat-blind and flatlining on the couch with a throbbing migraine, he'll try to kiss her on the lips.

"Pass the stamps," Joe says, flicking back the loosely braided hair that dangles down his spine like a grizzled cat tail. Whenever Joe squirms, Gus feels the creature claw up his own back.

Joe yanks away the cereal bowl between them when Gus pitches the stamp coil over.

"Don't steal my Cheerios," Gus slaps Joe's hand, pulling the mournful face that makes him look like a plumpish fifty, though he's only thirty-six.

Joe licks oat dust from his grinning lips.

"You chew like an Indian," Gus snaps.

"You smell like rat piss," Joe hoots, stomping his lizard-skin boots. His cheekbones, heavy lined with sun and age, are soft as kid leather.

Marlee enters, slumps down next to Gus, who is quietly nibbling at the edge of an *o*.

"You got my cigarettes?" she asks Gus, folding herself inside a long black knit sweater that exposes only her face and feet.

"You smoked 'em Tuesday. Better cut back."

She pulls out a bottle of nail polish from her jeans pocket and begins painting a hot-pink helmet on her big toe.

Marlee and Gus grew up on the wrong side of sane, so they're next-door neighbours. Nuthouse Knobs. Crackpot Criminals. The Deranged. Marlee came in off the streets, the thing men fucked behind dumpsters. Now, she's on low-grade watch at the home. Not that she'd ever go through with it, but one rainy afternoon she swallowed a half-bottle of toilet cleaner just to clear the stench from her throat. The last time Gus acted out—packed his life up in an old hockey bag and hitched the Don Valley to his brother's place—Donny sent him back on the Greyhound from Peterborough, pronto. That was two summers ago. He's been good all year.

Mrs. B. returns with a glass of water in her hand, gesturing to Gus with her wristwatch. He nods, plucks from his silver pillbox two skinny whites that he washes down in a long gulp. He'll be slo-mo soon, bleary by dinner.

The rice is one item on the plate. The rice is yellow and smells like buttered bones. The red peppers curl, sodden and sad in their oily, garlic swim. Gus pokes his rumpled fish at the kitchen table, feeling his organs flip. He spikes a red pepper that he sniffs, drops and then pushes the plate away.

"Come on, Gus," Mrs. B. says, dropping her own fork.

Gus lowers his eyes.

"Last time."

She sighs as she rises to fix Gus a peanut butter sandwich she glues together with clover honey. With a quick flash of her blade, she splits the sandwich four ways.

"Okay," she turns, dropping the plate in front of him. She taps the table. "Eat what you can."

Gus's torso sways, his arms remain motionless at his side.

"Come on, Gus." Mrs. B. says, rapping the table with her knuckles. "Take a bite."

Gus squeezes his head, muffling the edge in her voice. He sees his mother's fingers tap-tapping the cigarette on the lip of a blue glass ashtray. She is butting the stub out, covering her ears.

Joe finishes the last of the cod while Gus looks down, begins sorting patterns on the yellow linoleum in the kitchen, kneading his plump cheeks with his fingers.

Mrs. B. slides her chair over and pulls Gus's hand away from his face. She rubs her thumb over Gus's raw red knuckles and lays his hand down on the table.

"It's okay, hon. Save your energy. Donny's coming tomorrow."

Donny's greasy jeans are tucked into oil-stained workboots. In the home's sparse living room, he paces between two brown curbside couches with water-stained cushions. He checks his watch. Crew's on site. Fuck. Christ. Piss. In his aching jawbone, he feels the hammer of hydraulic pumps and half-dug trenches. He's got the engineer's change orders. Cost overruns. Goddamn job is killing him. Looking up he sees Gus lumbering slowly down the stairs, still wrapped in his white terry-cloth robe. Big as a hollowed oak, premature belly spread. Donny shakes a full prescription bottle at him.

"Don't skip out on me, Gus. You know what happens."

Donny watches his younger brother's eyes dart across the room and drop, taking inventory. Gus freezes at the sight of Donny's workboots.

He bunches the terry-cloth belt in his palms, squeezes

the ball, then lets the belt drop like a fishing line to the floor. Gus pulls it back up, watches it fall again over his slippered feet. Donny pats the dusty couch cushion, coaxing his brother over with a smile.

"Look, Gus, we can't do our usual pizza run this aft. Got a date with a wrecking ball."

Gus bunches the belt in his lap, blinks wet, wandering tears. Donny wraps his arms around his big old stump of a baby brother, tries to hold the roots down, keep the disease from spreading. Root rot. Runs in the family.

Gus sobs into his brother's neck. "I want to come home."

Donny holds him close, tries to stop a lifetime of trembling. Five years, six episodes, a thousand pills, and dead-end dreams between them.

He can see it in his brother's puffy eyelids, the grey, candle-drip skin. New meds are doing a number. He looks more like her now. Same mess of auburn hair, same staple-sized crease below his chewed lips. How Gus loved to bite and chew his bottom lip while they built expansive basement cities out of cardboard and old sheets that Gus later trampled when Donny refused to make him mayor. Donny looks over his life like a cross-sectional drawing, his mind moving from room from room. He pictures his mother sitting back on her floral couch, the dim glow of her after-dinner cigarette, eyes going in all directions. And Gus at ten years old, past the biting and moodiness, withdrawing into his mumble mouth in the kitchen, doing an after-dinner puzzle in the same pajamas he's worn all day. While Donny fucks off to his buddy Cheevie's house for double dessert. Cheevie has Nintendo on the set, a mother who never once tried to pry open a bathroom door with a chef's knife. Smooth exit, just like the old man.

Donny loosens the belt around his brother's waist. "Gus, we can't. You know Pinky's happy as horses with the house all quiet."

"Fuck Pinky," Gus mutters, turning abruptly, sopping up tears and spit with his fuzzy sleeve.

What's he supposed to do? Gus left them broke with all his therapy and specialists. His brother wandering for days then begging for more money on their doorstep, sending his wife for depression pills. Pinky won't let any more of his bad blood in. Last time they took him back, Gus sold Pinky on the Internet. Amazing how many lonely farts will drop the price of a used car on a mail-order Chinese wedding. Gus posted her picture on a dodgy-looking website advertising "Exotic Lucky Asian Brides." Pinky was wrapped in white-and-pink wedding chiffon, a purplish-pink orchid in her hair, something bite-sized dangling on the end of a shrimp fork. Gus wrote that she was petite, submissive, ornamental. Some old goat paid Gus a fifteen hundred-dollar cash deposit in a coffee shop, leaving with nothing but a marriage licence application and the promise to spend eternity with "Pinky Cameroon Sparkle."

Cheap Chinese takeout, Gus said to Donny, flashing his wild smile at the front door, handing over a wad of fifty- and hundred-dollar bills. Donny could tell Gus was on a mounting high, had seen him go from glue-headed to God in a matter of hours. His head a red planet, light screaming through his skull. Gus said the meds were like sparks shooting off. Flash fireworks, followed by the inevitable hours of blind panic. Then it was like gravity had given up on him. His head floated in air, thin as the atmosphere on Mars. Claimed he was only trying to pitch in. Pinky threatened to move out.

Gus threads his belt through the loops in his housecoat and ties it like a tourniquet across his bicep. The familiar phrase keeps rattling in Donny's skull: Think you can save your brother? Can't even save your marriage, useless fuck.

"Pinky will come around," Donny says, trying hard not to look restless, though Jesus Christ, he thinks, the guys will be leaning on shovels, fucking the dog till he gets back. "Her dad's covering my new equipment loan."

Donny tries to offer an encouraging smile.

Gus starts to flap his arms, extending his neck, a whooping crane in a stiff wind. Donny holds his brother's arms at his side. Gus wrenches away, taunting.

"Pinky's got a face like the back of a shovel," Gus bellows.

"Shut it, Gus," Donny orders, trying to wrap his arms around his brother's shoulders, hold his burden tight. "I know it's disappointing."

Gus rises, shouting in his faux-Asian accent. "Twyme, twyme, money-back gawantee." He flaps and turns away. "Fuck Pinky."

"This is bullshit, Gus."

Donny can hear stirring in the back room, drawers open and close. Mrs. B. is on the phone in her office.

"Not forever," Donny says. "Give me some time."

Donny met Pinky in one of those mahogany and brass steakhouses with the deer antlers mounted above the bar. She was serving rib-eye steaks to men who chewed the fat over commercial real estate deals. Turns out her dad owned the place. Owned a half dozen apartment complexes and a US home-care franchise. Her family was an empire. His was a broken tenement. Pinky moved through the room, pale-blue moons dusting her eyelids, still as a watercolour. He knew he wasn't worthy but asked her out anyway, tumbling over his broken syllables. She was working part-time, preparing for first year of law school. He was wedged into steel toes, lean and strong, the hungry eyes of a man on a mission to be more. On their fifth date, he made a nest of his long arms, cupped her bird bones inside, and called her My Lily Hands.

Donny pulls Gus's hand away from his brooding face, turns to see Joe pound down the stairs toward them.

"Go away, Tomahawk Chuck," Gus shouts up at him.

Joe marches over and grabs Gus firmly by the terry-cloth shoulder. "Smoke break. It's noon, polar bear, let's migrate," leading him toward the front door.

Gus twists and breaks free, tumbling into a coffee table.

"Everything all right out there?" Mrs. B. calls out from the office.

"Under control," Donny says. "Sorry, clumsy today."

Donny trails his brother to the front door. Joe raises

a dismissive hand, motioning for him to stay put. Donny nods agreement and stuffs an envelope filled with pizza money inside Gus's housecoat. Joe shoots him a puzzled look, stomping his feet.

With barely a nod to Donny, out the door they march.

Native guys float, they had told Donny. Mohawk or Cree, toeing twenty-storey beams, steady rivet gun in their hands. It was all bullshit. Joe strongly preferred the ground metal framing, but Donny needed him, his most reliable steel-joist man, to inspect a support brace on the fifth floor. Crew said he must've had a rubber backbone the way Joe bounced down in one piece. Whatever was on his mind back then never came back. He couldn't manage on his own, so Donny found him a place with Mrs. B. he could afford on permanent disability. Once Joe settled in, Donny figured it would be good enough for family so dropped Gus off with a couple of gym bags, two weeks after his brother had set fire to their shower curtain. Abandon ship! Blame Pinky? Sure. He was fucking free.

On-site by late afternoon, the front-load driver shouts down to Donny, "Okay to take another run?"

Donny nods, directing traffic. Raising its toothy bucket, the driver steers the front-loader through tire-sucking mud, shattering glass and beams on a downward strike. Whining like a beaten dog, the low-rise splits. Burying his toe in sharp debris, Donny thinks, This is the job. Bid was strong. Overhead decent. If he can hold the margins, maybe he can afford to build an extension off the house in the fall.

Give Gus his own entrance. Donny returns to his truck. He roughs up his estimate pad, knowing his numbers never add up. Not counting the new pickup, the payments he's still covering on the second mortgage, he's hardly pulling down a profit. Pinky will never go for it. Her private practice hours are brutal. Her parents would probably pull the loan. To them he's nothing but a mid-level contractor racking up bills and a growing beer gut. Fuck it. He'll find the money. Set Gus up in some studio apartment close by. Take him out twice a week, get his meds back on track.

Donny knows the drill. Pour concrete slab, pound the building out, pad an invoice or two. Take his commission off the top. Offer me an extra buck, he'll tell the subs, I'll throw in the townhouse complex too.

Things Gus will do for a dollar:
- Clean the kitchen floor with a soapy grey mop.
- Commit to Cheerios in the morning and finish them.
- Buy Marlee and himself cigarettes when she gets her Thursday cheque.

After his brother leaves for the site, Gus pulls two turtle blues from his pillbox, his arms heavy rubber fins. He plods to the bus stop, watches the number twelve roll up. He stubs out his cigarette and climbs the stairs. Staring down at the fare box, he watches the coins tickle the steel throat then spit out a paper tongue at him.

"Alberto's Pizza," Gus slurs like a drunk directing a cab.

Brusquely, the driver motions him to the back of the bus. Gus sits in the last row, cracks his pillbox, and swallows another white. Blearily, he watches Bookbag climb on with two friends at the next stop. They sit at the front, but she waves back at him. Gus can't lift his sweaty hand. They rumble on for ten minutes until Alberto's red neon lights up. He yanks the cord.

At Alberto's, an alert hostess ushers Gus to a dimly lit back table. He's blinking fast. Skipping ropes and twigs start to stretch and snap in his gassy head, his body in a flat spin. Seated, Gus stabs a fork into his leg so he's lucid enough to order his usual Hawaiian Special. When the silver tray arrives, a large pie, thick crust smeared with pineapple and ham, he dips a wedge into his Coke. He orders a coffee, adds six sugars, then pockets the spoon. The table is pivoting, but he needs to piss.

Along the restaurant corridor, Gus counts gold diamonds fringing the emerald carpet that he follows all the way to the men's room. He teeters before the urinal next to a bank of stainless steel sinks. The burly man next to him bounces on his toes. Staring at him, Gus bounces too. The man zips. Gus pulls slowly at his fly. The man calls him something Gus can't grasp. Gus unleashes random words bouncing in his muddy mouth then grabs his own crotch, fumbling furiously.

The stout man drops his shoulder and drives Gus hard into the mirror. "Pull that faggot shit again, and you're dead!" he shouts, before walking out the door.

"Don't you cry," Gus says, seated on the bathroom floor, pounding his inner thigh. "Don't."

He digs his keys into his thigh as he sits, trying to stifle tears.

Gus finally rises, enters the middle stall, and unfolds the tabloid paper someone has left behind on the floor, carefully draping it across his lap. When he's through emptying his loose bowels, he scoops out his shit with the newspaper.

"Stuff in here could bring me down," he mumbles, folding the mess up on his way back to the table.

When he returns, the manager is waiting to escort him out. Obediently, Gus walks toward the entrance.

Rain flooding the streets outside is gunfire in his head. He slaps at his skull while he waits for an overcrowded bus to stop.

Donny watches his right boot sink to the top of his woolly, red-striped socks. Looks like the sewer lines might be a problem, he considers. Water ingress. A negative grade means death-by-defect, his grandstanding engineering prof always reminded them.

For a mean minute Donny is twenty-two, wearing the same dirty wool socks he'd slept in all week. Late for structural engineering with Sullivan, the second time that week. Modelling assignment overdue. He doubled back to the apartment to get it. Almost out the door and on his way, when the phone rang.

"Gus has gone off again," said the day manager at the YMCA. "It was you or the cops."

Donny found Gus bleeding and sore, curled up at the end of his bed at the Y. Claw marks at his brother's throat and wandering, empty eyes. Donny packed him into a cab. Another trip to the pound. Join the psych ward hounds who paw at their faces while the orderlies urge them to sit up, don't shout, stay calm, keep away from the glass. Don't leave Gus alone, crammed into that goddamnmother-fuckingplace overnight again, he thought, but had to drop him off with the docs anyway. Next day, he showed up to hear about the sucker punch, found his brother's head covered in a gauzy mesh. The treatment team sat him down. Donny said: Fuck you. Doped up. Tied down like a dog. As good as killing him. Doc said: Irreversible condition. Risk of self-injury. Gus was winding up an anxious, hallu-cinating patient with his run-on mouth, so the man took a swing at his demon. Gus never raised a fist. Donny signed his brother out, crawled back to his roommate Cheevie's with a six-pack under his arm. Gus spent two days sleeping it off on the couch, while Donny and Cheevie got wasted to Van Morrison and bowls of freezer-burnt chili.

It was their semester at sea. Three young men on the summer prowl, a taste for Belgian brew on their lips. The Dukan boys, tough-jawed, beefy where it counted. Gus was swimming in blond university women who fell over themselves for a chance to kiss his boyish lashes. He was even-keeling it on meds, auditing Ancient Greek from the last row of the lecture hall, a chattering ballpoint in his restless hands.

"You engineer the roads, I'll rebuild Rome," Gus liked to say to Donny, his steel eyes flashing silver whenever when he mapped out the Persian empire with mac and cheese.

Gus was golden on the right meds. They found a doc

and pay-what-you-can therapist. For the first time since Donny could remember, Gus was witty, sharp-edged, towering above the jocks in university busy bragging about their foosball tournament records and marathon fucking. Sharing beers with his baby brother in the pub was the best life Donny could have invented. Then the call came. Their mother's garage door was frozen shut. Pills on the seat and the car mat. She had drifted off into an eternal sleep with a trunk full of groceries.

Wasn't long before Gus started skipping his meds, buying rounds at the bar for strangers then slipping out before the bill arrived. It was a G-force drop. So Donny packed up for Peterborough, left Cheevie with two months' rent, and moved Gus out halfway through spring term.

On the job site, Donny's cell is ringing that special tone. Holding up an index finger to the impatient engineer, Donny thwacks his muddy workboots against his truck.

"What? I can't hear you." Donny barks into his cell again.

The engineer stomps off, rustling the papers in hands.

Gus has confessed to leaving his shit (Mrs. B. says excrement) on the table at Alberto's Pizza. Donny listens, but the phone keeps cutting out so he asks her to repeat it.

"I can't just leave," he shouts into the phone. "I'm the fucking guy in charge," he says, instantly regretting his tone. He punches the truck door, feels the sharp acid taste of warm Coke backing up in his esophagus.

...

Beetles storming his lids, something loose crawling. Riding back to the HMS *Shitstorm* from Alberto's Pizza, Gus paws his eye socket, fist deep, until he sees lime-coloured streaks. He slides the bus window open and breathes away the lingering stench of sweaty fish seat that's making his stomach churn.

At the next stop, the bus door opens with a shudder. Bookbag waves to Gus from the aisle and sits down next to him with her shopping bags.

She's dressed in black, wishbone-thin, a pimply teenaged forehead. Gus watches her smooth back her raven hair, bunch a ponytail she never fastens. Her fingertips sift and sort, shooting thunderbolts through his brain.

Gus pockets his balled fist. He tries to focus on the brittle slogans screaming across her tits. No blood for oil. Draft beer, not war. Fuck yoga.

Seeing the bulge in her breast pocket, he taps two fingers to his lips. She slides out a Player's Light and hands it to him.

"You okay, Gus?"

Gus drives his palm heel into his cornea. Her voice, too shrill. He closes his droopy lids, makes a wish, opens—she's still there.

She gives him a friendly shake. "Gus? You good?"

The bus tires screech. He wants out. The rain drives a fast-rhythm beat into his chest. He slaps the bus window, picturing himself climbing the stairs of his mother's house, hands locked around a pair of scissors.

He sees his sister Emma twisting the curling iron too close to her cheek. An orange ball bursts from the rod, ashes dusting her gingham blouse. Her mouth opens—a thousand night birds shrieking.

"Let go, let go," he mumbles.

"Gus, I don't understand what you're saying," Bookbag says. "You have to go?"

He pulls out the spoon he's stolen from the restaurant, licks the metal, and sticks it to his chin and settles back into his seat.

"Cool," Bookbag says, sitting back with him, "like a shiny goatee." She rakes her fingers through her tangled hair.

"Savemesavemesavememoneybackguarantee." After a while, Gus's mouth begins running on bus rhythm.

Bookbag pulls Gus's hand from his face, gently turns it over. His whole body vibrates while she smooths the padded skin. "It's okay."

Gus's baggy body slumps down in its seat. Together, he and Bookbag look out the rain-spattered window in silence, watch the hanging duck breasts glimmer along the gluey sidewalks of Chinatown's dim-sum drive.

"This is me," Bookbag says, rising uncertainly. "You all right to get back?"

Gus hauls her back down. She stiffens when he slaps something into her hand. A wad of crinkled bills unfolds in her palm. Gus is rocking in his seat again.

"Okay, okay, I'll keep this safe," she says uncertainly. "Four more stops then pull the cord. Make sure. See you tomorrow, okay?"

Gus watches Bookbag climb down the stairs, light up, blow a silver plume through the open doors. He fans the sulphur sting, feeling sharp metal boxes clang and clip the corners of his skin.

Mrs. B. is waiting for Gus in the doorway, knowing better than to make him talk. She escorts him to his room and settles him on the bed, where he lies back, burying his hands under his armpits. His eyes are bloodshot.

"Trouble comes," she says, patting his leg then pulling her arm around his waist when he sits up again. "Blame genes or blame Jesus, just don't let it get you down."

She rises, offering to call the nurse down the block just to check in.

Gus shakes his fast inflating head.

"Donny's got you in with Dr. Lee on Monday. You like her. You'll be feeling much better in a couple of days."

Gus sits back on his bed, keeping his spine straight, while he watches the floor beams split, a floodlight fall over the room, shattering him into a thousand pieces.

Two heel-clicks, three stomps down the hall before they hear Mrs. B. call up, "Lights out."

When Joe knocks on his door, Gus doesn't answer. He swallows two white pills, letting the night swarm slowly under his chin. Metal flies and bounces from the top of his skull. Knife-prick fingertips until his hands finally go numb.

By three a.m., his buzzing head won't quiet. Gus decides to slip downstairs to the kitchen to grab his apple-green cereal bowl from the cupboard. On the way, he notices Mrs. B. lying on the living-room couch, a wet facecloth pressed to her forehead. Gus fills his bowl with Cheerios, adds milk, and tucks the box under his arm. Creeping past Mrs. B., he sees her left hand jerk on her belly. He bends over her, kisses her lightly on the lips. Her eyelids flutter but she barely moves. He pads up to the third floor, to the end of the hall, closing the bathroom door behind him.

From the back of the toilet tank, he removes the pills he's been collecting. He drains the last of the Cheerios box, watches the blue turtles and *o*'s tumble together, the candies sink and toss in their oat sea. He shakes a few more pills into the bowl and with the restaurant spoon from his khaki's pocket, stirs the mess before shovelling it all into his mouth, craving a long, cement-headed sleep.

Mrs. B. is clutching the cordless when Donny arrives. The ambulance attendants are balancing Gus on the stretcher as they descend the stairs, Joe yelling at them to hurry.

Donny orders them to put his brother down in the living room. Reluctantly, the men set their burden down, the sheet fallen, draped diagonally across Gus' chin. With all his force, Donny lifts his brother's torso from the stretcher, works his way down the arms, stomach, feels for the broken soul bones.

Sirens silent, the paramedics pull away from the house. At the living-room window, Donny stands next to Marlee, who is digging her freshly painted nails into her skin as the ambulance rolls away toward the intersection.

Donny motions to Mrs. B. that he'll be right back, needs to get the cell from his truck to call his wife. He closes the front door, making sure he hears the solid click. In the truck, he steers straight for an after-hours bar. Then, head swimming in booze, he drives all night until he remembers.

On his way home from his buddy Cheevie's house, he's pie-stuffed and pleased with himself after winning drunken Pong on Nintendo. Light on in his sister's room above the garage when he drifts through the front door. When the acrid stench reaches him downstairs in the hallway, he begins to mount the stairs two by two, tumbling knees first on the landing. He rises, stumbles toward Emma's room.

From the doorway, Donny can see Emma is standing by her bed, her hair locked in a curling iron set flat against her skull. Smoke and sparks jump from the brittle strands of Emma's hair. The metal rod is singeing her skin. He can smell burning meat. His mother is shaking the girl, yelling at her to stop moving. Everyone is screaming. Gus is on all fours next to the bed, struggling to stand, his right hand closed around a pair of scissors to set Emma free.

Head swimming with Cheevie's dad's cheap rye, Donny blinks but his legs won't move.

Soundless cries, Emma coughs twice.

His mother shrieks, giving Emma the old fingernecklace from behind, her hands locked around his sister's fragile windpipe. Donny touches his own throat. So drunk he can hardly stand.

He watches Emma punch out weakly with her left arm.

Gus is back on his knees, too hoarse to scream.

It won't stop.

Not when Emma falls forward, her right cheek and forehead clipping the nightstand.

Not when his mother tears the curling iron electric cord from the wall, knocking the ceramic lamp to the floor.

Parked on the demolition site, Donny sucks in a chestful of diesel. The smell comforts him, in a quiet way, as dawn breaks between glass and steel, bathing Yonge Street in fractured yellow hues. He bends to tighten his bootlaces, then rising, deliberately smashes his unshaven face against the side-view mirror.

Gus and Mom and he and Gus and Pinky and Joe and the sharp, bottomless world tuck a rusty hook in his mouth, hoisting him over the city twenty storeys. His swooning face a wrecking ball, Donny cracks a bloody fat-lipped grin, the momentum in him growing, knowing now he'll never be able to avoid the crash.

If on a Winter's Night a Badger

I'm not the kid you picture when you think prodigy. Call me the last luminous presence at Middle of the Road High School situated at the end of Suburban Sprawl Lane, right next to a wood-chip playground and two crumbling plots of green artificial turf. And though some of my achievements have been noted, I do have my detractors. Last week, without provocation, Ronnie and his rugby thugs dumped two full plates of spicy beef enchiladas in my lap at the school caf. They keep threatening carnage.

Big sis protects me, because she's ravenous, rash, and heavy set. She's in her room right now rereading her favourite soppy romance novel about a lovestruck hog badger who stalks his own predators and shreds them ear to ear until the right female sow soothes his lonely heart. I need to tell her Ronnie hauled me naked from the gym locker room today until I begged for my stinking sweats. She'll hiss, she'll snort. But Badger will take care of business.

Badger calls me Alexia though I am boy with boy parts and she is girl with badger parts, like sharp forefoot claws and a musky growl. She's woods-bound most nights, but there's a sliver of light under her door now. I peek in. Sis is too absorbed in her book to listen, her eyes turning nut brown while she reads. Mom says it's like a spell she's under, this tail end transition from pup to full-blown badger-hood.

"Your sister needs space right now, Alex," Mom advised, daubing two drops of oil on my cage-door hinge this aft.

So why am I the one she's locked up, sometimes from dawn to dinner, to avoid our petty sibling fights? Mom calls me impulsive. Misguided. Alienated. Ha! More like masterful. Last night I shot up Captain Dung and three alien universes on level eight. Take that Nerdromancer6 high score!

So the cage. It's comfortable enough in here. A six-by-eight basement model with a stainless steel sliding door and discrete sanitary tray. I've got a mini bar loaded with Snickers, the supermodel channel on TiVo, and time to pen thoughts in my leather-bound man-memoir, so I'm pretty much set.

My curfew's at ten p.m. That's when our nocturnal Badger roams free—the woods, the school caf, anywhere she can binge on food scraps or brawl with a twitchy squirrel. Think I'm bad-tempered? Badger is flat out unpredictable. Mom's worried we'll claw each other's throats out one of these days. With all the crap we've been through this year, she's probably right.

Like last night, we're sitting around the dinner table, Mom and I are chomping on a veggie pot pie while Badger scarfs back a pocket gopher. No seconds? Sis lets out this epic wail, begins clawing through the tabletop polish to the wood grain below. Glasses shattered. Plates flew. These days, everything sets her off.

I tiptoe. I tolerate. But with Mom, it's always: "Turn that dreadful Dengue Fever music down, Badger needs her rest." "Hide the Hattley's dog and open a window, your sister's secreting."

Notice what she doesn't say? How was *your* day, Alex? Your sister's a handful with her horrid moods, way to hang in there, champ. When Badger trapped a northern brown snake, she sucked out all the venom and deliberately stuffed the leftover skin sack under my pillow. The skin was wrapped up in my favourite red Dengue Fever concert T-shirt. Animal! Mom doesn't say a thing. Badger is this godlike presence here, while I go unnoticed—the singular third person in my own epic adventure.

And I'm not the only one who's pissed. Yesterday, Mrs. Drudd from next door angled her wobbly cart in the grocery store, trapping Mom and me in frozen foods. She blew up over Badger.

"They're just snuff holes," Mom explained. "Badger likes to dig."

Drudd started a red-faced rant about falling property values. No more field mice on the stoop, no oozing backyard carrion, or the city will drive us out for good.

We've had two compliance notices already. The third and final notice will force an imminent eviction.

"Keep that nasty Badger indoors," Drudd ordered, "or good luck finding another transit-accessible middle-class neighbourhood to ravage." Then Drudd added that if Mom had a man around, maybe her problem child would learn some discipline.

Mom went Richter from the waist up. "Keep your mouth shut in front of my children," she said and pulled me behind her like I was a child.

Finger-poking Drudd's discount pork, she added, "Remember that thick stew I brought over last week? After a bloody feeding, Badger always leaves me the entrails. Surprise. No filler!"

Drudd combusts. "Your teen's a terror. Keep that *thing* inside or you'll be on the streets so fast it will make her tail spin."

When Mom is finally asleep, I pick my cage lock and slip upstairs to see if Badger has received my book bait.

Quietly, I push on her door. Sis has dug herself in behind a barricade of my mother's old tote bags and cardboard boxes and is propped up on her bed by two firm pillows. Next to her on the nightstand is a big bowl of rippled chips. Between her paws, she is holding my gift: her favourite Hog Badger romance novel tucked inside a powder-blue gift bag. My perfect bound, hardcover forgery—high-end laser printed and glued to the spine of the updated edition I found—means Badger won't realize until the last few pages it's not quite the happy ending she remembers.

Badger pokes her snout inside the bag. Yeah, go ahead. Give it a good sniff, sis. Smell that? It's our burning bond. Badger needs a new story-shaped bridge over the yawning void of her lonesome, mooning, pudgy existence. Change the story, change your life, am I right? I've seen my sis in action. My tragic version will stir up such sadness and injustice, she'll fall into a consuming rage. Sis will go postal. And I'll channel those killer instincts toward Ronnie.

Sis sharpens her claws on Mom's emery board, filing each tip to a razor point. Crouched low, I see her slide out my apology note. *Sorry for the tail snipping incident. Got this special edition at the store for you. Friends?*

Greedily, sis pins back the title page, opens to page 1, and begins reading about how her hero Hog Badger is leaving surprises for the local posse.

〰

 Pointing his flashlight beam along the snowy forest trail behind the school, the posse leader halts. His armed troupe gathers around him. Caught in his spotlight is a six-foot, gutted beast, draped and lifeless across a blood-speckled snow pile.

"Wolves?" a man in a "Go Leafs" ball cap says, poking at the furry mound with his snowmobile boot.

"Too big. Look at all that gut flab," the leader replies.

"Cougars?" says another, tucking his shotgun barrel under his chin.

Who would do this? thinks Go Leafs. They've seen tragedy in their hills before—a group of three-legged racers downed by a toxic batch of pot-luck coleslaw at a family picnic — but nothing like this: a squat, flesh-coloured, woolly-looking mammal lies face down.

The leader boot-kicks the mound over, finds its huge belly is shredded.

"Damned Nocturnals," the posse leader shouts as he slides out the suspect's calling card: a mangled mouse tail tucked inside the envelope.

"Starts with rodents and roadkill, then they wipe out our whole family," a posse member says, staggering backward.

"Be trouble back in town if we don't waste one," Go Leafs agrees.

Hearing a rustling above them, a cluster of glassy-eyed posse stop. Cocking their rifles, they raise their barrels and take unsteady aim into the treetops.

Breathing hard above the treeline, Hog Badger raises his pig-like snout, smelling sweat and booze wafting up from below. He can't believe it. He's not the only small game in town. There are greedy, nastyass omnivores all over these woods. Why are they coming after him? Sliding along the slope edge, he escapes, burrowing under a snowbank, his nubby white ears vanishing into winter's night.

❦

Badger lays her book down with a chisel-toothed grin, marvelling at the updated story. I watch as, with her tiny tail tucked underneath her, big sis begins to coo. It's February, after all. Love month for badgers. She knows things will be heating up soon for her hero. In the next chapter, Hog Badger meets a sweet honey, makes cute badger babies. Hot, hot, hot!

Not.

Just wait for my exquisite plot shifts, I think. Badger's mood will plummet, her delicate hormones will dip in despair, and my mind-melding authorial control will begin. Shock and awe, baby. It'll be off the hook. She'll be so sad and vulnerable, I'll guide her into destroying Ronnie. Believe me, I'll be more powerful than any Sectoid Commander.

"Lights out," Mom calls out in a thin voice from her bedroom. She's been working two jobs, looking as broken-down and pale as Dad did before he died.

Badger pricks a rippled chip from the bowl. Squeezing her belly chub, sis lets out a low moan. She's put on a ton since summer. Curves in awkward places, extra tufts between her ears, always Daddy's little princess. Why bother to compete? Me, a thirteen-and-a-half-year-old male with advanced intellect, chicken-fed but scrawny. Badger, sixteen pounds of low-slung carnivore with a darling white head stripe. No contest.

"No one's gonna love me like this," Badger bawls, then buries her snout under the pillow. I feel a stab of pain in my chest, until she spikes another rippled chip from the bowl. Fatty.

Good. Now that her curiosity is piqued, and her sappy expectations are high, it's time to collect my thoughts in my man-memoir.

That's right. The narrative of a conquering hero. He's

the one who understands the cruel order of the universe and finds a way to put himself first.

Vexed: The Journal of Alex P. Jones, a Major Minor
Time to explore life's synchronicities, O Reader. We're bond-building now. I'm going to give it to you straight. Think life doesn't play favourites? You and I know that's a steaming crap taco with shit-flavoured salsa on top. I hauled garbage and cut lawns while Badger rototilled the backyard. I mastered Newton polynomials, while Badger bombarded the house with her butt juice and bad breath. Soon sis will be heartsore and mooning over her soppy book, while Ronnie's enemy line keeps on advancing. Lonely Street is the road we travel, O Reader. So try and keep up. The only journey for us is forward. Settle in, and sit up straight. We're on track to destroy Ronnie, with a little help from a pissy Badger.

At school on Thursday, Mr. Trask parks himself in front of my desk that is covered with glass beakers and a Bunsen burner, about to offer his dumbed-down science demo. I stand and watch. Amateur hour, as usual.

"Go ahead and light it, Alex," Trask urges me. Better known as Mr. Junk Science and rugby coach to Ronnie and his thugs.

All eyes are on me and the unlit Bunsen burner. Drawing the rusty old flint lighter, I squeeze. *Piff.* Again. *Piff.* Another flame-out. Insults and mockery erupt from the class.

"If you're too afraid to light it, Mr. Jones…" Trask snorts, making a big show of pulling out his personal spark lighter. Man's been gunning for me since I stumped him about compound melting points during the intermolecular-bonding-in-solids module presentation I made.

Vwoosh. The blue flame climbs, hot, luminous, like Suzie Brett and me at lunch. Atomic intensity. Now all of that's cooled, since Trask's rumoured "hands-on" experiments with Suzie. He offered her extra credit to help him set up for this Friday evening's science fair soirée. The subphylum sleaze.

When Trask moves on to his canned talk about combustion, Ronnie steps in front of me, and swings his arm back, smacking my crotch with his three-ring. I double over but manage to grab my steel ruler like a sword. The rugby lugs grab the ruler and gut me with their elbows. So when Trask looks away, I unscrew the liquid-filled baby-food jar I grab from my backpack. Trask glances over at me, snatches the jar away, giving it a sniff. Without a word, he confiscates my backpack, the jar, and orders me to the office.

You may have science, Trask, but I have nature. And she's about to get evil all over your ass.

Badger's in a mood when I get home. Irritable bowels. Cramps. I don't know; I don't care. She stinks. Mom instructs me to go straight to my cage after dinner. Now that Drudd has turned Badger into a shut-in, she needs more room to move. Fine, fine, I tell Mom, then crack the cage combo once she leaves for work.

I knock. Badger hisses. I barge in anyway, tell her to forget Ronnie for now and focus on Trask, who needs a good savaging in the school parking lot on Friday night. Use the full inch-and-a-half canines, I say. Go seriously subcutaneous on his ass.

Badger slumps against the radiator.

"Come on, sis. It's time to take out the Trask!" I nudge her with my foot. "Think of Mom. Trask has got me in trouble at school. Mom doesn't need any more grief. And think of all that fatty meat afterward."

Resting a paw on her chubby belly, she emits a foul smell so putrid it should be flammable. With one swipe, her curved claw leaves a trail of beaded blood across my wrist.

Like it's my fault she's tubbing up, forcing Mom to work overtime to keep us in groceries. Truth is, Badger's entering a state of torpor soon, Mom says, her body processes slowing down so she'll be able to survive on her own fat. I poke at Badger's belly chub with a pencil. She's going to slow down. We've got to act. I tell her if she bats Trask around for me on Friday evening after the school science fair soirée, she'll probably shed a pound or two. Badger bares her razor teeth, growling. I retreat to the doorway, where I watch as she cracks open my tragic Hog Badger tale.

Go ahead and read, sis. You'll get all worked up and nutty over life's cruel injustices and take it out on the world. Revenge is a dish best served hot-blooded.

I decide to slip back downstairs into the cage, grab my fine-tip black Sharpie, and air out the old man-memoir.

...

Vexed: The Journal of Alex P. Jones, a Major Minor
Survival of the male species? Perilous. Tonight it was
greens and gopher bits for Badger. Mac and cheese with
beefy franks for me, please, I asked Mom. No way, she
said. Wieners are made from emulsified meat and that's
gross. So Mom fixed me this heap of nutted pilaf. Here I
am on the doorstep of manhood and I'm stuck choking on
bird balls. Nothing but smog in my troposphere, I tell you.
Like all those SUV drivers tearing the ozone a new one.
They don't give a crap about me or anyone else. My head
is going freaking supernova. All I need is one night. One
explosive night in the suburbs. Trask and Badger will meet
this Friday, become an inseparable duo for one ravaging
instant that annihilates time. Are you paying attention?
Eyes on the page, and away from that viral video about the
tiny lemur eating a rice ball. Stick with me. We're gonna
raze this thing. Once Badger fully absorbs my version of
Hog Badger fantasy fiction, her own hero's journey is going
to stray far off course. And reign terror all over the long
winter's night.

Hearing Badger screech, I perk up. Better abandon your
expectations, sis. Let your eyes fall heavy on the page.
You're going to become incensed at the latest plot turn.
I've made sure of it.

Posse hunters hot on his tail, Hog Badger zigzags through the woods in search of his hillside hideout. Passing a shallow, frozen pond Hog Badger thinks he hears a hottie pop up behind a fallen log fringing the water. Approaching slowly, he lets out a throaty churr. She disappears beyond the wooded ridge.

It's a trap!

Fluffed up and hissing, the Nocturnals are staging a revolt. Coyote emerges, surrounded by wolverines and a sleepy Kit Fox. They corner Hog Badger, driving him against a plump blue spruce.

"You're reckless," Kit Fox barks at Hog Badger. "You put us all in jeopardy with your stupid antics the other night."

"So I slipped a mouse tail into a manila envelope on the trail. A lark! Just wanted to rile them all up. They're so dumb and twitchy when one of them goes down. Come on guys, I'm a lover not a fighter."

"What about the human kill?" rejoins Coyote. "Posse's after blood now that you've gutted one of their own."

 "My claws are dull as democrats," Hog Badger protests, showing off his blunt tips. "It wasn't me."

The Nocturnals press forward, jaws open and salivating.

"Seriously," Hog Badger pleads. "Could have been that greedy Woodchuck. Guy thinks everything is a joke. That squat fellow was already ravaged by the time I got there."

Coyote howls. Hearing the advancing posse approach, the Nocturnals scatter, leaving Hog Badger defenceless.

Pushed to the east by the advancing posse, hemmed in by the Nocturnals on the west, Hog Badger flees far north. Panting hard, he scurries in search of a new hillside hideout, far from the rifle shots and boozy breath. He knows the Nocturnals didn't buy his innocent act. They realize he's a ferocious hunter, has got a nose for blood and the anal glands of a shit-kicker. There's no returning to the life he had. There's a mark on his back, and he can't escape it.

❡

I hear a high-pitched scream upstairs, then the unmistakable sound of Badger sobbing. I slip out of my cage and sneak upstairs to my sister's door.

Sis makes this scary growl-click with her teeth.

"Where is the courtship, the canoodling?" she shrieks, sifting and shredding pages. "Where's his badger honey? All those suckling cubs!"

Sis claws at the pages in vain. "He'll be dumpster diving. Forced to live on cat food," she wails. And I scramble to a hiding spot down the hall, when I hear, "Oh merciless world," then the sound of a heavy object hitting her wall.

Once Badger has had the chance to calm down, I find

her rustling around in the kitchen. I stroll in to find sis stuffing her emotions.

"What's up, beast breath?" I say, casually pulling up a chair.

"Despair," she says, holding a bagful of houseflies. "Annihilation," she adds, and starts popping the insects in her mouth like peanuts. Sick.

"Yo, so sis, did I tell you? It was hot dog day in the caf today. Plenty of all-beef leftovers and chucked sunflower seeds to help you fill that void."

Badger moans.

"Check it out tonight. Caf is deserted on Thursday nights."

Sis snaps a fly head between her incisors. Not even paying attention to me.

So I turn up the volume. Tell her I visited Stempson's hardware store after school. Share how he rudely ignored my attempts to explain the importance of fractal geometry in building flame assault rocket launchers, after collaring me for stealing a cheap four-inch toilet flange hook-up. Then he spotted the four-foot length of PVC pipe I had stuffed into the back of my jeans. Along with a pilfered trigger assembly.

"So I go all Master of Disaster on him," I tell sis, doing a jumping kung fu kick by the stove.

Badger growls at me.

"Stempson's on the school board with Drudd, you know," I inform her. "Think they're conspiring to squeeze us out. Better gather some energy."

A hungry look crosses Badger's face.

"Wonder what that nastyass Hog Badger would do?" I say, lightly, elbow on the table, chin propped up with my fist.

Before I even have to remind her to bite Trask at the Friday night science fair soirée, she's shimmied up the living-room curtains to the windowsill. I race to the open window, see her plop down onto the driveway. Steam curls from the nostrils of her tipped-up nose. She's headed to the school to fill her belly with white buns and salty luncheon meat. Go ahead and mess up that school real good, sis. Just as every story needs the right set-up, every conquering hero needs a fall guy.

This chapter of my life is unfolding exactly as expected. The next one will set things right forever.

Mom is staring into the open fridge when I roll into the kitchen Friday afternoon to drop the urgent school notice on the table. She sets down her coffee cup and picks up the letter with the words "School Breach Last Night" typed in bold across the top.

Mom reads aloud, clicking her tongue about the break-in at school Thursday night. Food and garbage scattered. Vandals tore apart most of the furniture in the cafeteria.

Almost on cue, the phone rings. I hear Mom gasp on the line for several minutes. She hangs up and marches straight to Badger's room.

I trail at a stealthy distance.

Mom squats down, eyeballing Badger who is cowering under the bed. I crouch down behind Mom, out of sight.

"Mrs. Drudd called." Mom is rubbing her eyes. "You know, the woman who started this whole city eviction process *and* the head of the school board's safety committee." Mom waves the letter around, amid swirling dust bunnies. "They found some smudged five-toed prints around the vandalized cafeteria."

Badger slips further into shadow.

"I told you to stay indoors."

Badger's white head stripe is barely visible now.

"She wants you chained up like a common dog," Mom chokes up on the last bit.

Badger busts out from under the bed, hops up on the mattress, and burrows under the bedsheets before Mom can grab hold of her.

"They will drive us out," Mom says, her hands trembling.

Badger tunnels in deeper, purring anxiously.

"We're not done talking, Miss."

Mom checks her watch. From Mom's side of the call, I know she's got to attend the emergency meeting Drudd has called. The principal is up in arms. City manager's even showing up. School destruction will cost thousands to repair, and there's no more room in the budget. Someone will have to pay.

"Don't you move from this house tonight," Mom orders Badger, who is nothing but a lump of shame in Mom's throat right now.

To be a hero, I remind Mom on her way out to the emergency meeting that last month a family of raccoons snuck into the school through an open window in the boiler room. Who says it wasn't those ring-tailed, five-toed bandits making that mess in the caf? (Reasonable doubt, baby. It's a beautiful thing.)

Okay, so maybe I do feel a little sorry for sis. After Mom heads out to face Drudd, I stick around long enough to watch sis pull the faux romance novel off the night table, and dig into the story, her beady eyes wet with worry and regret.

⚘

Mating season has come and gone. No rest or love for the Hog Badger. Bony, half-starved, he rubs up against the trees, leaving his scent in an effort to lead astray the bloodthirsty posse. After a long fitful journey, Hog Badger stumbles upon an abandoned den and digs a hole at the entrance, large enough to trap passing prey. Settling inside for some uninterrupted sleep, he awakens to a grunting sound outside. A large, stumbling, six-foot furry mammal, reeking of smoked sausage, has tumbled into his trap. Famished, Hog Badger flies at the exposed throat and belly. As he sinks his canines again and again into the blood-matted fur, the desire to keep feasting consumes him. He trots further out and up into the hills. Under a full moon, the night clear and cold, he begins scouting for more prey, when multiple shotgun rounds blast out across the hills. Hog Badger stiffens and collapses, oozing blood from his long pink snout.

⚘

When I hear Badger's bedroom door slam shut, I crawl upstairs in semi-darkness and crack the door. Badger is looking out her window.

I know where sis will be headed. Despite my mother's warning, my lonely, love-starved carnivore will skitter into the cold to tame a hunger she can't name. She'll smell the buffet lineup at the school for the science fair soirée and be on Trask like flies on an outhouse turd. I better get moving right now.

From the coatroom of the science fair soirée, I watch Trask hold court before a long row of lame-ass project display boards. When I brush his shoulder in the moving crowd, I manage to slightly nick him with my penknife. He looks up, angry and confused, so I speed out the door with my coat over my arm, get hooked scrambling over the chain-link fence. I have to strip off my red T-shirt to get free. I drop down on the icy sidewalk, throw my coat on, and beat a path home. Once I slip inside my cage, I wipe off my greasy hands with a moist toilette.

Soon, Trask will be the last man to leave the science fair soirée. Badger will watch Trask head out to his car, get a faint whiff of blood, and sink her teeth into his juicy paunch. This is going to be awesome!

I sleep like a baby Friday night, so don't even hear Badger slip back in her room. My head is clear, my mind calm, when I get up early Saturday morning.

I fill up on a protein shake while Mom is doing the Saturday morning grocery run. A car door slams outside.

Shorty, in a too-tight blue uniform, and his partner Groucho emerge from their police car and ring the bell.

A serious incident at the school last night, the cop with the fuzzy moustache tells me at the door. "Alex, right? Is your mother at home?" Groucho asks, looking over my shoulder.

I shake my head. "How do you know my name?"

"Listen, son," he says, ignoring me, "the school will be closed on the weekend, no sports or extracurriculars, and probably Monday and Tuesday as well."

"Why?" I make a witless gesture, feigning ignorance.

"We found snow-dusted paw prints around a seriously wounded victim outside the school last night. Other prints lead up into the wooded trails. They're the same five-toed prints we found the night of the school vandalism," he says, and strains to look past me into the house.

"My sister's a roaming badger," I reply calmly, "what do you expect?"

A high-pitched chur emits from the kitchen. Hearing claw clicks across the floor, the officers barge past to find Badger eating blackberries at the kitchen table. When her white-striped face turns toward them, I see a bright berry hang from her lower lip. She slurps it up, scrambles down the chair, and breaks for the laundry room. The cops follow fast on her tail. I trail the cops, watching Badger dive under a stack of cotton sheets. Her white dorsal stripe disappears in a thick cotton blur, and her two round eyes poke back up. The tall one, I can tell, is fighting the urge to hold her and tickle her soft grey underbelly.

I stand at the doorway, ignored.

"Really hope you catch the guy who hurt our beloved

science teacher," I mutter while the cops are groping around for Badger, scooping up towels and underwear. "Bad luck for Trask," I continue out of earshot. "Did you know he threatened to assault a student? So what if that student brought little bit of solid fuel to class? Stuff was sealed in a baby-food jar. What's the big deal if this wunderkind was building a super cool DIY shoulder-fired rocket launcher to rid the world of vermin and miscreants like Ronnie and Trask? That's what men of action do. Truth is, Trask was weak willed and bummed out. Failed marriage. The recession. Global water crisis. All those IT jobs going overseas. Yes sirs, guess he finally ran out of hope. But honestly, who tears out his own throat with the tweezer apparatus? Anyway, I just hope Mr. Trask is in a better place right now. I mean, places."

Cops are too absorbed watching my sis burrow under a pile of fluffy pillowcases to listen. Badger pokes her head up from the basket. A silk pillowcase flap is draped across one dewy brown eye. The tall cop cocks his head, giving his moustache a tweak. Must be a dad.

Badger bolts down the hall and out the front door I've conveniently left ajar. Giving chase, the cops end up slip-sliding on the icy driveway, and both collapse into a heap behind their squad car.

"Hope she's okay in this freeze-up," the tall, mustachioed cop says, finding his feet. He turns toward me and wipes his hands.

"We just needed to ask her some questions. Mrs. Drudd from next door says she covers a lot of territory. There's a violent predator in our midst. And nobody knows the backwoods better."

"Sure, sure," I say, thinking Badger will be fine, as they drive off. These days, the winter is her best friend.

Vexed: The Memoir of Alex P. Jones, a Major Minor
Are the best years of my life ahead of me? It's a question I ponder when the Snickers crash hits me like a falling meteor. Dad believed things would always turn out for the best, but what good did that crap do us? He gave us a reason for hope. We got hosed. No one gets out alive. That's right, O Reader, stop believing in life's fiction and confront the flaming turd of truth. And don't just sit there dragging passively behind the plot. This is my memoir, my story, not some crappy drugstore novel where the clumsy action rises midway then dumps you on your ass. And stop foisting all your dreamy romantic resolutions on me, too. Your need for redemption is your own sad story. Who said that the past is a tapeworm, constantly growing, which I carry curled up inside me? Super gross. Forget it. You're pinned to my own progress now. So get in lockstep, O Reader. Are you a prisoner? Is this a cage? Are we imprisoned together? Hardly. We're all stuck in our own steel-reinforced cages after all.

Badger is busy heaving her unpleasant musk through the house when the cops return Saturday afternoon to deliver the news that the victim, Mr. Trask, didn't make it. As Mom and I stand shoulder to shoulder in the doorway, taking in the shocking news, she covers her mouth, while I blink away tears of joy.

From out of nowhere, Drudd lunges for me between the cops. "Badger's responsible, I can feel it in my bones."

"Boy's just lost his science teacher," Groucho orders, his arm shooting out to stop Drudd in her tracks.

I do my best tear-duct well-up. Drudd sputters on with her wild accusations while my mind drifts, contemplating spicy fries and supermodels, the antidote to everything at my age.

"We'll handle this, ma'am," says the tall officer who escorts her back across the street.

Yep, Trask should have known. If you're the last guy out after the science fair soirée on Friday, you'd better check your pockets for a coil of blood sausage and your forearm for a slight nick. And if in your haste to get home, you stumble into a freshly dug, hip-deep hole near your shitty minivan, you'll probably end up with a nasty groin injury. And if a limping man in the pitch-dark with a pocket full of blood sausage is mistaken by a tormented, lovesick, far-sighted member of the family *Mustelidae* (née Badger Jones) for prey, he might find himself face to face with his own mortality.

And I wonder if, in his final, ravaged seconds, Trask stopped to examine his pitiful life. Before his body drained of excess cellulite, assorted platelets, plasma, and hemoglobin, did he ponder his role in escalating this conflict? Bogus A grades for rugby jocks. All those rumoured hands-on experiments with Suzie. In his final hour, did he crave redemption? Absolution? Contemplate life beyond the grave? In his spiritually barren stupor, did he even wonder what comes next?

One down. More enemies to go. Sunday morning I am eating my favourite toasted honey-and-bacon sandwiches in the cage when, through the vent, I hear Badger moaning softly in her room.

Mom is still in bed, exhausted after this latest turn of events. Drudd is keeping the town on edge. Badger is omnivore suspect number one in her view, but there's no substantial proof. Sis has been roaming for weeks around these parts without any serious human incidents, plus the prints were already compromised by snowfall. We've been back and forth to the station to tell our story. Without hard evidence linking sis to the killing, no arrest can be warranted. Even so, we've heard a rumour that Drudd is threatening to form a vigilante team to haul Badger in.

So when I hear the doorbell ring after eating my sandwich, I figure it's just crazy Drudd about to go off on me again.

I open up. Groucho Marx cop apologizes for the early hour.

"My mom's still sleeping," I tell him. "She's really stressed out. No thanks to you guys."

Keeping his voice low, Groucho says, "I'm sorry, son, but we've found more evidence at the crime scene."

Watching me carefully, he hands me a lumpy manila envelope. I reach inside, pull out a length of torn left sleeve and collar from my red Dengue Fever T-shirt. Damned chain-link fence!

"Lab says there are trace blood stains on it," the cop tells me. "I'm afraid they belong to the deceased, Mr. Trask."

"Cuff the boy! Cuff the badger!" Drudd rages from down the driveway, her arms waving madly. She starts blasting accusations, advancing on us at the doorway. "I was at school with the safety inspectors. Ronnie said he spotted you lurking in the coatroom on Friday night. Said you hopped a fence wearing a red Dengue Fever shirt!"

Groucho pulls her away from me.

I sniffle. Try to look meek and wide-eyed. "Dengue Fever is totally mainstream. Sick jams. Everyone at school's into them." I hand the torn fabric back to the cop. "Not even mine."

"Monster!" Drudd shouts.

The cop orders her back home, but I can hear her pounding on the door when Groucho steps back in, saying, "Look, son, I have to ask. Where were you Friday, the night of the science fair soirée?"

Vexed: The Memoir of Alex P. Jones, a Major Minor
Tired. Sore. Like I've got a head full of flu glue. Did you get
breathless, too, running upstairs to answer the door with
me just now? Did your heart seize when that cop slapped
the manila envelope in my hand? Dispel every thought, O
Reader, you might have of failure. I've built stink grenades

from hairspray, shot rockets through mini malls. Maybe, O Reader, you're sitting on a cramped bus, thinking, when is that boy gonna get past the blowing-up-shit phase of his life? Feel me? Our simultaneous desires are mingling. Right now, you are crossing that artificial turf, watching the action unfold beneath a zing of electric lights. I can hear you breathing with me, O Reader. Without my strong, reassuring presence, you're helpless, like some sucker waking from a dream, the image lost again the instant it appears. Here's what I remember: Dad was flat on his back, eyelashes gone, head bald, tubes going everywhere. They had cooked his insides with chemicals until his mouth was too raw to speak. Then they marked him up, tattooed his skin, shot him up with radiation. Cancer ate him away anyway. Life after was a tunnel none of us could see through. Mom moved us to the suburbs, scaled things back to keep us afloat. So go ahead, cue the violins, brace for a shitstorm, and stop believing in the warm-and-tinglies. Like Badger discovered, it's gonna hurt you in the end.

Mom is frantic. Police call her on Monday to say they have found a second set of DNA on the Dengue Fever T-shirt fabric. Cops are asking me to volunteer a strand of my hair to test it tomorrow. All the local teens are being tested, but mine is top priority.

Mom's sister from Winnipeg has decided to fly in to help Mom through the latest family crisis. I take advantage of her distraction.

We've got to act now, I'll tell Badger. Share how Ronnie

is trying to frame me for Trask. There's only one move left. Dead men can't talk. Ronnie needs a prompt exit, and we can set him up as the one who ravaged Trask.

When I slip upstairs to share my plan, I find sis in her room, clawing apart her romance-turned-horror novel page by page, even gnawing on bits of book spine.

"Nothing matters," I hear her sniffle, followed by another loud ripping sound.

While she's pricking and pulling apart the last chapter — my triumphant third act Hog Badger death sprawl — Badger lets out a piercing cry. Glued to the back spine is a thick wad of extra pages.

"An epilogue!" Badger screeches with delight

Shit. I didn't check when I doctored the updated version. Not even I saw that coming.

"Yee-ka-ka-ka-ka-k-Yaa," the eagles cry, circling high above the posse, who are boot marching toward their bloodied kill. "Our hills are free of the Hog Badger," the men chant in unison. Dazed, listless, Hog Badger hears the faint sound of snowmobile boot crunching and lifts his head. He's not even hurt. Snout up, he inhales the odour of cheap whiskey and rolls around in the snow to wipe his chin of the blood from his earlier kill. Looking for a defensive weapon, Hog Badger digs through his den. Finding nothing, he roots around the fallen beast outside, locating something he remembers flashing below the blood-matted fur.

A spark lighter.

No one will expect a winter forest fire, he thinks, rubbing flint across steel. All I need is a spark.

❦

"He's alive!" Badger shrieks. From my cage, I can hear her drop her book to the floor.

No. No. No! If Badger loses that fury and fire in her belly, she won't destroy the evil snitch Ronnie and eliminate nosy Drudd for good. It's Monday, and the cops want to test my DNA tomorrow.

Time for plan B.

Ronnie and his rugby boys will be eating at their usual pizza place tonight. When they're walking home, around ten, I'll swoop down and blast them with two pounds of ground round. Badger will catch the meaty scent and be feasting on those bad boys by midnight.

Mom is so wiped out, she'll sleep right through it. I'll leave a garden claw in Ronnie's hands, then tuck a suicide note inside a manila envelope.

Good. I've got Superglue, enough blowback-action to split a tree stump.

I'm rocket ready. Except, no manual trigger thanks to Stemple!

Never mind. Got the flint lighter from science class. Got a surly sis with a fat complex and a fierce overbite. Spark. Smoke. Boom!

Slipping upstairs, I find Badger quietly purring in the hallway. It's freezing out, and there's a gust of wind coming down the hall. Before I can unleash on her about killing Ronnie, Badger's beady eyes shoot me a fierce, shut-your-trap look.

She gestures toward the front door that's been blown open and says Mom is sleeping soundly for the first time in weeks, so get my scrawny butt into the hall and shut it.

Okay, okay, just to keep sis on side, I go.

Melty snowflakes are blowing in, forming penny-sized puddles on the hardwood. The wind gusts in, and hail strikes my cheek when I reach out for the doorknob. Around it hang the remains of my red Dengue Fever T-shirt. The one the cops found at the scene.

Badger clicks up behind me and cocks her head, all sassy like. She's sporting her I-knew-you-were-up-to-something-all-along face.

"Gimme," I snarl. "How'd you get that?"

Badger just bares her teeth.

In a flash, she's gone and returned with the rest of my T-shirt clenched between her jaws. She is sawing at both the torn sleeve and the rest of the fabric with her poky incisors. Bits of collar poke out of her mouth before she ends up turning the entire T-shirt into an unrecognizable, saliva-soaked mess. Finally she trots up to me and spits out the gooey pulp at my feet.

For fun, Badger gives my ankle a nip.

Sis has been protecting *me*?

A slow, aching sadness crawls from my gut to my stopped throat. I can't find any words.

Looking at my sis, I think back to the day my parents found her freezing and emaciated in a back field, brought her home wrapped in towels. Sure I whined about competing attention, but I came around. I'd bury yard mice and voles in the backyard, she'd find them, and we'd do it all over again. Dad chased her around, buried her droppings, loved her like crazy. Maybe I did blame her when he got sick two years later.

Sis is dew-eyed, too, as we stand facing each other for a long time. Night falls and we're still standing there, listening to our mother's breathing, soothed by her long, restful sleep. When Badger finally nods to me in the hallway, I grab my ski jacket and we step outside.

The moon is a pinprick in Badger's eyes as we travel across town, tromp along the snow-packed school field, and head up into the wooded trails, on to where the forest grows silent and dim.

In the pitch-darkness, we make our way to a clearing and lie flat on our backs, spewing vapour clouds from our mouths. Gleeful, we make *zwish, zwish* sounds as our legs and arms wing back and forth against the packed snow.

Night angels, O Reader.

In the gathering darkness, look up high. See the tree branches bow, their limbs muscled with snow.

You, stretched out on the couch or plumped up on your bed with a back pillow and your big expectations of what's to come.

Listen. Let your body sink into the soft, snowy night.

Yes, I'm talking to you.

Keep your spine flat, your legs and arms loose, keep sweeping the ground. There. Feel that snap of cold on your cheeks. Taste the lingering sweetness in the whiff of pine-scented woods. Look higher. Count the soft-glowing river of stars. See the bright planets, like dazzling dots hovering high above the horizon. There's Venus. There's Mars.

Relax. Concentrate. Listen.

You're tired of being left alone in the dark.

In the dissolving moonlight, under a starry wilderness, the only thing that matters now is to continue reading. Don't let your attention shift. The fragments and fallen crumbs will pull you apart, may abandon you in places. Read on. The good part is coming.

Monsoon Season

Monsoon rains will flood the main roads by fall, but it's early June when Jess lies bloated and raw in bed six on a shared ward of Phuket International Hospital.

Morning rounds, four days after surgery. Dr. Jemjai arrives, bending from the waist, palms open, the way a magician reveals he has nothing to hide.

"Any pain today, Jess?"

She feels like a slow-tortured French prisoner in some noir European thriller, a brooding smile pinned to her mouth.

"Like someone just shoved a pickaxe up my pelvis."

"Let's have a look," Dr. Jemjai says.

Gently, he probes her abdomen, a two-fingered touch as if patting down a row of garden seeds.

"Stop." His hands too close to her hipbone. "Please."

When he lifts her gown to peel away the dressing, her stitches are bloodied. She feels wetness spreading beneath her bottom, imagines copper-coloured stains seeping through to the cotton sheets below.

Finally, he nods to her. She breathes deep. "Wait," she says. Deep inhale again. She closes her eyes while she slides two tight fists beneath the sheets. He parts her legs, checks the stent in her swollen vagina.

She is a fucking French crêpe, folded in two. Pain radiates from her bowels, her stomach, oozes out between her teeth.

He orders the nurse to push morphine.

"Any bowel movements?"

The nurse replies *suai*, shaking her head.

Jess knows *suai* means either bad luck or beautiful, depending on the rising or falling tone. Her bowels were fabulous from the sphincter up but never beautiful.

Jess forecasts the well-researched negative outcomes in her head. A rip? Necrosis, slow tissue death, choking off her blood supply? No. An infection crawling in, ten days before her scheduled flight back to Toronto.

She thinks about her life before the doctor. Lost girl in a death march, then the collapse. Has he just split her body apart, or sewn it together?

"When will you know?" Jess asks, pressing his hand.

"Tomorrow," Dr. Jemjai replies, patting her wrist. "We'll see tomorrow."

On her first day at the Thai guest house, Jess awakened, cotton-mouthed, dry heaving into a wicker basket beside the bed. A knock forced her to her feet.

"Feeling o-kay today, Miss?"

It was the pretty Thai hostess last night who had checked her in. No, she was not okay. Definitely not. The long flight. Bloated stomach. Her whole body in a sweaty revolt from the inflight meal. She felt like ... What was the Thai word? *Khee nok*: bird shit.

She accepted the bamboo tray carrying a bowl of clear soup, little slivers of ginger floating on top. The tingling warmth settled her roiling stomach. She slept heavily into the afternoon, awaking in time to accept an invitation to join the others downstairs for cake.

Trailing the succulent scent of sliced coconut, Jess made her way downstairs. She glanced in at the formal dining room that looked out onto a circular reflecting pool sprouting lotus flowers. A dark teak table stood in the centre, framed by three walls, all lined with silk-cushioned wooden benches.

Once she stepped inside, a seated woman rose at the far end of the table. She held her hand out, introducing herself as Fran Günter.

"I'm from Stuttgart, it's in the south," Fran said, her square, pink face sitting on her neck like the rubber tip of a pencil. Fran's tone prompted Jess to straighten her spine. When Fran gestured for her to sit closer, Jess pressed her eyelid to stop its nervous jitter.

A third guest arrived, introducing herself as Jo-Ann, an American from Virginia.

"Call me Jo-Jo."

"I'm Fran Günter. This is Jess."

"So when do you all go under?" Jo-Jo inquired, without waiting for the answer. "I'm going on a Phang Nga Bay cruise with my lover, we'll tour the temples. Ten days later," Jo-Jo smiled, stretching her vowels, "everything changes."

Jess wedged her hands farther down between her thighs.

Just then, the young hostess arrived, laying out tea and coconut cake on gold-rimmed plates, followed closely by a tall Thai woman in a tight-fitting turquoise dress.

From her magnificent high-heel tower, the tall woman smiled, did a full twirl so a river of cinnamon hair plunged between her shoulder blades. Her long legs draped to a perfect patent-leather point on the floor. Between them, Jess saw not a bump or bulge.

"I'm Lydia," she said, and her hands floated up to her fine-boned cheeks. "Look at you. I'm so happy you're all here. Welcome to Dr. Jemjai's Guest House."

"You're gorgeous," Jo-Jo blurted out.

Jess snorted, muffling her mouth with the cloth napkin. She leaned forward, in love with Lydia's heart-shaped mouth. Though the pills had softened Jess's face, swept with dark bangs to soften her harsh jawline, next to Lydia's beatific beauty, she was a gorilla in the mist.

"Where are you from?" Jess asked.

"Suphan Buri," Lydia smiled. "A farm in Central Thailand."

Lydia told them that when her family's rice crops were ruined by swarms of plant hoppers, she went to work in the Bangkok bars. The first year she managed to send enough money back home to save the paddy fields. Four more seasons of rice-stem borers and the only way to help her family survive was to stay. She met Dr. Jemjai at a lecture he was giving on best practices in Thailand's gender reassignment clinics.

"I walked right up to him, told him that a monk had told my father that I would bring the family honour as a girl. He offered to perform my surgery if I could help him run the guest house. That was five years ago."

Fran cleared her throat. "My father ran coal mines in the Ruhr Valley." She made a gesture of wiping her hands clean.

Hating the bleak mines, she pursued a career in journalism as Arnt Werden. When she was exposed as the son of a wealthy German family, her disgraced parents tried to chase her off with hush money.

"Did you run?" Jess asked.

"In these heels?" Fran joked, pointing to her slingbacks. "I took an assignment covering exploited migrant workers from Cambodia and ended up wandering into a field of orchids in Doi Saket. They grow cattleya hybrids. Lavender-blue orchids with frilly petals and slate-blue lips. Vivid blue lips, can you imagine?"

Jess took a slate-blue bite of her coconut cake, felt the petals fall to her feet.

"I saw poor workers struggling in the fields. Violence in factories," Fran said, keeping a hand on her chest. "Why should I hide? For myself, I had everything."

Jess thought of the working girls at the bar and Robbie pouring out free shots for them on Fridays. Fringed with feathers, Robbie's face beamed behind the bar when she told them to put their suffering on a layaway plan and lit up a glowing row of B-52s. God it was so easy to fall in love with Robbie, Jess thought.

Despite years of vitamins, hormones, liposuction, and laser therapy, Jess had never held a real lover. A crude, midnight circle of one-night stands, sure. Men who'd fuck anything in a short skirt, yes. She was their shape-shifting, Queen Street trannie. Fuckable. Transgressive. Freak. Subject, object, verb. No agreement.

"We're all works in progress, right?" Jo-Jo said and touched the bridge of what Jess could tell was an expensive aquiline nose.

"Okay, ladies," Lydia said rising. "I know you're excited. Maybe a little scared of the dilations, the diarrhea…"

"Shoving a shunt up our cunts," Jo-Jo added, then turned to Jess and shuddered. "Twice a day? Nasty."

Lydia wagged a telling finger at them. "But what the girls usually want to ask is, Will my coochie make me come?"

"I want a vagina, like any woman," Fran interjected.

"Like Eamy, that sweet Thai Ladyboy who made up my face at that Boots makeup counter. Said her old Swedish boyfriend paid for her boobs."

Lydia folded her napkin twice. "Some *kathoey* stay with the *farang* for money. That's how they can afford to live and talk like women."

"Well, I say if every fuck is closer to losing the prick, lose the prick at any price," Jo-Jo chimed in.

Jess felt as if a long knife trimmed her soul. She was all concealer and three-layer cover-up, pencilling her lips to erase the rough outer edges of her life. Still, she bled. Robbie was gone, probably for good. Toronto was an indifferent stranger.

While they chatted, she mentally extracted her organs and laid them out on the table. Heart, lungs, spleen, liver, plopped down and seeping. She counted each one then tucked them back beneath her skin. Okay. There. She was all there.

Lydia stood, apologizing for an early exit. She urged them to keep talking. And not to be shy about exploring their vaginas—how they fold, curve, contract.

"Keep taking your meds," Lydia advised, turning back. "The pills will play tricks in your head, but remember you're already brave enough."

For days, Jess and Fran lingered around the reflecting pool, taking short dips, mapping out a year-after reunion in Europe. Fran insisted Jess return to bathe in the Andaman Sea. She knew the owners of a beachfront bungalow, and they could stay there for free.

That night Jess dreamt she was wading out in sheltered Kata Noi Bay beach. Black clouds rolled in, the wind whipped up, battering the palm trees, bent and shivering toward the sea. She drifted out, the tide flooding her ears, she flailed, swallowed waves, then the scene went black.

When her body surfaced, it wore her mother, Margaret's, face.

Nine days after surgery, there are forms to sign. Prescriptions packed in a neat white sack. Jess waves goodbye to the orderly who slips a rubber doughnut beneath her bottom and wheels her to where Dr. Jemjai is waiting in the hospital ambulance bay. On the way, they pass a billboard featuring two Thai nurses in tuck-waist dresses with white winged caps. "Phuket. Let your baby be born in paradise."

Paradise Lost, Jess thinks. Satan wore a satin lace teddy; the serpent slithered inside to keep warm. Pandemonium!

Dr. Jemjai gives Jess a reassuring smile, while two attendants lift her into the back of the waiting ambulance.

It will be a short hop from Phuket International to Bangkok, then an overnight stay for the early morning long-haul flight back to Toronto.

Climbing into the back of the ambulance, Dr. Jemjai tucks a note inside her carry-on.

"For your physician in Toronto."

Jess tilts her head toward him. When he holds his hand out, she closes her eyes, allows her cheek to fall heavy in his hands.

"Drink more water than you want to," he says. "Use the creams. If your legs become tender or swollen, seek medical help. Immediately."

Jess takes hold of his wrist.

"I can't feel anything below the waist," she admits.

"Good," he says, shutting the double doors behind him.

Wisps of cigarette smoke twine through Margaret's nest of curly grey hair. She picks up the old red kitchen phone with the annoying buzz. The line is crackly, but she doesn't dare hang up.

"Terry?" she repeats, hears a murmuring crowd at the end of the line.

"Yes, I'm at Bangkok airport."

Margaret presses the phone harder against her ear, feeling her chest tighten. She has lived through teen turmoil, his tough-on-the-outside talk, but the voice. Her son's low tenor is now soprano smooth. Not soft on the vowels, not a lilt, but a young woman's voice. A gun flash. The moment her son goes missing.

"What happened?"

"Didn't you get my postcard?"

Player's Light dangling between her fingers, Margaret walks over to the refrigerator.

Greetings from Phuket. She turns the card over.

Hi. I'm in Thailand. There are stray dogs everywhere. One lady went out to rescue a lab from a flooded water buffalo field. She got so sick a few days later they had to cut her legs off. Not the dog, the woman.
P.S. Sorry for the long disappearance.

Margaret reads and remembers Terry, only seven years old the night she got the emergency call. An older German shepherd hit by a tow truck. Could she come? Harold was away again on business, wouldn't be home for a few days. Margaret tucked her son, with a juice box, in the back seat of her Datsun, and off they sped to the clinic.

A young couple was cradling their battered dog in a sleeping bag when she arrived. He was cut straight through the underbelly, a ragged slice from gullet to mid-stomach. Her hands were shaking when she placed the dog on the gurney to examine him.

She found Terry a blanket and tucked it around him on a sofa in another office.

It wasn't long before she led the owners back to her surgery to break the news. The shepherd's head was tilted sidewise on the table, a draped sheet across his lacerated gut. The bereft couple retreated to their car while Margaret shaved the dog's leg and filled the syringe. Her sleepy son ambled in at some point, pawing his eyes, refused to leave. Margaret pulled the sheet around the dog, laid him sideways on the fleece-lined sleeping bag she spread across their laps. Terry found one of the dog's paws and held it in his small hands. He stroked the fur tufts above the collar.

Margaret cooed, "Good boy, you'll always be loved."

Even after needle pierced skin, when the shepherd's breath grew faint, through the last muscle twitch, her son held on.

"My postcard? Did you get it?" the voice, a stranger on the line, asks.

"Yes," she says, folding the postcard in half. Margaret expels a sharp plume of smoke through her nose. "Are you in trouble?"

"Had surgery. There were complications."

"Oh my God, Terry. Are you all right?"

Silence.

She thinks about when Terry stopped talking altogether. He was thin and twelve and being shoved and boot-wedged into school lockers. Margaret temporarily exchanged her vet's licence for a recipe box, sent him to school with

fresh-baked banana bread. At home, her life became sens-
ible, Saran-sealed. Terry seemed happier, Harold more
rooted, staying at home for longer stretches between work
trips.

They found crack in Terry's room at sixteen. He was selling, not smoking, he swore up and down, but they didn't
believe him. By then he was wearing off-the-shoulder black
T-shirts, a David Bowie glitter phase that left him bloodied
at school.

One night Harold arrived home from an underwriter
conference, took the red-eye back to get an early start on
the weekend. He found Terry making out with another boy
on the basement couch, their freckled backs covered in bites
and scratches. The boy with Terry had flushed skin, red rings
around his eyes. Out of his mind.

Harold erupted, ordered his drug pushing, punk-rock
glitter girl out.

Terry pitched his clothes in a suitcase. Margaret had no
more energy to stop it.

Margaret taps the spoon against the rim of her coffee
cup. "What's going on?" she demands, drawing smoke up
through her lungs, holding the burn.

"Will you come?"

"I'm your mother," Margret replies, firmly. She hears
Harold's car pulling up the driveway; a car door slam.

"Yes, you gave me life and intermittent asthma. What I
need now is a pickup at Pearson."

Margaret dumps a saucer into the sink. She takes a deep
breath. "I'll borrow Emma's car. Mine's kaput."

"What about Harold's Lincoln?"

The doorbell rings.

"It's easier this way, Terry, believe me," she says, walking over to the front door. She pulls back the sheers to watch Harold in the driveway. Margaret glares when he slams the trunk, balancing a load of empty moving boxes he'll use to haul out the remains of their twenty-eight-year marriage.

"Thai Airways, flight 783. Two p.m. tomorrow."

"Hang on, hang on, Terry. Someone's at the door."

The doorbell rings and rings, a sharp, quick, staccato rhythm.

"Stubborn bastard," Margaret mutters and then, muffling the phone in her hand, mouths through the side window, You're late, at her soon-to-be ex-husband. She watches Harold jiggle the doorknob furiously.

"Shouldn't you be writing this down?" Jess says.

"No, got it. Thai Airways, 783. See you at the airport, Terry." Margaret hangs up. She stands, watching Harold struggle with the knob, then slowly slides the front-door bolt back, leaving the chain.

The next day Margaret searches the arrivals sign at Pearson. She finds the baggage claim and watches for a half hour as impatient travellers tow away the last of their luggage.

She circles the empty conveyor then reverses her orbit, looking in vain for Terry.

God, she could use a cigarette. She checks her watch again. What version of Terry will she see? Her brilliant drop-out with the sleepy hazel eyes? Her baby-faced son with the beautiful, long lashes?

The passengers stream by. Terry is nowhere. Finally, a flight attendant taps Margaret on the shoulder, delivering Jess in her wheelchair.

Terry's eyes are sunken back, his thin face is pallid. Margaret looks him over then nods to the attendant. She bends down to meet her son's eyes.

"I'm okay," Terry says, his voice breaking.

Margaret examines Terry's long hair. Beneath his stretchy, apple-green sweater, her son has breasts.

Terry tries to push himself up from the wheelchair. Margaret hooks her arm around his waist to steady him. Weakly, he stands, but his eyes roll back. He goes limp in her arms.

The last thing Jess recalls before blacking out is a German shepherd riding the airport escalator.

She awakens on a futon in Harold's office, minus the desk, filing cabinets, and Harold. Margaret stands over Jess, holding a small silver tray with a single mug of black coffee and two tea biscuits on a side saucer.

"What have you done?" she says, dropping the folded note with Dr. Jemjai's medical instructions on the tray beside Jess.

Jess tries to sit up. She can't begin to say.

"What happened to you in Phuket?" Margaret shouts, turns, and bangs her way back down to the kitchen.

Jess pulls her feet over the mattress, rises from the bed, taking short, deliberate steps down stairs to the kitchen.

Margaret is pouring the dregs of the coffee pot into a

chipped ceramic cup. She takes one sip and dumps the rest down the drain.

Jess pulls out a chair, about to sit, then thinks better of it, afraid to rest without her rubber doughnut.

"I should have called."

Margaret lets her hands fly. "You know, I always thought you were gay. You hated those ruffians next door and played around with my eye makeup. But this is … this is …" Margaret gestures wildly in Jess's direction.

"Sick?" Jess offers.

"Extreme. Even for you."

A wave of nausea hits. Jess feels her head tilt back, the room pitch forward. She steadies herself on the chair back.

"Well, at least your father's not here," Margaret says, tossing her toast crusts into the garbage. "He wouldn't survive it."

"Left?"

Margaret nods. "Sat there, took out a spoon, and started pile-driving his oatmeal back and forth. Finally told me it was all over. Packed two suitcases and vamoose."

Jess feels liquid trickling down her left leg. Blood? Urine?

"I'm sorry."

Her mother is glaring. "Harold leaves, you come back as Cher. Think that makes you a woman?" She blots her mascara with a tissue from her sleeve.

Jess feels a sharp ache spasm up her inner thighs.

"Gonna need some time with this, Terry."

"It's Jess now."

Margaret rips apart her wet tissue. "Jeeesus Christ."

"Give me a week, then I'll go," Jess offers.

"You stay, I'll go," Margaret replies, tearily exiting the kitchen.

It's the same goddamn tragic farce, muses Jess, mumbling. Martyr Mother: a one-act drama. Margaret played all the parts.

Jess manages to avoid her mother for almost two weeks. They are magnetic poles: she in Harold's office, her mother at the movies, she upstairs, Margaret out for groceries. Each of them following their true north, pointing anywhere but home.

She was the boy Margaret and Harold had raised. An only child. The product of unconditional love and pure sacrifice, Jess thought. Or maybe love was just an idea. Not just about what you could see, feel, and touch. Love had conditions. Love stormed into rooms, demanding answers. Fed on wild expectations, love was always starving, afraid to lose out. Maybe Robbie was right, she thought. Love was the greediest bastard she knew.

With the house to herself all day, Jess closes the bathroom door behind her. Butt sore on the toilet, flipping through her instruction sheets, she takes the dilator in her sticky hands. Jess thinks then about her how her hands shook the first time she dialled Dr. Jemjai in Phuket. He told her he could make her *Neo-Vagina* look any way she wanted. He could emphasize the lips, so her *Neo-Vagina* would resemble a pouting face. Did he really say pouting face? His assistant sent her links. She clicked and cried, her palms tacky seeing the before and after. The transformations were clinical, remarkable, but the patient faces remained hidden. Blocked out, bodies detached, like they were caught in a criminal act. She knew all about trespasses. What about the bloody resurrection?

The great burden of her body rushed through her life like metastatic tissue. One organ, spreading to the rest of her parts. She was the penis in a one-act play. Had a penis personality. A penis future. Hostage to an abnormal cell, her body cut and cut again, splitting her in two. Female, or male? What if you were a morphologic mistake? she thought. What if you were more?

She was in a dream when she spoke to Dr. Jemjai the second time. Vaginoplasty, clitoroplasty, and labiaplasty had come a long way, he explained. Moist, elastic, hairless — these were the benchmarks of his profession now. He spoke about flaps and grafts and good vascularity. A hot blush washed over her cheeks when he told her the internal erectile tissues would leave her with orgasmic capabilities. He would leave the prostate intact, to preserve the clit's spasm, keep the throb alive. The diagrams he sent looked like the tampon instructions she read as a boy with delighted horror in her mother's bathroom. She saved money, accepted a loan from Robbie, and when everything fell apart at the bar months later, finally booked a flight.

Dr. Jemjai's office had sent materials, carefully walked her through each step. The doctor would take grafts from her scrotal sack, remove the testes, and invert skin from her penis, saving the nerve bundles for sensation. A penile inversion with flap technique. Her *Neo-Vagina* would be totally normal. Stop, she told him. No more technical specs. She wanted to hold onto the word *Neo-Vagina*. Turn it over on her tongue. An unexpected ache swept through her. Her head and heart couldn't catch up.

Legs splayed like a Russian gymnast, Jess takes a deep breath on the toilet. Knees spread, fingers slick, she works her way inside. Holding her dilator like a pen, she lubes the tip, holding it at a downward angle. She double-checks the angle in the pocket mirror. Careful, she says, spreading her labia, pushing the dilator gently along the gummy pink wall, every quarter inch a miracle. She removes it again. Don't force it, she thinks, just relax. Probing depth and diameter, the dilator disappears a little deeper, filling Jess with elation and fear. Will she tear up, bleed out if she pushes too hard? She checks the depth mark. Another half inch. Progress. In a few months, she'll work her way up to the six-inch dilator. Here's the measure of a life. Inches give her meaning. It's been over four weeks since her surgery—a lifetime since she shared Dr. Jemjai's guest house with Fran.

Her pants bunched around her ankles, she gently removes the dilator. Pressing her knees together, her whole body convulses, thinking about Fran. Is she on her own? Is she folded up in some grass-roof bungalow praying for morphine? They had tried to speak twice a week since the surgery, always with Margaret out of earshot.

They had joked about it, but each already knew the answer.

"No. Do you miss a lung tumour?"

"No. Do you miss acid-wash jeans?"

The penis was passé. *Neo-Vaginas* were about to take off, Jess said, cheering Fran up after a bad patch of spotting.

On the spot, she made up commercials in a TV pitchman voice Fran loved.

Need a flawless look for that exotic Berlin clubbing? Try Neo-Vagina. It's like lipstick between your legs!

Try the racy new Neo-Vagina. German-engineered perfection under the hooded flap.

Back in their Thai guest house, they'd planned a one-year-after celebration to parade their post-op, post-modern chic right down the Champs-Élysées. When Fran decided to get a tracheal shave, the calls stopped. Jess consoled herself, thinking that even with a local anesthetic, Fran could be raspy and hoarse for a long time.

Standing up, Jess feels a sudden fullness below her waist. Her legs are weak. Are they swollen? Oh God. No. Her breath accelerates. Can't. Get. Enough air. In.

Pulling up her pants, she heads for Harold's office, picks up the phone. She starts to dial 911, hyperventilating.

"Terry?" Margaret enters the room with her shoes on and a bag of groceries.

"A clot!" Jess bursts out.

"Not likely," Margaret says, taking the receiver from her hand.

"False alarm," she says calmly into the phone. "Bye-bye now, operator."

She settles Jess back onto the bed. "Breathe in through the nose for two, out through the mouth for two."

Jess tries to speak but her mother gestures to keep still.

Margaret makes a show of filling her own lungs. Jess extends her arms out, beginning to cry.

"It's anxiety. Terriers are terrible for it. A Jack Russell once bit off my fingertip when I snapped my clipboard too close."

Margaret begins rubbing her son's shoulders. "Your father had them too. Anxiety attacks. So bad I got him to wear a rubber band." Margaret points to a spot on Jess's wrist. "Nasty client email. *Snap*. Prostate rash. *Snap. Snap*."

Jess laughs.

"You're all right now," Margaret repeats, and rubs her son's back in slow circles.

Jess feels her entire body go slack, wanting nothing more than to curl up in her mother's arms.

"You're all right," Margaret says, in a soothing tone.

Jess presses her palm to her racing chest.

"Okay," Margaret rises abruptly. "Girls are coming over for bridge tonight. Make yourself scarce. We wrap up at eleven."

"I'm sorry," Jess says, holding her breath.

"It's all right," Margaret answers. "You'll be on your own soon anyway."

Disappearances. Jess is used to them, she thinks. Especially in five-floor mazes like this one, where salespeople make brisk, efficient escapes whenever she comes near. *Attention shoppers: Grotesque mistake in women's privates, plus two-for-one on ladies low-rise thongs.*

She remembers how a security guard once escorted

her out from the mall after a senior pitched her purse at her in the women's change room. Seeing her on the escalator, teenage boys pointed, fist-pounding each other. Men glared, reddened faces overcome by the unexpected. Ravaging. Bitter. Monsoon.

A boy stands on a white sandy beach next to his dog, which is snapping at waves. Cool air rushes inland, the wind shifts, heavy rains begin pounding the shore. A boy is there; suddenly, he's gone, the tide sweeps him away. No one goes in after him, Jess thinks.

She pops the stand-up collar on her sunflower-coloured cotton polo, smooths out her scarf, and wades into sale racks. Two more weeks without setbacks. Cinderella has lost her balls, now she needs a gown. Sifting through a dress rack, she pulls out a white scooped-neck DKNY blouse from the rack. "*Dinky* is right," she grimaces, then spots a simple black sleeveless wrap dress, some tan slacks, and heads for the change room.

"Take any one," a saleswoman gestures, looking down as she sorts a pile of clothes. Jess hooks her dress up and then, about to draw the curtain across, comes face to face with the masque of death.

"Jess?"

"Ursuline?"

Ursuline. From her Queer West days. Pity-filled, Viking-faced Ursuline, still sporting her Hurricane Katrina bangs.

Jess steps out of the change room.

Ursuline examines her as if inspecting a sweater, a cheap poly blend, looking for flaws, pulling at loose stitches.

"Wow. Haven't seen you since Robbie's."

Robbie's Play Palace had been an underground drag bar off Church Street, where trannies and hipsters paraded their chains and puckering PVC. Sweaty crowds gathered on weekends to watch Miss Demeanour play two shows nightly. Robbie stood behind the polished brass bar, sporting electric-blue Alice Cooper hair and a pet boa named Seymour. She pushed signature cocktails and, tucked inside her blue napkins, pushed a little E.

Terry came into Robbie's three nights a week, stood alone by the bar, dressed in soft chiffon, throwing shade against the burning night. Robbie took notice and tucked Terry under her wing. Terry began doing Robbie's makeup. Robbie turned Terry loose on her wardrobe. Within two years, Terry was calling herself Jess, ordering estrogen and anti-androgen pills through Robbie's US connections. Jess began to distribute candy bags of E for Robbie, pocketing a profit. Soon, Jess could afford to make herself over. First, her pimples disappeared, then the facial hair. Her chest, once covered in chestnut wisps, grew smooth and soft. Jess became fatter around the hips and calves, prone to barfing, sometimes in public. Suited up in a chenille skirt, she was no longer the terrible mistake her parents had made.

Somewhere between the fatty hips and sweater sets, Jess fell for Robbie. Maybe it was the hormones. Or Robbie's fuck-you demeanour. How she heaved her breasts over the bar, handing out her signature blue-ball cocktails ringed with cocksucker candies. Or her extraordinary Jamaican and Chinese mix with blue-black hair and pewter eyes, the fathomless deep of a wishing well. "Make a wish," Robbie said one night, winking as she caught Jess staring across the bar too long.

"You left in a hurry after Melody," Ursuline says. "Blasted off like you were on some one-woman mission to Mars."

Police cars. Yellow tape. Spotty mascara. How fluid and fast her old world had slipped away. Then she was floating, an earthly alien.

Jess blots a tear, but says nothing.

Ursuline directs an impatient customer inquiring about sale sweaters then turns back to Jess. "Everything went to shit so fast. She was a headline for two fucking days. Nobody wanted to go out after that."

Melody was Robbie's dream girl, a bottled honey blond with a henna tattoo across her wrist and a permanent pucker. Her pantyhose were found next to her in a bloody puddle off Bloor Street, sometime between the bar closing and sunrise. Just like that, Robbie boarded up the bar, sublet her apartment, and left. No one knew where. Maybe to stay with friends in the US.

Jess moved to the Annex, crowding in among the hot and hungry U of T students. Too lurid for their pansexual play, she became their ticket to little green pills. In a local grunge bar, she sold a dozen pills to a man in a smart suit who offered her a weekend tour of his townhouse. She stroked his lust all night, giving him another taste of his adventurous youth, oblivious to her own pleasure. When the pills and the whiskey began to wear off two days later, Jess awoke and saw that her rough skin, swept of primers and creams, filled him with remorse, even loathing. Maybe it was the comedown, but she knew that if she didn't leave the city then, she would be incapable of happiness.

"So, I have to ask," Urs tilts her head. "You went through with it, right?"

Jess holds up her clothes. "Look, I've got to get back."

"By all means, go. Like we were the problem. Not you," Ursuline sneers, tossing Jess back onto the pile of polyester. "Well, I hope this works out for you."

"And I really hope you find a stylist," Jess snaps, reaching out to stroke Ursula's dirty-blond hair, "because this shag is animal cruelty."

Jess turns abruptly toward her fitting room. Stepping in, she drags the curtain across, her hands lost in an uncontrolled fury shake. She glances at the full-length mirror, tries to gather the pieces of her refracted self: face, chest, legs, a blue tide retracting, leaving bodies strewn across the beach.

"By the way," Urs says, sharply, as Jess hurries past the dressing-room counter on her way out. "Robbie's back in town. Didn't she call?"

Jess lurks like a prowler at the end of her mother's block, watching the bridge brigade hurry back to their North York townhouses. Entering the front door, she hears her mother crash-landing coffee mugs in the dishwasher. Quietly, she slips upstairs into her mother's walk-in closet to try on her new dress before the full-length mirror. Pressing the tight-fitting dress to her hips, she frowns. Damn fluorescent lighting. Too much scoop, off shade, not enough shimmer.

"Back it goes," she declares.

She scans the rows of blocky jackets and mismatched skirts and tops in her mother's wardrobe. Thumbing through a dreary line of polyester, Jess spots a long, elegant black A-line zipped in plastic. Tugging on the zipper, she smells sweetness on the sleeves. Lily of the valley.

Slipping the dress from its hanger, Jess inches the mid-length over her shoulders and it falls easily across her hips. Admiring the open back and V-neck in the mirror, Jess doesn't hear Margaret arrive at the doorway.

Her mother walks over to her dressing table, plops down, holding a bottle of Merlot in one hand, pinching the rim of a half-empty glass in the other.

Jess reaches for a cover-up housecoat.

She emerges from the closet, drawing the belt tight around her fuzzy, pale-blue waist. "Sorry," she says, fanning out the frayed trim of her mother's old housecoat. "Do you mind? Bloody cold in Harold's office."

"Harold's a cold bastard," Margaret muses, smoothing a tangle of hair. She drains her glass and reaches for a brush, the bristles swarming with grey strands. She runs it awkwardly through her unruly nest.

Jess notices her mother's puckered elbows, the soft wattle beneath her chin. Overnight, her mother has become an old woman.

"Girls are telling me to get back out there," Margaret says, dropping the hairbrush on the table with a sharp clatter. She tugs on one eyelid. Reaching for more wine, she manages to swipe the bottle with the back of her hand but rights it before it topples over.

"He's getting married," she says and rubs her eyes. "Harold called me tonight, and I let him have it while the girls were ravaging my cinnamon buns."

"Maybe you should lie down." Jess points to her mother's swollen ankles.

"Not sleepy," Margaret grunts. Her eyes drift, clouds slipping over a translucent moon. She rises, roams about the room, picking up objects, turning over frames to lay the photos face down.

"Found himself a younger lady underwriter," she says, scanning a silver-framed wedding photo she tosses into the waste basket. "He's been fooling around on me for a year."

Margaret reaches across the dressing table, refills her glass, downing another long swallow of tobacco-stained Merlot.

"*Gin Kii!*" Jess shouts, and grabs the glass from her mother.

"Give me that."

Jess holds up the glass. "*Gin Kii,*" she says, then returns the glass to her mother.

"What are you doing?"

"Practising my wedding toast. Heard it on a Phuket beach. Means Eat shit, bitch, and watch your back."

Margaret manages a smile. She drops the glass, moves unsteadily toward Jess, who steps just out of reach, feeling a stabbing pain snake up her left leg.

Margaret stops, grabs her own breasts then lets them drop. "Am I not enough woman?"

Jess braces when her mother takes another tentative step forward, reaching out awkwardly. She holds her mother by the waist trying to keep her steady.

Margaret buries her face in the collar of Jess's soft housecoat. Their lightly pancaked cheeks touch.

Jess feels her mother's body fall heavy over her. Together, they sway in grief's slow, steady rhythm.

"Tell me something sweet," Margaret's breath is moist on Jess's neck.

Jess leads her mother to the bed, tucks her under the sheets. Pulling away, she hears a hoarse cry, feels Margaret's life tightening around her.

"My son is prettier than me," Margaret says, her voice trailing off as she turns her head on the pillow.

"Close your eyes," Jess whispers.

"I told Harold you're home. He's going to invite you to the wedding," Margret mumbles. "Slip some potassium chloride into the champagne toast."

Soon she falls asleep, snoring deeply.

When Margaret awakens, Jess is gone.

Two floors above the traffic stream, in her sublet on Queen Street, Jess dials Fran in Stuttgart. The voice at the end of the line is thin, vaguely hoarse.

"I had some trouble with the Percocet," Fran admits.

Fran's voice is an electric current running through Jess's fingertips after so long. Listening close, Jess thinks she hears a sob on the line, but it could be the connection. She knows a tracheal shave is risky. Stretching the vocal cords forward, then clipping off the excess. It could raise or lower her pitch. Not as extreme as going from Johnny Cash to Julie Andrews, but you never knew.

"Glad you called," Fran says.

Jess hears the clipped drawl, knowing Fran is too tired for English at this hour. A call the following week is suggested before Fran's voice trails off again. Jess hangs up, resolved to leave Fran a message every other week, knowing a return call may never come.

Two months settled into her new place, Jess slips into her first hot bath since before the surgery. Spreading her legs in the chipped claw-footed tub, she probes her shallow depth with wet fingertips, the nerve endings raw, electric. Her body soft and sudden and soon. A deep quiver. Her face flushes.

Jess pats herself down with a towel, pulls on a camel-coloured sweater dress. Around her neck she knots a bright green paisley scarf, letting her hair curl carefully around her neck.

Her phone buzzes. Robbie.

"Carmellina and Baz want curry. We'll meet you at Saffron's in a half hour."

Feeling loose but awake, Jess brushes her cheeks with pale cream blush. Before heading out, she drops a bag of cherry-flavoured cocksucker candies into her purse.

Rain, rain, blue and yawning. Jess pops her umbrella on Queen Street and takes a swallow of air, trying to loosen the low pressure storming her brain. She swings her black bead-and-sequined clutch, satin-lined with a kiss clasp, an unwitting gift from her mother, pilfered from the locked box in her walk-in closet. In a white-noise trance, she strides along, watching young faces stare out from behind the windows of foggy, candlelit hideouts. Crossing Bathurst Street, the buzzing club crowds snake around the block. Young men in dark leathers and collared shirts shout out names along the velvet rope. Women in pointy-toe heels and low necklines pose, wrap their arms around each other, arms extended to snap a group mirror pic they'll post later.

Margaret can keep the gorgeous A-line, the gloomy mood from draining too much thick-bodied Merlot. Every season demands its bold accessory.

Jess turns up her collar, braces for the southwest rains to come.

WOOF

The day Bella realized she no longer belonged to the tribe of investment managers sacking Toronto, she filled her backpack with powdered eggs and freeze-dried noodles that looked as sickly naked as she felt.

By dawn the next morning, she had packed her office into a brown storage box. On her way out, scribbled "Eat shit" across the cardboard sleeve of a paper coffee cup abandoned on her boss's desk. Reduce, reuse, resign.

The last decade had been earnings forecasts and price patterns, gourmet Chinese takeout and grease-stained spreadsheets, followed by late nights feeling up the dimply lump in her left breast. First jelly-bean sized, then a rubbery popcorn mass just below the nipple. Her paper gown parted, breasts cupped and compressed, Bella sucked in a sharp breath when the technologist's cold hands brushed her skin.

On the scans, the white spot windmilled out from her chest like an exploding planet. Irregular, the specialist later affirmed, sitting across from her during the follow-up, using his fingers to navigate the planet's dense mass on the image. Hand pressed to her dimpled skin, Bella leaned back on the chair opposite the doctor's desk and swallowed a deep, soundless sob.

A surgical excision and three-drug cocktail came doctor recommended. Bella sat at her kitchen table scratching out hairless stick figures on a ruled pad, each curled into a sad, intersecting spiral, absent two nipples. Fuck it, she thought. If she had wanted to kill cells she would have set up on a busy patio with friends, ordered double Gibsons, very dry, garnished with chilled pickled onions, and stayed until she closed the place.

So she did one night.

Stiff happy-hour martinis flowed as freely as their laughter in the open air. Two pitchers of spiked raspberry punch followed. The sweet fruit and hot sun on her face reminded her of family road trips with leaky tents and fragrant forest walks, brushing fireweed with her tiny fingers. Weekends spent at the lake with her three best friends, swimming in dark waters as the sun fell, joining in guitar-strumming circles, their wild voices pitched and ragged around the smoky fire.

Sporting her new three-season hikers, Bella gassed up the car, tossing in her brother's old flannel sleeping bag as the restless sun inhaled then seemed to cast the apartment complex in a soft golden hue. With a glance at the map, away she roared, the engine grinding on her V6 hatchback, the mountain pine bathing her lungs in rosemary, something sweet wafting in from her dreams. Her hands grew numb on the wheel by the time she reached the foothills, her vision a blur of whorled branches poking out from the slopes. She drove on for hours, to what seemed like the ragged outline of a faraway dream, like the uncharted wilderness itself.

Arriving at the remote northeastern gates, she encountered the dour-faced park warden, who told her he was not at all sure about a woman travelling alone so deep into the backwoods. Bella shared with him her knowledge of SOS mirror signals, flint and steel fires, inventing survival training equipped only with knife, poncho, and potato. When he asked, Bella handed over a detailed map marking her expected route. He finally surrendered the permit, but not before delivering a stern lecture about bear activity in the area.

"Make noise. Sing. Clap. Especially near streams. Let them know you're there."

The trailhead began at the end of a narrow, winding rough road where she located the parking lot, not much more than a dirt clearing suitable for two cars. Folded trail map in hand, dry kindling zipped into her front pockets, Bella began an uphill scramble, following a flight of orange ribbons marking a trail that disappeared by the time she reached the second stream crossing. By late afternoon, black rains began pummelling the route. Her legs shook as she fought wet, rutted grooves, clambered up exposed slopes, the trail turning braided and muddy the higher she climbed.

Even at rest, Bella couldn't stop panting. Her lungs were two spent sponges refusing air. The alpine pass had looked flatter on paper. Sagging and stumbling off course for hours, Bella finally spotted a clearing wide enough to set up camp. Squatting, she brushed away pine branches, cursed the deadwood slivers that stabbed the tender flesh beneath her fingernails. Clip-pole-clip, the A-shape tent shuddered in the wind. Penlight clasped between her teeth, she unpacked her multi-tool, her Primus stove and pots, the quick-dry towel with its handy mesh bag, and some waterproof matches. In the last light, she gobbled a shit-shaped protein bar studded with chia seeds.

Bedding down in the wet, ravenous dark, she couldn't be sure whether the night howls were coming from outside.

On the fifteenth day of blustering winds, freezing rain slapped the polyester walls of her shelter all night. Bella awoke to a heavy sleet storm, her balloon hands covered in a pimply red rash. As she curled inside her shape-shifting tent, the moaning winds groaned, their soft, wandering tones the closest thing she had come to company in two weeks.

Not true. She had spoken, once, to a blighted black spruce; lichen draped from its branches like an old man's beard.

"Got a cure for feminine itch, old-timer?" she had asked the lichen.

"Fuck off," the lichen had replied. "You smell like toxic waste."

She waited out the storm for three full days. Wrapped in her sleeping bag, the decades circled her like a heavy-skirted fog. She had never visited Machu Picchu. Missed the chance to meet her Irish grandmother. Would never take up oil painting from some studio balcony on an Aegean island or run the Boston marathon or ride in the space shuttle. Between here and Mars, an infinite universe, and all she could feel was the absence of everything. A fungal dread crept through her. Looking ahead was impossible; the future kept peeling away from her like the cracked, flaking skin at her fingertips. Even her dreams became wistful, misshapen things. Bella was mumbling, temperamental. Thick-headed and coarse, she grew to the size and shape of every hole and heartbreak she ever summoned.

Determined at last to pack out with her bug bites and bear spray and delirious aches, Bella pulled up pegs.

On a final, sombre hike along the treeline, Bella thought she spotted a tall figure rustling up ahead through the poplars. He threw a mammoth shadow, larger than most creatures drawing breath in the high alpine. Her heart did a flip-lunge as she followed him. Palming slick leaves, fighting slopes that tore at her itchy calves, she chased after the rustle and snap. Around a rocky ledge she clambered, higher, then another scramble upward, her lungs afire as she navigated a steep ascent across a narrow slope, calling out, "Hello, Hello," in the swirling wind.

He dropped away from her like a bent knee.

Wet-boned, she let her body slide heavily to the ground. Hugging her knees, Bella cursed the storm, her throbbing calves. Then she leaned back against a wall of silver shale, and felt the mountain move beneath her spine.

...

Bella rises before dawn and shakes out her tangled mess of brown hair. Wincing, she pulls a head strap over her thick-matted scalp to don her headlamp. It's been three months since she quit the city. She's got no choice but to make another trip to the local mountain town for provisions. Along a slope entirely absent of light but for her narrow beam, she scrambles down the mountain, picking a long, unsteady path toward the trailhead. Bone sore on the steep, zig-zag march, her bandaged ear aches. She stops to inhale a biting breath of air. The bitter cold is coming, she thinks, sniffing. She'll need a down-filled, waterproof parka, insulated mitts, long underwear, plus more food stores to avoid being stranded on some cliff, dying of exposure.

Arriving in the parking lot, she dusts pinecones and debris from her car and then steers the hatchback toward the far-flung mountain town. At a tiny café, she treats herself to hot chocolate before checking email at the old post-and-beam general store. Four urgent emails load from her oldest friend, Cynth.

The last subject line reads, *I need you now.*
Bella clicks.

Please come back to the city. I'm in trouble. Can't explain. Will you come?

Draining her travel mug, Bella checks the email date again. Already three weeks old. It wasn't like Cynth to complain, not even when they had shared that tiny, thin-walled college dorm room. Still, it was already September. Bella needed to return to the mountain, before the heavy snow-falls made his windward slopes all but impassable.

This is serious, she thinks, reading over the emails again. And she hasn't seen her old friend in months, so Bella fuels up the hatchback and speeds back to the city.

Bella squints as Cynth mouths in the doorway, "I'm sorry," then leads her to a teal wingback in the crowded living room.

She sits, watching Cynth set down tea and a flower-shaped lemon tartlet beside her.

"What's happening here?" Bella says, looking around, puzzled.

She notices Cynth's husband first, then Raff, her brother, on the couch opposite. Her best friend, Louise, is leaning over a coffee table laden with mini quiches and a large fruit and vegetable platter. Dear God, Bella thinks, shaking her head at the sight. Arthur and her mother in the same room?

"Seriously, what's going on?"

Her mother rises, glancing over at Cynth for a nod of consent.

"Bella, we all love you," her mother says, rubbing her trembling hands, "but we're afraid you may be in trouble. You took off without a word. Three months and barely an email."

Bella shrinks in disbelief. Here goes her family again with the WOOF thing. Women who eschew social conventions. Abandon everything and book it for the airport. Outliers, her father loves to lecture. Wild Ones Over Forty, he likes to call them, summing up an article he read in a national magazine, citing two major studies with full-colour, illustrated charts. The gist of it was that, unable to face their disappointing futures or corrupt world views, WOOFs seek relief in reckless adventure. They wander freely for a time, aimless as cattle, but they always make their way back.

"We're here because we're worried," her father, Arthur, pronounces abruptly, gesturing to the room, then clearing his throat. "A WOOF can threaten the entire social ecology."

Bella lops a whipped cream pompadour off her lemon tart, licking her index finger bald. While her father continues to talk, she watches Cynth's border collie dine, paws up on the coffee table, shredding two bacon-filled mini quiches. A herding breed instead of a child, Bella remembers Cynth saying, after a second round of Monte Cristo coffees.

"Can you see it from our side?" her father asks, holding out his hands.

"It's selfish," Raff grumbles.

"We thought you were finally going to settle down," Cynth adds, as if Bella's slight were as deliberate as refilling the empty coffee cups around the room.

Her mother pipes in, "But you've always been so picky."

Picky we are. Picky women, Bella thinks, pressing the pulsing vein at her temple. Too discriminating. Too demanding. Like preferring her backpack to this plate full of I-know-better.

True, she has never married.

...

She did love Ben, an American lawyer she had met at an equities conference in Brussels. Not just in the heady hours of their London-to-Bruges romance-by-rail, but in the months after. Bella, Ben, and baguette, cycling through Alsace or contemplating a peek under the Pope's robes in Rome. Sampling cave-aged cheese and Barolo from their terrace, watching sailboats cruise Lake Albano. Afterward they had crossed a stone bridge and he stopped her midway, clasping her hands in his, and called her a reservoir for his dreams. Later, the long-distance calls, the business-class tickets. Back home, she stitched together their panoramic passions, had them float-mounted on her apartment wall. Had she ever been happier? If so, she couldn't remember when. The anticipation of their next reunion had stirred in her such a delicious longing that love seemed to hang in the exalted air where she walked. The secret was hers to savour. Save her, it just might. Love was the rarest of all disorders, she had thought then. Contract it, and the whole world could seem sacred again.

He was married, of course. Most of her messages went straight to voicemail. During their meet-ups in New York, she wound up wedged into his barely furnished Manhattan studio rental, the smell of bergamot and vanilla on his shirts. He finally confessed a wife and a need to escape sexual incarceration. Bella countered that sharing a bunk in his wife's prison cell wasn't exactly her idea of liberation; and by the way, Fuck off and don't ever call me again. After

two light-headed years, their romance withered on its in-
fested vine.

Bella watched her life slowly unravel with a kind of per-
verse pleasure, while she slid deeper into the muck and
mire. This sort of suffering was predictable, she thought,
even comforting, drawing the support of indignant friends
if she told them. She kept quiet. No, life's real calamities
always slammed into you sideways. She hated the end-stage
dating of the over-forty woman. Daubing on extra prim-
er and concealer, the cream blush and lipstick, always a
shade darker than usual. The too-fruity wine, the two-for-
one tapas shared with much older men who looked at her
as if they were ready to flush out a badger. She pictured
herself squealing in their slavering mouths and ordered a
single tequila shot.

More than once she returned home to wring out her
heart in dry vermouth, orange bitters, and a splash of
grenadine. Pink. Plunk. Perfect. Head back on the couch,
shoulders sinking in front of the TV, fingering the cursed
mammary mumps. Another late-night crime show on the
screen. Splayed out on the coroner's examining table,
the woman's parched body is a mess of tangled hair and
bruises, leaves and dirt beneath the fingernails. Think she
did this to herself? the detectives ask.

With a start, Bella refocuses on the room, watching her
brother angrily poke the air.

"You're in a rut, sis. Spinning your wheels. Come on
home and grow the fuck up already."

Bella feels the coarse hairs on the back of her neck rise. She squirms, rubbing against the wool fabric to relieve an awkward lower-back itch.

Look how they buzz and claw at the foothills of my life, Bella thinks. Even Louise keeps insisting she is something to salvage. Remember to knit scarves and shelter kittens, Bella thinks, sitting stone-faced in her chair.

Hungering after the last of the baby quiches, Bella leans forward while they chatter, grabs and gobbles a mushroom tart in a single bite.

Her mother raises her hands in a gesture of despair.

Everyone agrees she's been acting strangely for months.

Everyone's sorry for missing the signs.

Bella tugs at the stem of a large potted fern next to her chair. She can picture the glacial lake ready to unfold its winter wings, the morning sun draped over the ridge like a downy blanket.

He is vermillion. He is Olympus.

The late spring storms finally passed in the alpine. Bella climbed high above the treeline, stopping to draw crisp air deeply into her lungs. Looking out across a rising plateau at the snow-capped peaks, Bella settled her fast-beating heart. The moment flooded her with peace. The horizon was infinite.

Millions of years ago, there were no mountains here. Just the outer skin of earth shifting, then colliding, becoming plates, creating mass, until the ground had compressed, pitching up sandstone and shale, becoming the very stones upon which Bella's soul now rested.

A glacier had transplanted him here. "I'm from a family of drifters," he joked, while she tiptoed through wolf lichen, across alpine meadows carpeted in bell-shaped flowers that tinkled where she walked. Standing amid bright blooms, their pointed tips like a fine brush dipped in scarlet-coloured paint, she watched the tall flowers bend with the wind, casting a ruby blush across the mountain face.

He was soaring and serrated, his shoulders set wide and snow-capped. He claimed to have lived here for over a thousand years. So she stood spread-eagled against his mighty rock cliff, sidestepping across shallow footholds, hands bloodied, chest out, aching for air.

He was all ridges and tumble. A stable, solid, impene-trable mass. Picking her way around his saw-toothed peak, she grew taut in calves and thighs. Her back ached as she leaned into sheer rock, scaling the granite rock face, her arms wide, fingertips wedging into cracks so sharp they shredded her flesh. Pouches soon formed beneath her eyes. Wind hurled, leaving her skin raw and coarse as she scrambled around limestone ridges.

She trekked on. Set up camp, tore down, wearing her moveable shelter like a second skin.

Occasionally she thought she heard a cellphone war-bling in the wind, and later, in a sharp clap of thunder, she recalled the awful *bang-click-bang* of the MRI. Then her mind began to cast dark shadows. All the trails were over-grown, she thought, the rocky path impenetrable.

Keep moving, he whispered, when she slipped on a patch of loose shale or missed the mark, spraining her ankle on a giant leap from a thick-bedded plateau.

The summer came. Drifted.

When hard winds swept up his scree slopes, Bella dropped below the treeline, slept curled in his valley cradle, her mouth wreathed in mist. She bathed in the basins of cascading waterfalls, their icy drops like nimble fingers running down her spine. An indelible silence enveloped her, hung in the air where she walked. Bella could find no words for the weight lifting from her.

She grew dandelion fingertips, felt unbranched, twiggy, and lean. Her life a hollow stem, untamed, spreading grace.

When hunger devoured her on overnight expeditions, he urged her to nibble the inner bark of a balsam fir. She ground down the bark to make a bitter meal that carried her longer than any freeze-dried packet. Craving sweets, she wandered along the treeline through the twisted woods, found a patch of plum-coloured berries falling like pearls from a string. Swallowing a handful, she felt her old life slipping away.

What more could she want? To taste destiny in her dreams. To bleed her life history where he scratched.

Rushing headlong into autumn, she felt sand and silt flushing her veins clear. It was inevitable that the earth would shift.

Bella watches her work friend Kate rise from a leather armchair in Cynth's living room, elbows flexed, hands on hips.

"Bella, you left me. Not even a note goodbye. Then they hired some MBA at work, with big tits and eel teeth, to replace the CFO. She's ready to fire the entire floor over our latest losses."

Watching Kate's eyes fill, then her expression flatten, Bella's gaze drifts toward the open window.

"You left me alone," Kate repeats, wiping her eyes. "Don't you even care?" Her friend sips her cold coffee then slams the cup down, leaving it trembling in its saucer. "P.S. Everyone at work thinks you're a nut job."

"We're not here to label," Cynth chides.

She exits and returns first with more fresh fruit and cheese, then a selection of bite-sized toasts draped with smoked salmon, and paper-thin slices of beef. Setting down the last oval tray, she addresses the room: "Statements not accusations, okay?"

Bella thinks she hears her father mutter "WOOF" through his mouthful of brie.

"Maybe what's happening to you, honey, is like a syndrome," Arthur observes, distractedly. "Like IBS or ADD. A dysfunction of modern times. Not entirely your fault."

"If life is a signpost, this is your U-turn, sis." Raff nods. "We're fed up with your extreme bullshit."

Bella resists the urge to swat at the warbling refrigerator hum. Her knuckles are marred with tiny cuts, a swampy-looking tangle of hair falls over her ears, clinging to her cheeks. She leans toward the cool air wafting in from the window, feeling a sharp tingle, like stinging nettles gripping her spine. Her mind wanders along the wide-open grasslands, begins scaling the high alpine.

Louise repeats, "So, what are you prepared to do to save yourself?"

Backcountry prohibitions:

- ☐ Do not climb above the treeline when lightning strikes.
- ☐ Do not feed or harass wildlife.
- ☐ Never shortcut switchbacks.
- ☐ Do not urinate on rocks.

Foraging below the treeline in the mid-August heat, Bella stopped to stuff a sanitary towel down her climbing pants. How many women bleed out in the woods, she wondered, rubbing the rough, raw skin around her mouth. Collecting a few dead pine branches, she began to pick the mud from her heels, notched and nearly worn flat from all her footslogs. Sniffing the spicy scent of fall on the horizon, she grew wistful. How often had she followed the sure and steady path for approval, to feast on the fat of it? Fuck Aunt Flo. Fuck the Dow. Fuck her mother's manic repression: two graduate degrees, a seniors' trek to Vietnam, yet still afraid to offend telemarketers.

Hop-stepping side to side in front of her tent to better position the pad, she remembered a female comedian saying a sanitary napkin was the equivalent of a man wearing a hot dog bun to work. Across the stage the comedian had strutted, swinging an imaginary briefcase, stopping to adjust her bun-crotch every few paces. Ketchup.

Menstrual blood. Life spilling out between the seams, Bella thought. Forget bullshit regrets.

The audience had roared as the comedian went striding down the aisle. Adopting a deep masculine voice, she had pointed to the indiscreet bulge between her legs. "Can you see it, Al?" she had asked audience members. "Does it look okay from the back, Frank?"

Bella chuckled out loud, zipping up her pants in the liquid hour before dawn.

Back in Cynth's living room, Bella begins laughing.

Louise interrupts to ask what is so damn funny. Louise is no WOOF. She has two kids, the body of a porn star. A job in real estate, with custom signs and a corner office. Her sprawling ranch house is flooded with natural light, features an all-white European-style kitchen where once, just once, Bella shared a kiss with Louise's husband, Ray. He had pressed up against her in the kitchen while they were full of good port and cheesy shrimp puffs, Bella too shocked to thwart his advance. She pushed him away afterward, trying to ease the awkward transition. Louise was running late, off showing warehouse property to an out-of-town developer, when they got the call. Bella and Ray took a taxi to the hospital. In the waiting room, the resident drew Ray and Louise aside to explain about the ventilator. Bella watched them barter with God but finally lose their eldest son to a massive hemothorax. She remembers the grief pile the couple made in the waiting room while she hovered near the nurses' station, her boozy breath masked by blue mints, shame spreading in her, crossing the territory of uninhabitable grief.

"I know the urge to escape," Louise says, rubbing her hands as if closing a deal.

"WOOFs end up suffering because they are without a purpose," her father explains. "Where is all this leading you, hon?"

"This is Middle-East crazy, sis," Raff says, arms folded.

Louise tries to conjure a smile, her eyes downcast and dim. "Stay with us, Bella. Don't go back alone, or you'll be wearing a fleece-lined straitjacket by winter."

Watching Louise, Bella has the urge to boil some white willow bark to ease her pain. She looks hard into her old friend's tired eyes and sees stands of trembling maples, their limbs spilling crimson leaves.

At the end of a late-August day, Bella noticed the alpine grasses were spiked golden brown. The nights had grown thick soles, went trudging across the hard earth, stamping cold into her aching bones. Her fingers and feet were swollen. She began to feel tired even on short treks and by mid-afternoon craved a bottomless sleep. Fists curled up beneath her chin, elbows tucked tight against her ribs, she felt the growing lumps beneath her armpit and collarbone.

Darkness sipped at her soul. Coyotes patrolled at dusk. Wolves roamed the open slopes. Retreating to a hidden limestone cave, Bella lay awake for hours, fearing the firelight could not warm her. A brutal sorrow choked her dreams. When she closed her eyes, her life was a flickering shadow against the wall, a trace of the woman she had meant to be. The encroaching nights, the pang of diminished hope, and lost chances ran loose and treacherous in her brain. She was prey, and he was anchored. His mass was no compass.

Come back to the city with me, she begged him. I'm naked. A sitting duck here. Please.

He asked her if he were to quit this place, how would the moon know how far to rise? There were rain shadows to cast, valleys to carve. For longer than she had roamed the earth, his jagged ridges had been a platform for the brightest star in the sky.

Bella began scratching the earth with her worn rubber heel. "Here," she said. She could not find her way back. "To this state." Her boots had not even marred the mountain face. By morning, the trail would be snow-dusted, not even a bare trace of her footsteps remaining.

He replied that all along his back were twisted scars, and these trails were old wounds that would lead her back to him.

Bella strapped her arms tightly against her chest. Feeling the tender flesh along her breastbone, the skin growing rough and thick, coarser than even a month previous, she began to shake, feverish. When she buried her pale face in her arms, he sent down a fine bedrock spray, a gale of laughter to wipe away her tears.

"Forget it. Just let me be," Bella said and turned abruptly from his spiked ridges, setting off down his rocky slopes.

On a sombre walk through the woods, Bella had trouble squeezing breath from her lungs, her lumbering legs growing heavier with each step. Resting for a few minutes on a rock, Bella saw the yearling bear climbing over the log before she could react.

Clap. Make noise.

Run.

The startled mother reared on hind legs. Bella felt the magnificent paw graze her cheek. The trees were growling as she took three faint-headed steps backward. A huff-pant. Chest wide. Another low growl seemed to split the earth open at her feet. Her legs collapsed, Bella stumbled back, her body careening off balance, spilling backward through stunted trees, then into a knot of prickly bushes on the wet slope, before tumbling down into a muddy ravine. She awoke with a faint smile, on a mossy green pillow, touched the fine blood bead running across her cheek; the cold seeped into her like a soft, psychedelic rain.

Cynth reads aloud from the guidebook. "After the encounter, the Participant will acknowledge her behaviour. If she admits it, pack a bag and escort her for treatment. If she denies it, the consequences must begin immediately."

Bella holds her hand up, requesting permission to use the toilet.

"Follow me," Cynth says, as she leads Bella to the smartly decorated powder room at the end of the hall. Her friend lays a gentle hand on her shoulder, tucking a glossy pamphlet into her back pocket. "It's okay. They know how to treat a situation like yours."

Door shut in Cynth's powder room, Bella gives a tired sigh. She unbuttons her shirt, holds her arms out at her side.

Feet set wide on the tile floor, her chest is fully exposed. She bares her teeth, rubs the back of her hand across her ruddy, wind-bitten cheeks. Holding her hands below the open taps, the sound is like a hot roaring breath in her palms. Bella rakes a hand through her matted locks, pulling from them a clutch of mountain heather, its white bells scattering across the bathroom tile.

"Ready, honey?" Her father knocks lightly, her packed suitcase in his hand.

Exiting the powder room, Bella returns down the hallway and back into the living room. She watches the room recoil as she grabs a bunch of grapes from the fruit platter, chews noisily, and spits the seeds across the table.

Raff jumps up. Louise knocks her wine to the floor. Her father reaches out for her. Cynth gasps, when, with a great heaving breath, Bella yawns, shakes their grip, and climbs out the open window.

The following summer, Bella treks along a lakeside trail to where a wide-winged glacier drapes across the jagged mountain face. Continuing up through the subalpine, she follows a rocky ridge that breaks toward a blooming alpine meadow. Her belly filled with bright berries plucked ripe from a thorny bush en route, she lies back in the purple field where mountain crocuses trumpet in a jazz of moonlight.

Hooked to her belt, a sealed map marking the hidden route to a high alpine crossing.

In her survival pack: a knife, poncho, and potato.

Last Down

Samuary.

That's what we called it.

The month Sam Feltimore carted out his brand-new cowhide, shipped all the way from Detroit by his divorced dad. Brown-paper packaged. Not even a shitty Christmas bow.

Coldest afternoon on the planet. New Year's 1981.

Ass-deep in snow on the backfield of St. Joseph's High.

First down.

And counting.

No one else from the neighbourhood can hack the cold, so it's just me, Pork-Eye, and Nick against the dead-end zoners, Sam, Prem, and Kevin.

Across the line, Prem's yellow turban winds above his head like a creamy malt. He caresses his beefy chest with gloved hands, then paws the ground between us.

"Sugar Mounds, you're going down."

"Shut up, Phlegm!"

I look down at my moundless number thirty-three and spit into the snow.

"Ready set." I *am* starting quarterback Tom Clements. Capacity crowd in my ears. I'll drop back into the pocket and roll right, unless there's a scramble, in which case I'll hit Nick going long.

I look left. All fibreglass and flames along the scrimmage line, helmets spray-painted with a lightning-streaked W, a rough and ready R: Go Riders! Go Ticats! Go Bombers! Go Argos! Winning teams spray-painted over the losing ones, because after the Cup anything goes.

"Stand back and wince, Dickhead," I yell at Prem, who keeps taunting me with his rabid tongue-flicks.

"Sack this," he shoots back, grabbing his crotch.

I look over at Yani, who is draped over a coat pile on the sidelines, a legal thriller wedged between his mitts. He yells at Prem, something about his missing ball sack.

"Hut one. Hut two. Hit me, P-Eye."

Downfield, Nick sprints, slips on a patch of ice, then cuts across, waving at me like he's flagging a rescue ship. I launch a tight spiral just ahead of his defender, and the ball sails right into Nick's arms and dribbles through them again to sink missile-deep in snow.

Prem trots up to me while I'm wiping down the football with a tea towel tucked in my jeans. "You're like a female puppy today. Can't hit a target and you smell like shit."

That's when Yani decides to help Prem find his missing ball sack.

Samuary.

Practice. Push-ups. Don't hesitate. Long into that after-noon, I could hear my father's voice in my head. Step into it. Relax, May, open your shoulders up. Remember, ninety degrees at the elbow and armpit.

All day I threw bullets against the pale winter sky, found the open man on the field, could see each play unfolding long before we even clapped out of the huddle.

What happened between Yani and me in those last weeks of December, I've never been able to master.

Two years ago, Yani showed up at my high school all twitchy and brooding, refusing to remove his Jets toque at assembly. He was fourteen, a year older than me in grade nine. New kid. Nasty mouth. Instant attraction.

I volunteered to buddy-walk him around school. Soon, we were patrolling the hallways, wearing our screw-you armour. I wasn't pretty-popular like my older sister, Amy. Never part of the please-give-us-tits-by-summer brigade. But I could do fractal geometry and advanced algebra in my sleep. Yani was pure brain monkey, wicked with words. Approach him without a wry joke about test-tube babies and he'd bite.

In our black-and-white world, Yani was this baffling, bulging grey matter, with his laboured hop-step and a Jets toque soon to become more famous at school than a Bee Gees's beard. Our quest was greatness. At least in our own minds. I went from being a somewhat recognized five-foot-nothing pixie-cut jock or brain (depending on who you asked), to being part of an infamous duo. In our dawning teen years, this was a serious second wind.

When Yani came down with double pneumonia the next year, he stayed away from school for eight weeks. I wandered around cursing Christ Almighty, but it was Gordy who ended up needing resurrection.

"He was only down for a sec," I protested to Principal Charon. Tried to explain how Gordy had found one of Yani's long-missing Jets toques, had gone limping down the hall like he was one of Jerry's telethon kids. Gordy hadn't counted on my rough start in French Roman Catholic school, where kids had sold baggies of hash at recess or got assaulted on safety patrol duty while wearing their subtle orange belts and sashes. I knew my Tabernac from my Criss de calice and definitely my Osti de tabarnak de calice. I could say the Lord's Prayer in French and curse it in English, and no cretin like Gordy was ever going to mess with Yani. *Maudit marde!*

When I told Gordy to quit, he forced my arm behind my back. I swung around, striking out wildly then slipped from his grasp, squeezing his hand so hard Gordy literally squealed.

Two eyebrow stitches and a sprained wrist later, I got hauled into Charon's office. Man was shark-eyed and short-fused, so much so Yani and I called him Heir Emperor, to the left of Genghis Khan. I had seen Charon openly berate a social studies teacher because he had both his ears pierced and wore pants so tight if he leaned over, we joked he might split the atom. Charon pulled out a rattling bottom drawer that he kept filled with confiscated pocket knives. Withdrawing one with a fake wood-grain handle, he leaned forward, unfolding the blade in his hands. A girl with such excellent grades, he admonished, his eyes forecasting my ever-diminishing prospects.

"He mocked a disabled kid."

"Yani's not the issue."

"Gordy's a manipulative freak."

"He's got a gash above his left eye," he said, gesturing to his own furtive brow, "and you're getting a three-day suspension." He began writing something serious in a leather notebook.

"Welcome to Stalin's Gulag," I huffed, mostly under my breath, and sat back.

So the principal's blade flashed in his hands. So I pulled my chair closer to his desk, letting the steel legs scrape across the vinyl floor. He was so tall, twisting that sharp blade in his hands, but the disparity worked in my favour. He tried to joke at first. Said he had a kid in there last week with a broken pinky finger and told the boy it was easier to cut off the finger than to set it. I looked up into his eyes, then down at the open blade he kept testing in his palm, and finally leaned forward and placed my fingers flat on his desk.

"Go ahead," I said, fanning my fingers wide. "I plan to write a book about you one day."

Yani was my triple-weave Kevlar companion, my Batman cape, my mission. His presence gave me courage.

All over the TV, men were aiming shoulder-mounted machine guns at each other. There were soldiers, some as young as Yani, hobbling across scorched earth, blowing up decimated villages. Tanks and helicopters flew over hillsides, missiles landed in places I couldn't yet identify on a map. After dinner my parents talked about Saddam Hussein like he was a recurring character in some serial horror flick. While they moaned about the oil crisis that December, Yani and I were busy building a brick wall. On one side stood the world, on the other Yani and I, wild with indignation over Cheron and Ethiopian famine and saccharine mainstream pop, and growing comfortably numb to Pink Floyd over a half-mug of stolen vodka from Yani's father's basement stash.

Meanwhile my older sister, Ames, was going to graduate in a few months and go backpacking with friends to summon the ghost of Jim Morrison at Père Lachaise. I couldn't abide my sister's lack of athletic grace, her desperate need to triumph on student council. The two of us fought so hard my father started calling us the Iran-Iraq conflict. While I was wedged into the purgatory of a grade eleven classroom, she was getting ready to see the world.

Escalating struggles had become an obsession. I had gone wild for the doomed Romanovs, with that crazy Rasputin and their sad sack of a hemophiliac son. Fell for men in fur hats and porcelain-skinned women roaming gilded palaces in St. Petersburg. Back then, revolts and revolutions were still twinkling and remote, exotic as the embroidered silver cloth that bound Czarina Alexandra's slender waist at her wedding. My own graduation plan was to visit the Winter Palace with Yani, to take in the Baroque architecture, walk the red velvet staircase, and pore over the gods on the eighteenth-century ceiling paintings before my sister ever set foot on the continent. During our blood-less coup, we would storm the palace just like Bolsheviks, and take home a souvenir Lenin pin. Yani, Lenin, and I were like leaders in exile, part of a revolutionary faction, an idea you couldn't split, until the fractures started forming in December.

It was three weeks before Christmas and everyone on earth seemed to think looking smart meant shelling out two bucks for a Rubik's Cube. I had orders to buy Ames a gift, and new locks for our front door weren't going to cut it. Leaving the mall, I spotted Yani on the other side of the street, stepping off the downtown bus. He was favouring his hip. It made my chest hurt seeing him try to stumble over all the plowed snow. When I called out, he pretended not to hear me. I ran over anyway.

Yani and I had been struggling. In late October we were hardly speaking. Not in the hallways. Not behind the chain-link fence, where we used to mock the stoners. Not at our favourite diner with the mile-high greasy fries and the missing toilet seat. I had made one goddamn mistake. His name was Finn.

Finn was only in my life for five minutes in mid-October. Our mothers had volunteered to drag us out to help at an annual charity drive for disadvantaged kids, complete with white cake, pumpkin vomit, and kids shrieking in pirate hats and black capes. On a break, we decided to go for a walk around the park to stave off madness. He was from a different school, had a bristly patch of blond fuzz on his chin, and a lisp that I expected tasted of sour cherry gum. Yani spotted us eating fries at our usual diner and went AWOL. He plunged into after-hours physics. Hung out with some Zork-obsessed dude named Letsky.

He took my calls. But his answers were often staccato, impatient, occasionally insulting. Apparently, I didn't understand the definition of sacred. The diner was not our hallowed ground, I told him, and Finn had spent most of the hour sucking on ice chips after burning the tip of his tongue on a french fry. Anyway, I never saw Finn again.

"Hey," I said, out of breath as I reached Yani, who was still struggling with the plowed snow.

Yani pulled his toque down so low he resembled one of Pac-Man's ghosts.

"Whatsup?" he said, coolly, like nothing had happened between us.

I knew Yani's dad had recently moved out and was shacked up with Anna, who worked in the principal's office and did the books for Yani's father. I had called him. He didn't take the phone.

"How is your mom doing?" I said in a voice too pity-filled for him to bear.

He drove his cane into a foot of fresh snow. "What did the normal baby say to the test-tube baby?"

"Your dad's a wanker," I answered automatically.

"Exactly," Yani observed, looking away.

"It's a real goddamn tragedy," I replied, trying to find the right distance.

Yani just kept poking deeper holes in the snow mound around him.

"Come on," I gestured toward the mall. "Let's get some Cokes."

"Look," he said in a robotic voice, waving his cane at the rush of shoppers. "Tiny…computer…chip…in…brain… must…spend, spend, spend." He tapped his temples.

Giant lacy snowflakes began falling across our shoulders. We were in a classic Russian novel. There was a family scandal. A doomed friendship. Looming exile. It was almost Romanov.

"Got a few quarters for the arcade," I offered, tentatively.

Yani declined, saying he and his mom were headed for his aunt's house for a few days so he needed to get back.

"Maybe he'll come around. Make it up to you guys?" I said.

"Well, you should understand betrayal," he replied so sharply it was as if someone had run cold tap water up my spine.

"I've been here this whole time," I pointed out and wouldn't let him leave until he eased up and agreed to come mock the grade niners with their spectacular feathered hair wings at the school Christmas dance the following week.

He grunted and made a Pac-Man whirring sound.

"Game over," he muttered, turning around, and tapping his cane in the direction of the westbound bus.

Christmas dance. Last one before the holiday break. Glory days for green-and-red crêpe paper, blue hair gel, and hallway bitches in baggy knit sweaters. Lurking near the stage, I watched three boob bunnies in floppy Santa hats hop toward the shaggy lead singer, who was strumming a cover tune on his cheap Yamaha guitar. Definitely not excellent.

Adrift in my sister's sateen gypsy blouse I fanned out my pencil arms in the crowded, overheated gym. Yani and I had been counting down the days to freedom, practising our best Clint Eastwood lip snarl for our upcoming *Escape from Alcatraz* movie marathon at the repertory theatre. Scanning the gym's darkest corners, I found Yani doing his usual back-bleacher sprawl, showing off his derisive smirk for the crowd. He was wearing his ripped Ramones T-shirt, eyes squinting like he'd just broken out of an alien seedpod. I waved at him. He returned a look of unfettered dread about being there, something between post-apocalyptic annihilation and invasion-of-the-body-snatcher paranoia. Imitating one of the invading clones, I held my arm out and hissed. I gestured for him to join me. He nodded his head but didn't budge from his roost.

I had begged him to come. Even suggested wrapping his yellow cane in black electrical tape. "A caution sign," I joked, though no one needed the warning.

On the field at the park, even the men turned to watch me throw spirals. Here at the dance, sporting this

Frankenstein sweep of my sister's pink blush and blow-dried bangs, I watched the guys just turn their backs.

Except Sam, who asked me to dance when the cover band struck up ELO's "Turn to Stone," the fog machine spewing vapour across our sneakers. We hip swayed, a foot apart. A soft breath away from my ear, he shouted that his dad was driving all the way up from Detroit after Boxing Day. Then the band began a slow strum. Sam stepped closer, put his hands around my waist, drew my hips against his. A sweaty-sock-ball feeling climbed in my throat, his musky Brut making my behind-the-knee-pits perspire. He pressed his lips to my ear, asked if I want to see an action flick with him and his dad over the holidays. I nodded approval. We swayed, belly to pelvis, his hand falling to the small of my back. We inched closer. My face flushed. When the song stopped, Sam broke away.

"Five bucks more to tongue her," Gordy convulsed, stepping out from behind a wall of jocks, holding out a crumpled bill.

Sam hunched his shoulders, but he held his hand out.

"Just a joke," he chuckled, when I shoved him and slapped the bill from Gordy's hand. The slow dancers broke apart, encircling us, laughing. When I looked up into the bleachers, Yani was gone. Left me isolated as Mao's China. I finally spotted him in front of the girl's change room, just behind the gym's double doors. Seeing my drawn face, arms folded tight beneath the "No Exit" sign, he shrugged dismissively, flashed a reckless smile, and pointed up toward the prank we'd been waiting all year to pull.

Our favourite English teacher had brought in a *Time* magazine cover as a way of discussing modern writers grappling with the meaning of existence. The cover was solid black with a question composed of three words printed across it. Yani and I had the cover printed up large, rolled it up and taped it from the railings. Next to it, we painted an identical cover with the answer.

Is	Yes.
God	Charon
Dead?	demands job.

Shooting me a hard, furtive look through those glass doors, he smirked, mouthed something like "Fuck them," and gave the fire alarm a tug on his way out.

Samuary.

Second Down. And we're screwed.

Ten minutes left on the clock. Down by five points. The field is a trampled mess. The gloves are off. I can't feel the tips of my fingers.

My heart is on fire when I look out at Sam and Prem who know I need five yards for a first down, and they're not about to give me an inch.

"Run ten yards then curl in," I instruct Pork-Eye in the huddle. "Don't stop until you smell pigskin."

Faking a hand-off to Kevin, I hit Pork-Eye who curls outside by mistake and is shouldered hard by Sam, though he makes the catch.

"Out," Sam yells, raising his arms.

"Not a chance," I shout.

"Look," he gestures down at the makeshift sideline. "Both feet. Out of bounds."

Prem echoes Sam, who marches out a straight line between the catch and the two backpacks we used as sideline markers.

We look over at Yani to make the call.

He sits up from his sideline perch, eyes the two backpacks. With great drama, he raises his yellow cane to eye level, closes one lid like he's looking down the barrel of a shotgun.

Calls the ball out.

Christ, he's stubborn. He just wants his fucking pizza.

Maudit, merde.

You had to know the rules with Yani. I tried to keep his world together when things broke down at home. Through his eyes, I had found my strength, tempered my weakness. But the rules kept on changing. He expected unfailing attention, my unshakable loyalty, the bonds of an immutable friendship. Or maybe it was just me who did.

Christmas holidays were in full swing. Exams aced, classes out. Deliverance was ours. Yani and I had made up again when he gave me a mixed tape with handwritten liner notes by way of apology. We listened to it in his basement, over hot chocolate with a splash of crème de menthe that tasted like bitter mouthwash.

Hunkered down that night in our upper balcony hideout

at the theatre, Yani and I leaned back, popcorn tubs on our laps, heads tilted as the lights dimmed. Extra butter on top and no Disney bullshit, please.

Escape from Alcatraz loomed, as heavy as thunder, across the big screen.

We grinned, watched the camera slow pan across San Francisco Bay, zooming in on the island prison where Capone was once locked up; just B-block and his banjo. Onscreen, a brooding darkness hangs in the air as heavy rains slash the open waters. Clint disembarks from the boat, is stripped down inside the prison then escorted naked through the dank halls to his cell.

"Welcome to Alcatraz," the guard says, as he slams the cell door shut, inches from Clint's face.

All I had ever seen of the island was from San Francisco during a family holiday, but we never got any closer than Pier 39. Weather was wretched and tickets for the boat tour had been sold out for weeks. I refused to talk to my family the entire day.

Some kids go crazy for light sabres and aliens. For Yani and me, Alcatraz Island was a notorious thing. An elusive white prison-castle, seabirds circling above it, hacks in the prison towers ready to pick off escapees. And all the prisoners could do was look back at the mainland, in plain sight, yet over a mile-long swim in the bay's freezing, choppy stew. The Rock. And what the rock belched out. A skyline full of fog-bathed tourists, hippie-dippies, and fishermen selling fresh catches right off their boats. And all of it just out of reach.

The prisoners all had scars, pocked faces, and harelips. They made shanks in their bunks, dreaming up a new destiny then digging it out from their cells using sharpened commissary spoons.

When *Escape from Alcatraz* came out in the summer of 1979, we watched the afternoon matinee, stayed for the early evening screening, and repeated the ritual.

No one ever busted out of Alcatraz? Sure they had. We'd seen Clint do it seven times already.

"Adults only in the uppers," a pimple-pocked usher commanded, waving his flashlight spear at us.

"Nothing but gimps and grandpas up here," Yani smiled. He made a big show of hauling his dead right leg up over his left. The usher muttered apologies and retreated.

"See you later, man," we said, quoting the film. "Jinx."

Yani's bum leg came from some bug that had crawled into him as a kid in Winnipeg. Started out like some flu, body aches, his head burning up. Then his whole body swelled, his hips became so weak he couldn't get out of bed for six months. A year later, after he had recovered enough to return to school, his father had to uproot for work and moved them all the way to Ontario. Yani had no friends, an awkward limp, and a new life in the burbs. He told me it was like being sucked from the mother ship and hurled at Mars, wearing a cracked space helmet.

Yani and I watched Clint sprint twenty yards across the prison yard, dodging the roving spotlight. Here the music did an epic build-up. We smiled at each other, kernels plugging our gums. We'd watched this scene so often, yet always froze up.

Clint is shimmying down fifty feet of drainpipe, playing gravel-mouthed Frank Morris, a real-life criminal with a super-high IQ. His breath plumes. Light falls over his grim face. Fearless.

"They made it, you know," Yani whispered, digging a finger into my kidney.

"Drowned like sewer rats," I shot back.

"Never found the bodies."

"Three cons in a rubber raft made of raincoats?" I gave my popcorn tub a firm shake. "Please."

Clint tucks and rolls, barely evading the tower guards. The spotlight glances across his shoes.

"Froze to death in the bay," I told him.

Yani smirked and leaned over. "Oh yeah, I forgot to tell you. Guess what? Anna in the office says the school's adding co-ed touch football next year."

I nearly had a heart attack.

Yani snorted. "Short skirt, a little lip gloss." He shook imaginary pompoms in my face. "You could be starting cheerleader. Gimme an A!"

"Asshole!" I twisted his bony wrist.

Yani pinched my thigh. I fist-pounded his weak bicep.

"You're not a guy, May. Get over it. Buy a skirt. Grow some real tits."

"Think you'll ever get a date with that ugly fence post of yours?" I hissed. "Not even a dog-faced circus girl with chin pus and halitosis."

"Aw. Daddy's little boy is pouting," he jeered, pretending to pinch my cheeks.

And for some reason I pictured my dad and me wearing matching beige vests in our two-man aluminum boat, casting on the rod and reel TV show we loved to watch together. Arms over shoulders after landing a ten-pounder. Attaboy. Good man. I was the son my father would never have; the boy's absence in me like a phantom limb.

With all the force in my body, I landed two elbows in Yani's chest.

Yani dumped his entire Coke across my lap but neither of us bolted.

The thing you have to know about Yani is how hard he tried to fail. Class-cutting. Whining about moronic teachers and idiot jocks in a voice growing so tense and shrill it was like an electric guitar wailing in my ears. Anything to distract from that crooked stump. One minute he'd be red-eyed over his parents' fighting, the next a sullen lump of hate. Push the wrong button and he'd disappear. Then his loss was a translucent bruise spreading beneath my skin. I never knew how much it would hurt, once the trouble started.

Staring straight ahead, we watched three fugitives kick out toward the frozen riptide, their arms wrapped around a raincoat raft fastened with rubber cement. Into the foggy night, three men vanish. Drowned in the furious bay currents or having reached mainland; no one ever knew. None of the men were ever seen or heard from again.

...

Samuary.

Last down and long.

"No prisoners," I call out in the huddle.

"Had enough?" Prem asks as I line up behind Pork-Eye. "Better punt."

My head is a block of ice with teeth. Both snot-stuffed nostrils are flaring, like those black plastic gorillas with the removable arms that go *pop!* when you pull them.

Yani has moved in closer to the sidelines to catch the final play. He doesn't give a shit about the game, but I promised to buy us pizza because his Christmas was such a bust. He keeps gesturing with his hands how many hot slices he's planning devour on my dime.

Pork-Eye gives me the snap. I wind up, arm back for the throw.

My hand hovers mid-air, remembering the arc, cool air where my finger and thumb form a V. I lean forward, sailing too.

The ball pings high off Prem's right shoulder ten yards away.

"Interception!"

I sprint forward, manage to scoop up the wobbly ball in my outstretched hands. Breaking toward the sidelines, my boots slip-slide on the slick, packed snow. Three stooges on the defensive line are trailing me. I look back, am almost across the end zone when someone clips my boot heel, catapulting me toward the foam-covered posts.

"Don't move," Yani yells, hobbling toward me.

I can't. My eyes fill. My right arm is bent unnaturally under my hip. Where I clipped the post, my knee feels plump, fat as a pink grapefruit. The sharp pain in my stomach makes me want to vomit.

"I never touched her!" Prem protests, as the guys circle around.

"Jesus, May, are you all right?" Sam approaches me cautiously. Lying on my back, I can see his blond curls brush across the top of his eyebrows.

Salty tears. Like I've sprung a goddamn leak.

Struggling with his cane, Yani kneels next to me, holding his hand out the way Clint would, a mighty, manly grip that will take us over the wall.

When I try to sit up, Prem takes a startled step back, seeing my blood-stained lips.

"Geez, May, I'm really sorry," Sam falters, bending down and reaching past me for his Christmas ball. "But I gotta go. Dinner's early. Dad's here from Detroit."

Yani whips his cane across, striking Sam's shin. "Fuck you."

"Don't shove me, gimp," Sam blasts Yani, pushing him backward.

They tumble together, but Sam easily recovers. "Look, May, I'll call your mom."

"Don't," I implore.

"Okay," he nods. "I'm really sorry," and sprints away with his ball.

With a trick of his cane, Yani manages to return upright, and in a crouch, pull his arm around me and lift us, bearing most of my weight on his cane.

My arm is throbbing, a piercing pain shoots up my shoulder.

"Let's go, warrior," he says, steadying me. Gently, Yani shifts me around, so my back is turned toward the rest of the guys. My whole body shakes in his grasp. Keeping my right arm tight against my chest, we hobble off the field.

"I was like Gabriel going in for the clutch," I sob.

"More like your head went in cabbage and came out coleslaw," he says, and leans in to kiss my bloody lips.

Sirens scream through my dreams that night. Dazed, barefoot, still dreaming of Hail Mary passes, I wake up to sirens wailing outside my window. I hop toward my frosted glass, wincing as I cradle the weight of my new arm cast.

Flames pierce the blackened sky.

My mother rushes into my room. "Stay there, May," her voice taut and trembling. "There's a fire across the street."

She hurries out and thunders downstairs after my father.

From the window, I focus hard enough to see Mrs. Feltimore, wrapped in a pale pink housecoat, stumbling barefoot over a snowbank. A man in a uniform scoops her up and hustles her into his squad car. Her two young girls, with tussled hair, open coats over pajamas, are sitting up on stretchers. Another two fire trucks arrive. An ambulance follows. Neighbours slowly stray across their doorsteps to form a ragged line across the burning scene.

Shocked, still groggy, I brace against the railing on the slow climb downstairs to join my mother at the front door.

She hugs me. We both watch as my father sprints across the driveway, blankets crowding his arms.

Firemen fling off their masks to suck in fresh air. Shingles are flying from the roof. Two more firemen rush inside the smoke-shrouded house. Another ambulance arrives, skidding across black ice. My mother leaves me to grab the ringing phone, and I hop out the door without a coat, watch the entire Feltimore living room peel away like tarpaper.

When the toxic clouds finally lift, I feel numb, no pain in my broken arm at all.

Two months after the blaze, my father and I are shovelling the driveway for the second time that afternoon. Mr. Naylor from down the street drops by to talk. I drag my shovel toward them, lingering a few paces behind my father. Mr. Naylor is shaking his head, complaining about the record snowfall we are having, but I can tell he is itching for a real talk because he keeps glancing over at me and dropping his voice.

"Think it blasted up from the basement," he says, pointing to a random mark on the blackened concrete foundation where the Feltimore place had once stood.

He smiles over at me. Both men step closer together, looking out across the street.

"Wife heard he wanted her back for the holidays. Divorce wasn't his idea," Mr. Naylor speculates in a hushed tone.

"Heard they found a stack of open paint cans, loose

rags, an old TV plugged in along with the space heater," my father says, leaning on his shovel.

"Could've been my basement," Mr. Naylor observes, shaking his head.

"A short. One spark. All it takes," my father agrees, shaking his head. With his gloves, he pulls his toque way back on his forehead. His salt-and-pepper hair is plastered to his face. Even from where I stand, I can see him wipe the corner of his eye and look away.

"Such a mess down there, so much debris removed by the firemen, they ruled the cause of the blaze indeterminate," Mr. Naylor notes.

In a strained voice, my father adds, "Hear the boy's going to be okay, though."

And I can still picture him lying on the corduroy couch in the basement, inhaling thick smoke billowing through the wood-panelled walls. Sam, sixteen years old, holding his father's football.

Samuary.

Before bumper crop dandelions.

Before long hallway kisses and late-night TV.

Before I went from cropped hair to shoulder-length, for good.

Behind the scrimmage line, a flag is thrown. In my mind, the passing play marched back to the forty-yard line, to the thirty, all the way to that blaze-filled blackness. I still remember my eyes stinging, watching the firemen work. Flames pouring out the windows then clawing up toward the Feltimore's roof. Billowing smoke. Bitter cold. The blurring lines.

Salty summer taste on my tongue, I whip the lawn mower around the azalea bushes, keeping my cut line straight.

Eight months after the fire, across the road, men toss residual scraps of wood onto a rubble pile while a Bobcat hauls away the last remaining trace of fire on a street stained with suspicion. At the far edge of the property, next to the Feltimores' maple, the workers pitch their pinched cigarettes at a huge gravel pile.

In a few months, the leaves will turn mottled yellow, the tall maple screaming the landscape crimson.

In a few years, I will no longer trust what I've seen.

How I had stuttered at the police station when the officer asked me in the days after the fire. "What was the last thing you saw, miss? Someone moving toward or away from the house? Could it have been a fireman? A man's hand or a tree branch waving in the distance?"

"A hand or a tree, miss, which was it?"

The brusque officer kept making me repeat the story.

How I tiptoed through the facts, trying to make sense of that night. Crews and ladders and veils of smoke. Rubbing my stinging eyes as I hopped forward to the end of the driveway. Watching the flames grow, thick smoke like steel wool knotted up my throat, while my mother tried to calm the sobbing next-door neighbours. I couldn't make sense of the shadows. Was there a figure dodging in and out of the trees at the back of the house? The investigators tried to paint me a scene. "Think carefully, May. Take your time. I know this isn't easy. Was there a man beneath the snapped branches of the Feltimores' maple?"

"I don't know," I finally told the cops, breaking down. "It was dark. I was half asleep." Could have been nothing, my mind playing tricks. There were trucks, fire crews, people running everywhere. Maybe there could have been a man in a Detroit Lions jacket near the house. A flanker trying to find his opening. My mother finally stepped in, saying that I had had enough and she was taking me home.

How my heart sank with the sound of the officer's pen scratching his pad.

How we marched across the parking lot, my dad buckling me in the back seat like a young child. "Okay honey, it's all right. Let's go home." How we drove all the way home in silence.

I can still feel the heat of those jumping flames venting the Feltimores' roof that night, thick woollen plumes, then a wind shift, a short break in the clouds, clear enough to see.

Yani in his Jets toque, leaning up against the Feltimores' maple, his hand curled around the crook of his yellow cane.

The way he just stood there, watching like it was the end of a parade.

Prey

When Myra calls back the second time, I'm bent over the bathroom sink, examining the last floating hair tuft on my shiny sea of forehead in the mirror.

"Why aren't you driving yet?" Myra asks. "Dinner's in thirty. Can you pick up a French Syrah on the way? We're having Breton crêpes."

We are: Myra, Dave, Michel, Swan, and me; the crunchy nuts and smooth centres Myra likes to collect around the dinner table. I'm the minus-one accompanying the crusty French baguette.

I work the bathroom knob. "On my way."

At the liquor mart, I grab an Australian Syrah from the middle rack, something with a clown acrobat and a sale tag on it. Then I'm foot-dragging between magazine racks and bulk candy in the grocery store aisles. Into Myra's I stroll, past the hour of absolution, in my raunchy green hamper sweater, with a sack of hard rolls and my twisted brown paper bag. The group gives me a look that says, You're the last person who should be bringing the Syrah.

The night Rachel left me, I wound up in an alcohol-fuelled, flat spin on Myra and Dave's floor, slipping wheat crackers into a dish of chopped liver pâté. The fact that Myra has two cats makes that memory particularly painful. My mouth ran loose and fast all night. Kept hitting replay. Coming home from work, three missing coats on the rack. A lemon scent on the kitchen floor, all the windows cracked, the sound of blinds slapping the sill in our now deserted living room. My knees shook on the march of stairs, the sense of an ending sinking in. Rachel's big reveal was penned in a stained kitchen-counter note. Her suitcases had been packed for eight months. It took her a full year to summon the courage to go, it read.

Sucker-punched out of my last long-term relationship, I had sworn never to take the plunge again. Then Rachel. Beautiful in the way orchids are — sculptural, delicate, impossible to absorb in a single glance. My brilliant linguist. Also a Scrabble-playing shark, inventing words that started with Q and ended in Azerbaijani, keeping a sly, sexy curl on her upper lip as she scanned the board. My heart was this floating fist of pounded meat whenever she looked my way.

Both wedded for the first time in our mid-thirties, we had been wine, baguette, and brie in the park. Hot streak gamblers on the Vegas strip. The odds were stacked in my favour. Marrying Rachel, I was much more likely to spend eternity happy. Three times more likely to survive to old age. At a far lower risk of depression. Our wedding was held on a vast acreage in a friend's horse barn, long before rustic barn weddings were spreads in glossy magazines, with quaint Mason jar tea lights and mystic canapés. Before witnesses, we promised to love each other from this day forward—a bumpy dirt road, as it turned out, kicking up bad habits and old battle scars. She had escaped a spiteful man who berated her for returning to school, and spent a long time anticipating the same from me. Our tender places thickened like a coarse hide, pulled us taut, but in different directions.

She savoured small pleasures. Cooking herb-crusted halibut together. Head-clearing marathon runs through the park. I was itchy for a chance to uproot, something in me was always kicking at darkness, trying to shake something loose. She grew frustrated by my inability to hold on to steady work. All my grand schemes to battle climate injustice were just talk.

"Look at the rising sea levels," I said, "and all these California droughts." Signs of environmental apocalypse were everywhere, but she refused to look.

Instead, we fought over my bathroom habits and piling bills and the time it took her to prepare al dente pasta. We didn't have the chance to fight over Dan.

Dan washed up onto a southern California beach in May. After Rachel left me, I was spending weekends alone, trying to rediscover my fucking pride. This led me to wandering the seaside barefoot, a contraband beer in my hands, dragging my tired ass in cut-off sweatpants through miles of silky white sand. One Saturday, I noticed a small group gathering in the shallows in rolled-up jeans, wading out up to their knees. They were all pointing. Turned out it was a squid, with its eight listless arms wrapped in seaweed and two tentacles submerged under the waves. Watching him struggle felt like the worst sorrow I had ever known. One look into those huge, heartbreaking eyes, its body flashing in the water from pinkish to red to white, and I knew. Without me, that squid would die.

Do something, I thought, or the seagulls will ravage him by sunset. Move your feet, Mark. Rescue that goddamn squid.

For weeks, I kept Dan at home in a hundred-and-seventy-gallon cylindrical acrylic tank I had rented from an aquarium shop, delivered by three giant men who positioned it on a maple pedestal in my living room. Following the advice of marine science, I kept Dan fed on a steady diet of saltwater feeder fish. His body grew twice in size. Despite an ocean of predators and our cancer chemicals, marine creatures still cling to survival. Believe me, he was suffering. I had time on my hands. Rachel was gone. Had her own needs to fill.

At Myra's, I settle onto a couch with the other guests, scooping up sticky mounds of her famous baked brie with blackcurrant preserves. Cool jazz swirls in the air, the B-flat blues bubbling over our ears as everyone describes the worst part of their week. Swan suspects her new yoga hire is using her hatchback as a hotbox, giggling as she goes ganja on the child's pose. And Michel's big boss, the company's lead engineer, keeps knocking heads over the weak rivets in the steel struts. Voices bleat while the trumpets sing down our souls. It's a fire sale of a night—we can't give away the wretched experiences fast enough. And we should feel delirious here, serenaded by these swinging sounds, the middle-child generation living large on teacher salaries and tech booms.

Except me. Due to my ignominious exit from the Seventh Circle of Hell, otherwise known as senior direct-mail fundraising writer for the Climate Concern Campaign, Sacramento office. We don't acquire donors, we encircle trust. With your generous help, we'll help end global warming on this planet. P.S. Get a fucking bicycle, asshole. Clean energy doesn't need your dirty soul. P.P.S. Yes, you, you self-ish, pollutant-pumping, toxic prick.

I couldn't help myself. You try tapping into green guilt for two decades. Sure we had Gore and his snappy key-notes. But even David Suzuki had finally thrown up his hands, declaring environmentalism dead, because we were still fighting the same goddamn battles we thought we had already won decades ago. Christ, I kept having nightmares about Suzuki eating KFC from a plastic bag on an Arctic drilling site and trading baby sealskin for nukes while farting CO_2. Maybe I was unravelling. All it took anymore was an early blizzard and a TV skeptic debunking global warming to lose some of the monthly contributors. My joke rant letter ended up being sent to our entire thirty thousand-strong member list, pre-signed by a famous corporate board member. Next day, I saw doors closing all around me, and I wasn't behind any of them. On my final day of trust, the foundation had me escorted out via uniformed guard.

It was time to move on. Apparently, Rachel had realized it after only four years of marriage.

...

Dave, Myra's husband, fills a lull in the conversation by telling us about the new app he's building, the Ex-ecutor.

"Kicker is," he explains, grinning, "you can replace your ex with anything. A sci-fi alien bear with a bad overbite. A half-centaur with a nose like a hairy knuckle."

"Like that face-swap app?" Michel observes.

"Sort of, but there is also this crazy vibration before the whole screen goes boom for five seconds," Dave adds, making a mushroom cloud gesture with his hands. "Very gratifying."

"When the app goes beta," I chime in, "I'll swap Rachel out for a gun-toting duck with an inability to embrace uncertainty."

Dead air. No one even cracks a polite grin. Myra meanders back into the room and claps us all to the table.

When the crêpes are served — plump buckwheat triangles oozing gruyère — Dave answers the doorbell, surprising us all by welcoming Myra's yoga pal Lyle to the table. He's got a trapeze artist's gait, a thick part across his full head of wavy hair. Not a trace of mid-gut paunch. Posy bastard.

Jet-lagged and glassy-eyed, he apologizes for his lateness, mumbling something about delays on the slow train to Mumbai.

Ten minutes into the meal, Lyle begins assailing us about the world overseas. Child soldiers. Swamp crossings. Bullet holes pierce his blackcurrant-stained mouth. Guy wears his tourist passport like it's a purple heart.

"So, you're back from southern India?" I finally say, picturing his harrowing trip from the airport to his coconut palm-lined lux yoga retreat. I had visited Delhi and some Himalayan villages on a backpack trip with two buddies after college. Rachel had always wanted to see the Taj Mahal's mosaics and touch the ivory-white marbled walls to experience the perfect Mughal symmetry for herself. We never managed to get closer than Seattle's hypodermic needle.

"It really changes you," Lyle says, looking down at his plate. "Saw children wandering barefoot in slums smelling of soot and tar." He lets his shoulders drop. "Bathing in polluted rivers. Even the sacred Ganges."

"Ganges has a billion gallons of raw, untreated sewage floating in it," I tell him. "Birds like to circle above it to catch bodies popping up along the riverbanks because the poor can't afford cremation."

It was something I'd seen and couldn't shake. I still feel waves of grief and shock whenever clean water comes gushing out of my tap.

"The people are beautiful," Lyle jumps in, ignoring me, because who wants to wade into the corpse-strewn Ganges after a forkful of buckwheat and ham?

"Women in gilded silk saris, all that ancient architecture," Lyle reminisces for us. "The Gothic Revival railway station they built in the Bori Bunder area of Mumbai took my breath away."

In my boozy brain, listening to Lyle is like swilling a mouthful of skim milk and scotch, but I swallow hard, then turn to ask Swan about her new condo.

"Open concept. I can count the waves rolling in from my balcony," she explains with her usual beatific smile.

"Guess we're sellouts for an ocean view," I remark, wiping my mouth, because, I don't know, it's nine, and stuff with Rachel, and I can be such an asshole after a few glasses.

Dave shakes his head, interrupting. "We're planning to add a garden path and some kind of deck in the backyard. Anyone know a good landscape designer?"

"Do you know that the ocean has a floating garbage patch?" I snap back, harpooning another crêpe. "An eight million-ton trash vortex in the Pacific, twice the size of Texas."

Myra reaches out to touch my hand. "Let's keep it light tonight, okay Mark?"

"Refill?" Swan interjects, holding up her glass.

Myra grabs the empty wine bottle and gestures for me to join her in the kitchen. I hop up on the counter, tapping my heels on the bottom cupboard to the new beat in the living room.

Arms on hips, Myra leers at me.

"What? We're taking a toxic dump in the ocean, Myra. A three hundred million-ton plastic dump. Every year!"

She pours out a last swallow of Syrah into my glass. "We've been here before, right?" she says, raising her eyebrows.

I hold my arms up in surrender mode. When Myra leans in to pat my shoulder, I nuzzle into her soft, citrus-scented skin.

"Dangerous territory," she says, pushing my face firmly away. She cocks her head. "Rachel?" she asks. It's never a question.

"Spotted her in a Walmart parking lot," I say, holding my arms out in front of my waist as if I'm cradling a basketball. "Out to here."

"That woman has cruel teeth," Myra pronounces, shaking her head. She swings around to pull her last vintage red from the rosewood wine rack. "Listen, my cousin Beth's in town," she says, handing me a corkscrew. "She drives a hybrid."

"I've got a lot going on with Dan," I say, attempting to un-throttle the cork from its tight neck.

"What's up?"

I hand her the open bottle. "He died yesterday."

Myra draws me into one of her soft, swarming hugs. Her bare shoulders smell of sliced peaches. Just then an old Smiths tune comes wafting in from the living room. Morrissey's liquid baritone slides inside my skull, and I'm remembering one of our wedding dances, the way the nape of Rachel's neck had lit me on fire.

Morissey is moaning about something irretrievable.

"You managed to keep Dan alive for months," she says near my ear. "That's something."

If I don't breathe, maybe Myra will hang on longer, but Dave is calling her from the other room.

"So, can I text Beth?" she asks, breaking away.

"Did you know Morrissey's cat has feline leukemia?"

"Jeeesus, Mark," Myra replies, throwing up her hands.

Meals on Wheels pulls me out of bed three mornings a week. It keeps me busy. That way no one, not even Myra, has sorted out that I'm underemployed at the moment. Today I am packing up fifteen trays of Salisbury steak and potatoes, mixed greens, plus a tapioca mound compressed beneath crinkly gold foil. The tapioca tastes like boiled Kleenex, so I pick up two-dozen butter tarts to tempt my roster of seniors and shut-ins.

The ladies at the door always want to invite me in, grateful for a five-minute friendship. They tell me about their pills and toxic potions, as if each one has a personality. Their kids are away in Dallas or Sydney or New York or some place that doesn't smell of antiseptic bacon, coal tar, and hallway rot. Their faces tell the life stories they struggle to remember for me. Living through wars, they save everything, twist ties, old shopping carts, half of yesterday's meal they will wrap up for later. Sometimes, I can hardly get through my ten thirty a.m. to one p.m. delivery window. I ache for the men. Hair sprouting from their soft, slack orifices, sitting in front of their small TVs, forks shaking over slivers of wet meat. Hunched over at the door, they take their tray with a vague smile and lock up after me. They never last as long as the ladies.

When I return my insulated bags to the Meals on Wheels kitchen, it's after two p.m., and I'm in need of a mood changer. Time for YouTube and my last imported beer on the couch.

Walking in my front door, I stop dead in my tracks. Dan is flopping around the living room next to his tank, halfway out of the huge bag in which I had placed him for funereal disposal.

"Jezushchrist! You're alive?" I literally lunge toward him.

Sitting in a viscous puddle in the middle of my living room, his bulbous head pokes up from the punctured, fourteen-gallon kitchen bag. I soak up the stringy fluids around his body, which is turning a translucent pomegranate colour. His wide, misty eyes stare back at me.

You were gonna pitch me out like garbage? his drooping expression seems to say. A single Dan arm begins to curl around my couch leg.

"I thought you were dead!" I shout, fetching more towels, feeling dizzy and a little exhilarated as I return to sop up more fluids. Dan remains listless and silent, watching me. So I try to explain that the fresh krill I had bought him was supposed to keep him fed, full, and happy. That I was going to return him to the ocean, but then he took an unexpected turn for the worse.

Dan emits a kind of *glurp* sound. Goddamn it, he doesn't believe me. So I tell him the truth. That the acid seas were belching him out. That he was probably going extinct anyway. Then I hear a sort of *gluck-choke-suck* sound coming from his mantle. He needs an urgent sea-water flush through his gills. I grab him, slippery tentacles and mantle dribbling through my arms, and haul him off to the main bathroom down the hall. When I deposit him in the tub, he sprawls across the porcelain bottom, resembling a stringy grey mop, one arm tip slipping below the stainless steel stopper. He's growing paler by the minute so I race out and retrieve a bucket of salt water from the rented cylindrical tank I haven't yet had the stomach to return.

Sitting alongside the tub, I hold Dan's clammy body in the crook of my arm, bathing his mantle and gills, urging him to hang on. Absently, I start humming that Smiths tune about the pleasure of dying by your side. Dan slips away from me, poking his mantle up over the side of the tub. Across my black-and-white floor tile, he spews a cloud of indigo ink.

Shut up and save me, it reads.

"Myra!" I shout into my dumbphone. "Get over here now! Please."

A half hour later, Myra shows up with two specialty coffees, wagging a telling finger at me in the doorway.

"Who is she?" she says, on tiptoe, trying to get a look over my shoulder. "It's that folk guitarist with the Free Burma bandana from college isn't it?" she jokes.

"It was Tibet!" I shriek, my autonomic nerves shredding.

Breathing deeply, I place a hand on my chest to settle down.

I whisper to her in the doorway. "Look, I need to show you something inside, but you gotta be cool, okay?"

Myra grins as I lead her on toward the kitchen.

Before I can warn her, Dan pokes his head up from the double sink. In slow, deliberate movements, he drapes a long, spiked tentacle over the lip of the stainless steel basin.

Myra jumps back.

Dan crawls out. Drawing closer, he extends an arm pair that he manages to slip around her wrist before she realizes it and tries to shake him off.

Hello, I'm pretty sure he's saying. You the girlfriend?

His powerful suckers glance off her upper lip. Myra screams as Dan's arms quickly tighten around her throat. Neither of us can pry him off.

"What the fuck!" I shout, when Myra turns and grabs a carving knife from the cutlery block, swinging out wildly. With a reckless vertical swish, she manages to excise part of Dan's tentacle.

Dan slides back down onto the counter, retreating toward the backsplash, where he curls up into a tiny pain ball. Fluids, the colour of toilet bowl cleanser, begin to puddle around him, pouring off the counter's edge to the floor.

"It'll grow back," Myra sobs.

"That's a sea star!" I roar. "He can release his arm tips in a fight, but his two tentacles are for life."

While we're shouting, Dan drops down to the floor and muscles up my pant leg. He wraps one of his sucker-lined arm pairs around my neck, squeezing. A second arm pair twitches and glows near my eyes.

"Call the coast guard," Myra shrieks, like I've got marine rescue on speed dial.

"Let go, Dan," I beg, trying to pry him away, but his grip is formidable.

Myra begins racing around, opening and slamming drawers. Finally, she pulls on some silicone oven mitts and, using two metal spatulas, manages to pry Dan off me. Together, we transport him, gently, to the tub where I leave Myra and return with another full bucket of sea water from the tank.

"We need to get him to the ocean," I say to Myra, when Dan slides across the tub and squirts his inky lament across the tile.

Prepare for a lawsuit, motherfuckers.

After jamming a chair under the outside bathroom door-knob, Myra and I retreat to the bedroom.

"What do we do now?" I say.

Myra places one hand on her chest and calmly informs me that squid ink is much lower in fat and higher in protein than most alfredo or marinara sauces.

"Dan is not delicious."

"Soy-drenched, garnished, and draped over a bed of rice noodles?" Myra makes a show of spooning sauce over a plate. "I beg to differ."

"He's just out of his element."

"He's lost part of a tentacle. Probably half out of his mind by now," Myra retorts.

"Squid have survived for hundreds of millions of years without us," I protest. "Dan's blue bloodline is unequalled."

While we contemplate rapid rescue scenarios, we hear a loud whooshing sound coming from the bathroom. I crack the door to see Dan below the open tap, filling his mantle cavity. And before I can reach him, he seals up, squeezes, and jet propels himself out the cracked window.

All week, I double down on sedatives, do a daily grid search for Dan. Myra refuses to offer any help. She's probably angry over the pass I took on Beth or the fact that I lied about paying my mortgage on plastic and about having employment. The jig was up when I invented a final interview at an organic food co-op Myra knew had never existed in the city. She hung up before I had the chance to embellish about the employee free juice bar.

I pick up more krill from the bait store and drop two fresh crabs over ice into my bike pannier. An hour before dawn, I pedal back alleys and laneways, heartsick that Dan may be a rubber speed bump on some shitty side street by now. After a few hours of roaming, I hear splashes in a blow-up kiddie pool near a backyard shed. Cruising closer, I see that Dan is flopping around inside. Popping a crab from my pannier, I approach him, slowly.

"Buddy," I say, holding the food out. "For you."

Dan snatches the crab from my hand, runs his razor tongue along the shell, and snaps it up in his bony beak. Then he reaches out and tightens his good tentacle around my torso.

"How can I make this right?" I choke out, drawing what feels like my last breath.

He releases me, inking the sidewalk.

Oysters. Convertible. Road trip.

Over a beer at the legion, I ask my nearly eighty-year-old dad for the keys to his old hardtop Chevy convertible. Tell him I'm helping some friends move across the state. Since his second divorce, Dad spends most of his time on a bar-stool popping hard yellow candies and cursing his elbow arthritis. For the fiftieth time, he advises me to get a real job with benefits.

"A wife is nothing compared to a good pension."

"You didn't end up with either," I point out gently. And I don't even mention all the layoffs or his permanently wrenched right shoulder.

"You get what you make in life," he scoffs.

"Rachel's making a kid," I tell him. "And all I've got is a hairline receding faster than the Athabasca Glacier." I pretend to slick back my non-existent bangs to lighten the mood.

The old man drops his pint. "Change the goddamn channel, Mark," he says as foam splashes the bar stool next to me. "Rachel left you. It's not breaking news."

Dad takes another long swill of beer and slides over some folded money along with his Chevy keys.

"Bring it back full," he says and takes another swig of beer. "Be safe. Tell your mother hello."

To grant Dan's wish, I max out my credit card ordering a custom-built, eighty-gallon round, clear tank that I lay on its side, making the Chevy sag on its back struts. En route I'll stop to replenish the tank with full-strength sea water, making sure the salinity is just right, monitoring Dan's temperature.

Suitcase packed, I call Myra and leave her a rambling message about the journey Dan and I are about to embark on. We'll head north up the California coast to where the skies are clear, the sand is silky, and the tidal flows are like an all-you-can-eat krill buffet. We'll drop in to see my mother, and then I'll find a perfect spot to release Dan back to the sighing sea.

When Myra calls me back later, she instructs me in her jokey-caustic tone to pack hip waders, bring cash for the cheap motels, and consider a brain MRI. I tell her Dan is a vow I'm keeping, no matter what. Before we hang up, she tells me that Beth is back in town. Why not stop by for coffee before the big trip?

I finish packing up the Chevy, and skip Myra's to get on the road early.

Dan and I plot a meandering route from Sacramento to San Francisco and then along the Pacific Coast Highway in the pinging Chevy, heading for my mom's new house in drought-ridden Sandsblad, California. Tank water swishes across the dirty floor as we motor on. For miles, Dan remains silent, so I try to keep him entertained with classic Stones tunes. Dan's hearing is way too low frequency, so I start loudly reminiscing about my notorious exes from my early days. Jan the vegan, a fine rhythm guitarist, who liked to sprinkle her hemp pancakes with cocaine. And ethereal Celeste, who once fronted a local nineties band before becoming a highly accomplished periodontist. After years of pounding vocals, Celeste dumped me over the phone, told me to message her on Xbox if I ever wanted to connect.

Once I download Dave's Ex-ecutor app, Celeste will become a molting earwig with sick morning breath.

Dan begins blowing bubbles in his tank. "No," I say, "I have no need to share sharp, unkind words about Rachel." How she showed up at my street-fair booth wearing her save-the-whales smile and Roman sandals wound loosely around her smooth calves. Browsing my pamphlets in a blue sundress, she trailed the scent of sweet oranges and coconut. When I asked, she agreed to add her name to my petition, and I handed her a biodegradable fridge magnet with my number scrawled across it.

"Bold," she said, grinning.

"Bowled over," I replied, clutching my heart pathetically.

Two weeks passed. Pure agony.

What's worse than a grown man checking his texts on the half hour? A guy high-fiving the courier when Rachel called, three weeks after the fair, to invite him for pho.

Water splashes against the back of my neck. In the rearview, I watch Dan sloshing around in his tank. He gets it. He just does. Squid can see for miles, far beyond anyone else. He and his squid kin have spent their lives in places no natural light ever reaches. They understand the solemnity of darkness. Ask marine explorers to describe aliens and they'll probably evoke the mysterious deep-sea squid. Those giant, penetrating eyes positioned on either side of his bulbous head, like some creature on Mars. His complex DNA. His ability to withstand extreme cold and pitch-black seas. And yet light is as remote for them as Mars is from the sun. Stir not in murky waters if you know not the depths, Rachel always told me. Whatever the hell that really means.

By the time we pull into the driveway of Mom's new rancher in Dradsbad, Dan is slumped at the tank bottom. With only a cool sea breeze and the a/c sputtering, the car has been a bloody deep fryer for the last stretch.

"Hang in there, buddy," I say, reassuring Dan that soon I'll drop him off, and he'll have a whole undersea playground to explore.

Mom opens the front door and waves at me when I get out of the Chevy to stretch my legs. I can smell the coffee brewing from the driveway.

Mom embraces me, the scent of dark roast heavy on her skin.

Squatting, she eyes the tank inside the Chevy suspiciously. One of Dan's big, seductive eyes stares back at her from behind shatter-proof glass.

"Myra told me you'd become obsessed with a bottom-dweller," she observes, dryly. "I assumed she meant another musician."

"Wait a second. You just moved and changed your number. How did Myra know how to reach you?"

"I'm not El Chapo, honey. We talk."

Mom is seventy-two, but she can still cut it up. Myra was my college sweetheart, and Mom wept openly at Dave and Myra's wedding, before soaking up too many margaritas and ending up dirty jiving all night with the emcee.

Lifting Dan carefully from the tank, I keep my stance low, balancing his shifting weight as I enter the house and settle him on Mom's kitchen floor. With her permission, I quickly sanitize the double sink and fill it with extra saltwater from the tank. Immediately, Dan plunges in and starts playing with Mom's drain stopper.

"Can we crank up the air, Mom? Dan likes it super cold."

Mom turns down the thermostat. She pours the pot of

coffee into a white carafe and gestures toward the kitchen table.

"So, Mark, what's the news at six?" she asks, as we both pull out chairs.

"Got a new job. At the organic food co-op," I claim. "Senior manager, full benefits. Starts in three weeks."

"Terrific," Mom says, clapping. "So can you stick around for a bit, then?" Mom pours us coffee into her favourite china cups. "Could use your touch with the evergreens. They look like giant hairballs."

"I'll take a look on the way out. But I really need to get Dan back to the ocean."

Mom proceeds to complain about California's mandatory water bans. Not the need to conserve but the dire situation among leering neighbours.

"It's gone from tense to batshit crazy. Neighbours are hiding out behind bushes to drought-shame each other."

"Oceans are vast sinks absorbing our carbon dioxide. Fossil fuels keep choking the drain." I hear myself lecture Mom.

"I know, hon," my mother says in her soothing tone.

"Sea waters are turning to acid," I say, and shoot a sympathetic, knowing glance at Dan. "So what I'm saying is California's pretty much doomed."

"But, hey, coffee's good for us again," Mom replies, raising her cup cheerfully. She spoons out a blizzard of brown sugar into her cup then spills a small java puddle on the floor refilling mine.

I watch Dan slither out of the sink and drop to the floor.

"You know, I think we might need to get under this Rachel business."

"She's having a kid," I grunt, folding my arms. "She's taken to wearing these bright floppy hats and baring her growing midriff all over town like she's some kind of rare species of flora."

"You've been shadowing her?" Mom says, and casually drains all the liquid from her creamer into her own cup. She stirs and stares into swirling mocha, in silence a long time.

"I run into her sometimes. We live in the same town."

"Obviously the child's not yours?" Mom says, and her downcast eyes gut me.

And then the memory returns. Rachel rifling through the bottom drawer in the bathroom vanity, calling out to me, Did I see her new razor? I came to the doorway. She was towel-draped and had already slipped her one foot inside the foaming bath she had run. We weren't even going out that night.

My act was deliberate. I confessed to using her razor that morning to rid stray fibres from the cloth upholstery on our shitty basement sectional.

She just shook her head, declining outrage. When she pulled the curtain across, I could still see her naked shoulders slip under the bubbling waters. Hear her sigh as she submerged deeper, up to her neck.

I stuck my head through the curtain and shouted at her that she was wasting water. I may have said that she was a waste of water.

"Rachel wanted a different life," I tell my mother.

"What did you want?" she asks.

"Global waste-reduction, a drastic drop in greenhouse gases, a sign that we're not all going extinct," I almost shout, but what I mean is another story. A new beginning, or a different end, and something to make of the rot that's been piling up in me all these years.

My mother reaches out for my hand.

The climate-controlled air is beginning to turn my lips purple. I need a breath of fresh air outside, something to escape the cloying, sticky lung manipulation inside the house.

Avoiding my mother's gaze, I pull my hand away and watch Dan suck up some spilled coffee. Afterward he starts flailing around, shooting out tiny blue sparks of bioluminescence he uses to lure prey. I jump up. He's hallucinating. A terrible sign.

When I kneel next to him, he slips an arm pair around my ankle and spews black ink across Mom's freshly mopped tile.

California bites. Get me to the Rock.

As I am repacking the Chevy in the driveway, I try to reason with Dan.

Mom is shaking her head at us through the kitchen window, scooping up grey water from the dishes into a large bucket for the garden.

"Newfoundland's in eastern Canada," I try to explain to Dan. "That's practically on the other side of the world!"

When Dan holds up the stump of his severed tentacle, I almost vomit.

He's turning the colour of pavement. Dan's body is a marvel of undersea camouflage, capable of matching any shade it sees. When I look deep into those six-inch saucer eyes, I think they might just hold the colour of destiny.

How could I have not understood until now? Dan's been harbouring a dream. He's heard about the giant squid colonies that live on the coast of eastern Canada. For a billion years, these near-mythic deep-sea dwellers have been swimming in a universal mystery. He wants to dive among his old Newfoundland chums before his time comes.

"All right," I say, sternly. "But I'm choosing the motels."

During our first overnight stop, Myra rings me while Dan is enjoying his sea-salty Jacuzzi. I hit ignore and end up checking messages the next morning. Apparently, the aphids are suffocating her peonies, and the satiny sundrops along her back fence now resemble a mound of shrivelling, yellow buttholes. It's Myra's *mea culpa*. A cry for forgiveness. But I can't return now. I don't want to think about everything that's dying.

Dan insists we take the scenic route to Newfoundland, so we motor for five days en route to the Rock, an island of jagged cliffs jutting up from the North Atlantic like the back of an ancient, rough-hewn sea beast.

Sailing across on the ferry from Cape Breton to Port aux Basques, Newfoundland, it's blowhole city! A humpback rises from the water, then slaps his serrated tail against the Atlantic. Exhilarating! We finally spill out from the ferry's great white mouth and turn onto the highway. Using Dan's sensitive detection system, plus my GPS, we map a route toward Exploits Valley, where the giant squid can be reached via an out-of-the-way hamlet called Glovers Harbour, a town famous for its annual giant squid festival and dramatic iceberg spotting.

All I really know about Newfoundland is that last year locals spotted an iceberg four times the size of Manhattan floating off the coast near St. John's. Born in the Arctic, this one had broken free from a Greenland glacier, sailing away like a ghostly, thousand-year-old vessel, bearing its pale-blue mast. The massive berg travelled along the coast for days, whittling down like a pencil on the journey, on its way to disappearing forever.

After a refuel, we continue northeast and find the sign for Glovers Harbour. A pamphlet in the interpretation centre explains that one cold November day in 1878, the world's largest colossal squid was floundering in the surf near the town's sheltered bay, and fishermen hauled the 2.2-ton squid to shore. Later, the town became so renowned for the legendary catch, local officials decided to build a life-size, fifty-five-foot concrete-and-steel statue in its honour. Thousands stop by each year to get a close-up look at the writhing legs and two enormous tentacles now permanently frozen in mid-air.

We park on the roadside and follow a path down to the wooden dock, where blue-bottomed fishing trawlers and rowboats pitch and bob in the gusting wind. I set Dan down on the dock, and we both peer over the edge, look out in silence as ragged leathery waves unfold and stretch out beyond the bay, crash and collide into the turbulent open waters, before dissolving into the infinite sea. Looking down at Dan, I suck in my breath. Keep telling myself that it's all for the best. Dan's got his own deal with the future, and it's got nothing to do with me.

While I am trying to gather enough courage to say goodbye, I hear a splash. I look over and see Dan has slipped from his place on the dock and is plunging beneath the waves. His ruffling fin propels him in a diagonal line, a swimming bullet piercing the Atlantic. Then it's only me, and the wind-dragged waves rippling over the surface.

After a while, furtive clouds begin sweeping in over the bay. I rock back on my heels, licking a salty taste from my lips.

More powerful winds whip up, so quick and sharp, the cold cuts me open. Soon, the entire harbour is shrouded in ever-thickening fog, and I feel my throat constrict. With the wild, rocking motion on the dock, my entire body sways. I can't keep still.

What if Dan gets trapped on some hidden sea shelf? I think. What if the currents shift, leave him stranded and starving on some desolate beach? I slump down on the dock. What if the sharks get to him first?

Look at the storm, I think, feeling the harbour close in around me. We need to get the hell out of here. But Dan is gone. And Rachel isn't with me anymore. There's just this smell of salty air. A metal rowboat knocks against the edge of the slick wooden dock.

Maybe that's how Rachel felt. Tired of me fearing the

future, always wanting to turn back. Always trying to turn back. Storm-struck in the belly of a whale, busy swallowing all the light.

When I can't stand the frigid temperature any longer, I follow the winding path uphill back to the main road. On the way, I see a young man leaning against the giant squid statue, his ball cap barely reaching the squid's concrete underbelly. He holds one triumphant arm in the air, the other palm is brushing the bottom of the squid's siphon. He's posing for his buddy's camera, as if he's just landed the big one.

And I think about those Newfoundland fishermen. The ones back in 1878 who pulled their giant from the sea. Imagine the men hip-wedged against the rowboat's hull, leaning out across the choppy surf, trying to corral the squid's magnificent body with their thick-braided rope. Weak armed, the men kept hauling in the creature, his flailing squid body the length of a school bus. Hand over hand, they pulled the sleek form toward shore, the bulb of its head poking up from the water, his monster eyes as big as basketballs. How the squid must have landed in a heap on that rocky shoreline, two sucker-lined arms draped across the men's rubber boots.

I can see the ruddy-cheeked fishermen standing in a circle, shirt-sleeves rolled up to mucky elbows, spreading the squid's fins out like a tarp. An extraordinary creature laid bare, no longer a mythic tale from the phantom sea. Maybe an old man from the village emerged, with his lit pipe and heavy woollen pants. Patting the fishermen on the back, he squatted down, glanced into those elusive, giant eyes that once brought light to complete darkness, reached out to touch a tentacle, and allowed the mystery to slip from his hands.

When I bend over and grab my knees, my mouth tastes like a backwater cave spilling stomach brine. My mind is reeling with thoughts of Dan and Rachel and what comes next.

And I think, All our lives as predators, and not one reason to pray.

Gindelle of the Abbey

The kettle sings its wispy falsetto in the kitchen as you pull out the dark brown moustache from the locked desk drawer in the basement, coat the back with spirit gum, press lightly against the vertical grooves of your upper lip, letting the whiskers hang over, so you resemble not some aging metal rocker but a man descending, his eyes flitting toward loneliness.

Jemma would never recognize you. She's cocooned upstairs in a slumber so heavy not even the Australian face-roaming wolf spider you'd seen on YouTube would rouse her.

It's almost five a.m.

You should be at the corner of St. James and Second by now in your torn green flannel sleeping bag.

Forget the tea. Climbing up from the basement, in your father's tattered three-button wool coat, you stop at the landing, listening for floor creaks upstairs. Soundless. You pull the kettle from the heat in the kitchen, wrap up three blueberry-bran muffins in paper towels, and grab your keys.

On the drive downtown, lean, flat clouds skip across a sky the colour of an Arctic sea. In the rear-view, you smooth down the corners of your mouth, thinking human hair really does make the most convincing moustache. Though the last thing you ever feel these days is human.

Saturdays are for corrugated boxes and crayon-etched cardboard signs. You tell no one about these weekly excursions. Especially not Jemma, who thinks you are on your regular fishing trip to Orion Lake with Ted the philanderer. The two of you bouncing over the water, angling for northern pike that grow two feet long and sport a mouth full of spiked teeth.

Your own teeth are painted with nicotine-stain enamel. Over the years, you've learned how to use makeup brushes to create the right effect. Black wax for the chipped teeth. A base layer and blending shadows for your hollowed forehead and eyes. Wrinkles are something else. It can all go horribly wrong so fast. A few light passes with a black pencil and cream (just a touch) to build up the lines around the mouth. A lifetime of decay is what you're after.

Another rear-view check. Your face is the colour of a dried-out coconut shell. Lighting a cigarette, you take a few long drags then let it burn all the way to the stub.

A weak sun dribbles through the cherry tree–lined street by the time you park before a line of three-storey homes with gingerbread trim painted the colour of Easter eggs. Grabbing two green garbage bags from the trunk, you shuffle east, body bent like a pulled nail, walking an hour in second-hand shoes so large you have to keep your heels flat just to stay inside them. From the coat and the cigarette, your body reeks of tobacco and mothballs bathed in naphthalene. You'll drop the tackle box, wave hello, then strip down in the shower before Jemma gets a whiff of your exhilarating pits tonight.

Keep moving. There is a particular light you mean to catch. A stolen, silent hour on city streets, where no one notices, and no one breathes.

Scratching your balls with dirty knuckles, you make your way north. A sweaty early morning jogger looks over, startles, then speeds away from you on a diagonal sprint across the road.

Down toward the overpass, the city opens its mangy mouth. Man-shaped mounds soak up hours behind cardboard shelters, their faces hidden behind sharp, piss-fed shadows. Drained of colour, the city here is more vivid than any mushroom hallucinations you ever had with Eddie back in Moncton. In a while, sin will come strolling past you in torn nylons, trailing bottomless grief. A young man they call Pitbull is sporting a scraggy beard and torn T-shirt, leaning against a brick wall smoking a cigarette. He's so thin he could thread his own arms through the spent syringes at his feet. You light up and offer him a loosie from the crushed pack in your jeans.

Itchy to the tip of your very fetching moustache, your greedy eyes feast on these ragged faces. Some nod, though you're such a leering tourist, as sordid as your fucking moustache. A woman yells out from a narrow corridor. "Fuck you! Fuck off!" You want to hold all the sound. The rambling speeches. The dumpster lids crashing down from the alley. Jerking cars, their brakes squealing as someone floats across the road toward oblivion. Most here look as if their flesh were drawn in pencil, thick, heavy strokes around the mouth and ears, a certain hardness in the wrinkles that fan out to the edge of their cheeks. Their eyes are opaque. Not brown or green or round or almond-shaped or hooded with a glint of reflected light, but smudged into shallow sockets, blending in with the cracked pavement, the exact shade of decaying streets, as if erasure was a necessary birthright. The lingering stench of despair is so strong in your nostrils, you think you'll never smell the bottom of it. It leaves your heart hobbled in places. You want to save this whole goddamn world, one shallow sentient being at a time. The urge to abandon your life and disappear into these streets is so strong, your shame walks on four legs and howls.

"Motherfucking diesel surveillance moon candy on the cocksucking beach!" an old man shouts to no one, pushing a shopping cart with its thin, splitting metal ribs.

There are words in his beard, life jolting in his eyes when you offer him your coat. He stops then lurches forward, his skin bitten with scabs at the hairline, more flaking from the tip of his long nose. Ignoring your offering, the man keeps scanning the alleys. Inside this jumbled verse is a low-frequency hum you are sure no one else can hear.

Gindelle hears it too, you think.

When you reach the corner at Second Avenue, you wave and smile at the old woman, barely visible beneath a tattered green-and-white-striped awning. Her back against the wall of the brick-front building, she's balled up between a vacant Thai restaurant and the delivery door of a shabby antique place.

"You look like shit, Red," Gindelle of the Abbey croaks at you from her throne, two foam-filled green cushions that keep her bottom hovering a half-foot off the pavement. You grin, noticing her hand is still cupped in a queen's carriage wave.

"Firecrackers," you say, flattening your sleeping bag alongside hers. "*Bang, bang* going off all goddamn night in the park."

She calls you Red, though your tattered hair is streaked grey, a touch of baby powder rubbed into the midline bald patches. One Saturday Gindelle just leaned over and said, "You're like those red dots on a map. Always moving. Never in one place. Restless bugger, aren't you, Red?"

Judging from her puffy eyes, she's had a turbulent night. But her eyes have a perpetual glow, the way your mother's always do, making breakfast in the rented bungalow in Moncton, not far from where the prostitutes circle Victoria Park. You think you can hear your father bitching about the squawking crows from the living room.

"Get any sleep?" you ask Gindelle.

"Cops urged us to move along after midnight," she shrugs, wrapping a blanket around shoulders as thin as handlebars.

"Bastards."

"No. One of them brought me coffee. We shared a powdered doughnut, and he told me all about his wife's cyst. Told him one shot to the neck." Gindelle makes a squeezing syringe gesture. "Gone."

...

You found her sitting alone one Saturday under this awning. She looked up at you and pushed over to make room, offering you a stale biscuit from one of her tote bags. Guiding you around her sacred steeple with pride, you could tell she knew how to stake out a plot of land and build a life around it.

Gindelle's cape is stained with grease all the way from Saskatchewan. Something about a farmhouse and a fall. The grain farm she and her husband built was set way back on a dirt road. While she worked in the garden, her husband liked to sneak in and pluck the sweet red peppers, barely ripe from their green canopies, eating them like apples. When he dropped dead seeding canola, Gindelle tried to keep things humming. Almost snapped her back coming off the tractor. Chronic back pain, emergency rooms, pain killers, dirty overalls, loaded up on morphine. She finally quit the farm. But the heroin high she developed to sleep pain-free again? A woman her age? Who would believe it? Not the people parading past. Not even you. Later, thinking of Gindelle's life on the farm, her fall and this brutal, graceful landing—never a word of self-pity from her lips—you close your eyes and savour these Saturdays.

You rifle through your pocket. "A new bakery was handing out samples," you say, offering her a blueberry muffin wrapped in paper towel.

Gindelle shreds her cake with a short row of chipped lower bicuspids, her neck puckering like congealed gravy while she chews.

"What's up today?" you ask.

"Repair the chapel, then to the cloister for prayers," she crackles, pointing up to the split awning, her laugh an untamed elegy above the growing traffic hiss.

You swap stories on your side of the double lane. Crossing that road is like playing chicken, especially on weekends. Gindelle calls it motor-car bingo and has two broken toes to prove it. She was here before the office towers. Before the mall shoppers lumbered past her corner on their way to the food court and five levels of free indoor parking.

You tuck your garbage bags and your backpack behind the brick pillar by the antique store's delivery entrance, decide to patch the leaky awning with duct tape when Gindelle does her usual food court scavenge.

"I hate bran," you say, holding out your last muffin to her, then lighting a cigarette. Jemma bakes when she's anxious. Jemma is frequently anxious.

Gindelle tucks the plump muffin in her bag, folds her feet underneath her, the white socks and sandals barely visible beneath her scrawny bottom, though she sits tall as Jemma at her wheel.

From her potter's wheel, Jemma will spin clay into exquisite glazed bowls she fires in the backyard kiln. She sells the art she loves, sometimes shatters the work she doesn't. Her studio is littered with shards and curses. When she throws again and centres the lopsided clay between her hands, forging a hypnotic, spinning shape, so smooth along the outer edge that when she pinches it, the mouth opens and pulls the wobbling mass into something new; you could almost weep. Her potter's hand, her heart's extension, is cupped grace, was how you first fell in love. The promise that a world, once misshapen and broken, was fixable.

"Red, hand me one of them." And you offer Gindelle a cigarette and a light.

The spinning mess in your head could sully most of Manhattan, or Moncton, where you were born forty-one years ago, hating the river valley, the French you could never master in school. That fucker, Doucette. And you with your fighting temper and fake jiu-jitsu holds, choking your thick Acadian accent. You'd hang out in borrowed, long-finned cars, cigarette pinched between your teeth, ripping around Lewis Street with Eddie and your three best friends. Hair goop. Hockey-stick slashes. Selfish pricks. Eight bucks between you. You owned the city. You fucking hated the city.

Lost for a moment in that grainy picture of youth, you think, sitting here on the wet pavement, you're a ghost in your own glossy life.

Gindelle scratches her scabby elbows. She removes her ball cap, sports a snow cone of white hair atop her tiny head. Fifty cents in the overturned cap she sets in front of her to start the day off. You've got a few coins, too, you say. Skipped a meal or two so you could buy a Big Mac later.

A young couple strolls up to your corner. You watch the man's gaze lower to where you both huddle, then quickly cast ahead to a distant doorway. Window-browsers. Tire-kickers. They've got concerned faces, but not enough follow-through. You and Gindelle know to wait for the real action; the weekend shoppers sipping five-dollar lattés. Better yet, the charity canvassers sporting clipboards and hipster beards. Best is the old guys with wild hair and battle scars, often good for a few quarters, or a half sandwich from the sub place down the street.

As the day drifts, the city spills weekend explorers. Families emerge from parked cars. Teens ooze out of suburban buses. Couples push strollers hung heavy with bags, hurrying to catch the green light, racing Gindelle who is sitting high on her foam-padded throne. She's queen of these streets. Watch them throw coins at her feet.

By noon, the cloud bottoms are burnt aluminum pots. Gindelle tucks her blanket underneath her chin.

"It's really coming down now," Gindelle says. "There go our tips."

The rain flies into your doorway at a sharp angle, begins dribbling then slamming in through the awning. You push Gindelle's cart behind the pillar. A crash of thunder and you remember that flash rainstorm in Moncton the day you packed up the rental truck, threw in your hockey bag next to a used Fender telecaster, and you and Matt and Eddie, who made all his own skins and never played the song the same way twice, were set to jam all the way to the Big Smoke. Split gas. Skipped any towns without a truck stop. Kept your lizard Smoothie-Rich warm while his tail flicked out the open window, a fresh pile of leafy greens and crickets in a Ziploc for the road.

Then someone heard a shot, or maybe that's how you remember it now. Couldn't have been. The collision was probably six blocks away. You and Matt were waiting at the curb with boxes, mangling your beef jerky. Five minutes away, near the old fried chicken place, Eddie's front tire had skidded out and he fishtailed across the road, sliding into oncoming traffic. The only thing in Eddie's pocket was your number. Your father got the call. The thought of you and Matt standing like orphans on the curb stuffs you with disgust. Christ. Anyone could have eaten asphalt that day. You and Matt just sat at the kitchen table, capsized, blotting your eyes before your stunned mother. Next day, you tossed your keys across the rental counter, drained a half-bottle of whiskey with Matt in the woods, and neither of you said another word. No one had an escape plan without Eddie.

You excelled in science at Dal. Came home summers to fight with your old man, mean as any Moncton winter.

"Get a fucking job!" shouts a lanky kid on his long-board, passing your corner as you pack up in the rain. With a little hop, he does a flip, tumbles, cursing when his board falls away from him.

"Go shit yourself!" you yell back, so the kid comes toward you with speed.

He spits in your direction, but the wind returns a fat, slick gob into his eyes. He can't even see you. You're the looming threat to his invincible ride. An accident waiting to happen. Like Matt and Eddie and Moncton that day, then Smoothie-Rich ended up dying three months later, after a cold snap, and you hid in the garage, baggy-eyed bawling as you pitched a month's worth of freeze-dried grasshoppers into the trash.

The skater flips you off. You look into his bloodshot, watery eyes. Can tell by the skunky scent he's twelve feet high.

You are these Saturdays. Imposter. Trespasser. Thief. Smuggler of stories and a fake ID. Recorder of foot traffic, and one-line taunts, while the streets darken Gindelle's skin, steal life from her exhaust-choked lungs. You are circling the underworld with Gindelle of the Abbey as your queen. A dime bag of weed in your pocket for later, propped up against a metal newspaper box, you're free.

Thunder roars. A flash rips the sky in half; the light slaps the inside of your skull clear. The awning is useless, so you carry Gindelle's things with yours around the block and unpack the blue tarp from your duffel. She waits while you tuck one end of the tarp beneath the "cardboard only" dumpster, then slide the other beneath your duffel.

Into the sagging cardboard cathedral you huddle next to Gindelle, who touches the shiny nylon roof with its sad, sagging walls. Gindelle agrees to keep an eye out for cops, while you relieve yourself behind the Chinese import place.

"Bring me back a paw-waving kitty?" she says, winking.

You don't tell her that it's actually a Japanese beckoning cat, and the only reason you know this is because of your trip with Jemma to Chinatown for herbs. Jemma's acupuncturist had sent you both there for a fertility boost a few years ago, after yet another set of cramps and spotting. She had passed another rubbery piece of tissue into the bowl and you both retreated to your own corners for three weeks. You stayed in the spare room. And when she

215

decided to visit her mother for a week, you spent the nights traipsing across the east end.

When you return to the makeshift tent, Gindelle's lips are turning bluish, so you tell her to go warm up in the food court, before security runs her out. She promises to return with Shanghai surprise.

Alone, you text Jemma under the tarp. *Storm came up. Lake so rough we're holed up in a pub. Ted already pickled. Will bring home a chewy red. xoxo*

Jemma texts back. *Throw Ted to pike. Make it a full-bodied Cabernet. Two forks. xoxo*

Tin-taps on the dumpster drum you to sleep. When you open your eyes and step out, Gindelle is nowhere to be seen.

Leaning over a garbage can, Cleopatra approaches, is batting heavy lashes at you.

"Have you seen my dog?" she asks, one pinky hooked inside her jeans belt loop.

You have not seen her dog. Groggy, you realize the rain has finally stopped.

A yellow T-shirt slides off of Cleopatra's bony right shoulder. Raccoon smudges around her green eyes, tiny mascara flecks dot her eyelids. You notice her skin is sliced with small silver hoops in three places.

She holds her hands waist wide. "He's kind of barky," she explains.

"What's his name?"

"Made him a collar out of leather and twist ties," she says, looking down the alleyway. She walks a few feet toward the Chinese place and returns. Her tongue clicks, and she yanks a wad of gum between her fingers that she snaps back against her two crooked front teeth.

"Roddie," she tells you, scraping the gum from her front teeth.

"No dogs except us old ones," you say, realizing how creepy that sounds.

Eyeing the coins in your cap, Cleopatra tells you she and her boyfriend could use some money for dog food. You search her eyes. Six years of Saturdays, you know this girl is hocking one loogie of a lie.

"Where's your boyfriend now?" you say, casually rubbing your eyes.

Cleopatra points to a white van you had noticed circling the block earlier in the day. Precision Roofing is painted across it next to a corgi howling Roof! Roof! The van swings back around and stops at the alley entrance. Cleopatra waves. The van screeches. A spot opens up. Vanboy reverses hard, parks, and slams the door behind him.

He's tall, slack-boned, with a sloppy smile, like a runny fried egg. You notice a scribble of hair around his mouth. He's at least twenty-eight. Probably older.

"Fuck you been?" Vanboy shouts at Cleopatra.

You hand Cleopatra four dollars in change from your pocket. "I'll keep an eye out for Roddie."

She pockets the coins and returns to Vanboy. "He broke the leash," she grumbles, but her voice is wobbly.

You can tell. Cleopatra is living a life that will split her open by seventeen. You've seen it first-hand. Like that girl on Tamrack Street a month ago, lying across a pool table, dead after scoring pills laced with fentanyl. Instinctively, you touch the vial of naloxone dangling from an old shoelace around your neck. You keep it tucked under your black T-shirt along with a sterile syringe hidden in an inside coat pocket. You're a vampire in reverse, fighting off death by injecting life back into the next overdose.

When Cleopatra turns back toward you, she tugs at her T-shirt collar, revealing a string of plum-shaped bruises running from her neck down her left shoulder.

The back alley barks. Crouching, Cleopatra holds out her arms for a mangy hound-lab that trots up and flops onto her feet, smelling of rotting shrimp. His paws are sticky, a clipped right ear folds forward. When he begins nibbling at his own bottom, Cleopatra scoops him up into her arms.

Vanboy cuffs the dog's head, then holds his hand too close to Cleopatra's cheek.

Cleopatra twists away from him to shield the dog.

"Hey," you say, taking a bold step toward Vanboy.

He takes hold of one of her elbows, whips the girl out in the direction of the van. He sneers and shows you his folding knife.

From the far end of the alley entrance, there is a loud clatter. He sees Gindelle carrying her food court remnants in her hands. Vanboy looks back at you, sharpening his pinpoint pupils.

"Your old lady?" he says, shaking his head. "Fucking ugly."

Heat rises from your scalp. He's nothing but a low-level, scrape-it-together dealer. Not interested in any goddamn pennies. He's probably plying Cleopatra with drugs, luring her into service.

When Vanboy turns away, you don't say a goddamn bloody thing to the back of him. You watch them climb back into the van.

Cleopatra tries to keep the dog still on her lap in the van. She's staring out the side window. Your feet are made of clay. Coward. Fake.

Vanboy wheels into traffic, a lurch to beat the red. There's a bang, the shrill sound of metal scraping metal.

Mr. Kon from the noodle place is running toward the intersection with you. You find Cleopatra looking rattled in her seatbelt. You open the passenger door, escort her and the dog to the sidewalk, claiming the girl is your niece.

"You okay, honey?"

Vanboy is holding onto his unhooked left shoulder, screaming. Oblivious to anyone else, he is slamming the hood of the parked car he's managed to plow into.

"Fucking assholes!" he shouts into the empty vehicle.

He points at his own windshield while the crowds circle him.

By the time sirens whir into the intersection, you've moved your dazed Cleopatra to a safer place.

Where Cleopatra leans forward, the edge of the double bed sags, and the springs almost poke up under the sheets. The odour of bug spray makes you both sneeze. You ask again.

She recites the days of the week, backward and forward.

You drag your chair closer toward the edge of the bed in the no-frills hotel room. She is asking about Vanboy.

"He has a dislocated shoulder. He was sitting up on a stretcher, cursing the paramedics."

Cleopatra reaches in her bag, holds up her phone, and snaps your picture. "Pervert," she says, her hands shaking. She pitches the peach-coloured comforter from her lap, demanding to know more about what happened. To know about Roddie.

You guide her to the curtained window, point to a weedy strip of grass where Roddie is munching on kibble next to a silver water dish. He's tied up to a bench.

"Police found drugs," you lie to her, not for the first time. "Under the driver's seat," you add. "I had to act fast."

Cleopatra looks you over suspiciously. With her fingers, she brushes the top of her lip. You feel her heavy stare and realize your moustache is slipping. You pat it down again, but the whiskers keep peeling away from your bristly skin.

"What are you? Some fucking child rapist?" Cleopatra shouts.

"No, no." Your hands fly up, open palmed. "My car is a few blocks away," you say. Another lie. "Take you anywhere. Hospital. Shelter. Friend's house?"

Cleopatra finds her backpack on the floor, pitches it over her shoulder and heads for the door. Blocking the way, you promise to drop her off at the bus station.

"Buy you a ticket. No strings."

"Fuck you, porn stash," she says and snaps your picture again.

"Wait."

When she grabs for the door handle, you press the door shut.

You dig out a clip of twenty-dollar bills and hand her a few, backing away.

Cleopatra weighs the bills in her palm. She cocks her head.

"Seen guys like you," she replies, sliding the cash into her front pocket. She holds up the phone again and clicks.

"What if I send this picture to the cops?"

What if Jemma finds out you buy prostitutes soup on your lunch hour? That some winter nights when she's teaching her advanced clay-throwing class, you hop into the front seat with cabbies going nowhere. That you almost killed your father—he was drunk, you were almost eighteen and tired of his fists. Your old man had misjudged the forklift, clipped a warehouse rack at the end of a twenty-four-hour shift and ended up getting pinned beneath a load of steel tubing. The surgeon managed to save his arm, but the man he struck, the one who was bent over his clipboard counting rows, would never walk again. Your father was not the same man afterward. The distance between you and your father's grief became a gulf neither of you could manage to cross. Your mother held her tongue, made him breaded pork chops, taught you how to vanish.

It wasn't so much your mother's words as the dusty look in her copper eyes, the fallen smile whenever she glanced over at your father, permanently anchored in rose-armchair misery, sighing in a way that meant that's the way your life goes sometimes.

He'll hurt you, you think. Your mind is lost and lurking in the dark of this cigarette-stained motel room.

Cleopatra tugs again at her T-shirt, exposing her bruise-ringed neck. Seeing your alarmed reaction, she shrugs.

"Mall cops," she gestures at her neck. "Over a fucking hoodie." She touches her upper lip again and smirks.

"I can find out where they took him," you say, in a casual tone. "Stick around and we'll figure it all out."

Cleopatra brushes her lip again.

"It's a trial run," you mutter self-consciously, patting the dip in your upper lip. "Wife isn't sure about facial hair."

You ask her to wait another second and rummage around in the backpack, handing her a dog collar with a stainless steel clip and matching leather leash. "Got these while you were napping."

"Thanks," she says, then pats her front pocket. "He's a roofer. Laid off. An asshole sometimes. We're working it out. Fucked-up world, isn't it?"

"Can I drive you and Roddie someplace quiet?" you offer. "Please?" Because she's a comet floating toward your sun, and everything's hot and speeding up in your brain now.

She shakes her head. "A thousand girls like me out there. We don't need you."

Before Cleopatra leaves, she takes your moustache in like she's figuring out how to fix a crooked jigsaw puzzle piece. "Go home, porn stash," she says finally. "Maybe Jesus had it coming."

...

You pick your way back to Gindelle through men with slow shifting eyes. Near Second Avenue you watch an old woman trade threats with a man across the street. A wispy-haired old-timer, his skin the colour of spent tea bags, sits slapping at his neck, eating from a paper cup filled with sugar. You drop a few dollars in his lap and make your way to the fast-food place.

Gindelle beams at you below the green awning. When you sit down next to her, you hand over the grease-stained paper bag, because you know Gindelle is crazy for fries.

"Red, Red, Red." Gindelle smiles and munches. She pulls the burger from the bottom of the sack, lets out a squeal of delight when she lifts the bun from the patty.

"Extra pickles!"

"And double sauce."

She takes a bite, offering you the next one, but you wave her away, saying you've already feasted. Some lanky kid with long dreads dropped a ten-dollar bill in your hat.

Gindelle tucks her blanket around her shoulders and licks ketchup from the corners of her mouth. Instinctively, you touch your freshly glued moustache.

"Ain't life grand," she says.

Pulling out your sleeping bag from behind the pillar, you drag it next to hers. Fumbling with the zipper, you get a whiff of baked chocolate coming from the coffee shop three doors down.

"Where did you get to, Red?"

"Met an old friend at the Y."

"Too bad," she says, shaking her head, tearing away the last bit of meat. "You were gone before I could say anything."

"Say what?"

"It was so good," she replies, and pulls her arm across her chest in a pitching motion.

"What was?"

Gindelle unleashes her wild laugh that ends with an excited shiver falling across her shoulders. She giggles and points to the end of the alley, her eyes wide open. "When my big-ass Coke hit that van prick's windshield."

Jemma is dining on huevos rancheros when you arrive home, much later than expected. The concoction, heavy on the tomato-chili sauce, runs sloppily over her rye toast. She looks up at you, swallows a messy forkful. She licks salsa bits from her lips.

"How's Ted?" she asks, her voice straining for warmth.

"Left him passed out on his couch." You drop the Cabernet on the counter and pull up a chair. "Should have texted you again."

"I ruined the bowl with the inlaid clays," she says. Another forkful of chili vanishes.

While she slides her rye toast under a mound of the spicy sauce, in silence, you look around the room. Jemma has an inclination for *fin de siècle* movements, so your house is filled with images of wilting French women and decadent men in top hats. She likes to guide you on museum visits, dropping words like *rococo* and *dada* and *the grotesque* as you scan paintings signed by artists with furious-sounding names. Her dazzling mind is an elite gym and you're barely reaching the swing sets. You understand fluorocarbons and sulphur hexafluoride. A chemist for a company that deals in home insulating foams, not finger frostbite and foot rot.

She grabs her breasts and holds them together like pressed oranges, a pained look crossing her face.

"Sore?"

Jemma makes a plus symbol with her index fingers. She grabs the indicator from the bathroom and drops it on the table.

You look down, hold her tight, until the huevos rancheros fire up her throat again and she reaches for a glass of water.

"Can we?" she asks.

You nod. "Yes."

It's just pee on a stick right now, you think. You know urine contains human chorionic gonadotropin, a hormone produced when an egg attaches to the uterus. Conception after thirty-five was like winning the goddamn lottery, the gyno had said it right out. With her irregular periods, and your family history of diabetes, odds were slim to none.

You had both accepted the idea of childlessness. Jemma kept on spinning masterpieces. You held on to your secrets, imagining the vases growing ever-widening bellies.

She gives you a cautious smile, and you kiss her sweet, onion mouth. That tickle in her stomach is the sensation of molecules binding, but there's no reason yet to believe in a miracle. Her mouth, this spell, the long intoxicating night, is not the only thing you love unconditionally.

...

The beard arrives two weeks late in an unmarked bubble package. Jemma hands the package over with a puzzled look, giving the envelope a quick shake. You mutter something about Sean's laptop at work, a graphics card, some tech term you know will bore Jemma blind.

She shrugs and returns to her studio.

On the way to the basement to tuck the beard in your bottom drawer, you linger outside her studio, watch her small belly graze the wooden shelf of her mud-spattered wheel. She's wearing goggles, a white mask to avoid blowing dust. Mesmerized by the throwing, you watch how her fingers find the hollow, with a slight pinch a muddy neck wobbles, rises, then drops back into her spinning lap.

You think of Gindelle's loose throat and smile.

You tear open the padded package and pull out the expensive beard you've kept hidden for six months. The beard is a thing of beauty. Hand-knotted, Swiss-lace backing, a little scratchy, but a snug fit over your freshly shaven face. The packaging boasts "100% human-hair beard," next to a photo of a smiling young man inviting you to choose your transformation: pimp, emperor, or detective! And you can't decide which. Laying it down, you pull out a fresh bottle of spirit gum and begin painting your chin.

...

All along Second Avenue where you walk, heavy winter jackets are slung over chair backs in the restaurants and bars.

At the corner, you find Gindelle tucked inside her sleeping bag below the awning, with its messy patchwork of silver duct tape. She has a takeout coffee cup between her hands, is wearing the grey toque you gave her three weeks ago.

She smiles broadly, her lap wrapped in a skirt made of a rubber doormat. Gindelle is so beguiling, you think, bowing to her as you approach from the sidewalk.

She scans your too-trimmed bearded face.

"Pretty eyes, Red," she says and squints to get a better look at your face as you approach. "You look like a grey wolf," Gindelle laughs. "Missed you."

While you unroll your sleeping bag, she gestures up.

"Cold and clear tonight," she says. "On the farm at night you could see the Milky Way like a giant, hazy pinwheel. Sometimes even Mars, outshining all the stars."

"Ever want to visit?"

"Me and a bunch of little green men?" she says, tucking her arms back inside her bag. "I'm good here."

"Commute would kill me." You wink. Looking over at Gindelle you think no place more strange and remote than now. If you can just figure out how to stay.

A bitter wind tonight and Gindelle yearns, not for the single-room hotel further east, for thin sheets lined with bed bugs, but for this faded awning sheltering her from the tattered edges of night. Only when freezing to death is her only option will Gindelle finally relinquish her throne, she says. In the shelter, she claims she's nothing but a sad old woman with ghoulish teeth.

When you shake out the dirt from your bag and crawl inside, Gindelle gestures for you to slide up closer. Hip to hip, you trade heat, and she throws her cape around your shoulders, to stifle the chill threading up your spines. You resolve to find Gindelle another coat, something with satin lining and puffy sleeves, tell her a box went missing off the loading bay at the shopping mall.

Gindelle's bony fingers find your wrist and squeeze. You pet her arm. There isn't enough time, you think. Already Saturday excuses are wearing thin. Jemma needs more of you. Last night you held her hair back while she was hugging the toilet over the smell of raw chicken.

You watch Gindelle sway quietly, her legs tucked up close to yours, then she tips sideways against you. Her rattling breath against your thick-bearded chin is a force keeping you fixed to the ground. Feeling Gindelle's tired body against yours steals your next breath, makes you believe in this moment you can keep the world safe.

Gindelle starts to breathe heavy, a cough caught deep in her chest. She sighs and her whole body relaxes again.

You want to ask her about thresholds. Last chances. Where life begins. You would offer all the gold coins in your purse, pull the secrets from every locked drawer.

"Red," she says, "I'm tired," and falls asleep in your arms.

Polymarpussle
Takes a Chance

It was as if the silver poplars that ran behind my mother's house were bent forward all fall, their brittle limbs shivering with winter dread. By the time the November chill arrived, climbed inside my bone rack refusing to leave, she had been dead two months. Then cold and numbness came to me as naturally as sleep. I missed too many work days, gave up answering the phone altogether. My roommate finally called Alicia over.

This morning she shows up with a vat of minestrone soup and hugs me at the door. She whispers something about shadowy grief and how time gets tangled up in it and then slips a folded list into my hand. Calamus root, rose quartz, plus the new *Dreams of the Dolphin* CD. Alicia directs me to a tiny row shop at the end of a cul-de-sac downtown and makes me promise to visit this afternoon.

The sign on the purple door reads "Open, Hours Changeable." No one behind the counter. Good. What I came for I didn't really know. I unfold Alicia's list and shove it into a back pocket. What have you got for a hungry, pawing grief, I want to ask.

A musky scent drifts toward me from an Ali Baba's cave of trinkets at the back of the store. On my haunches, I poke around the crowded carved teak racks, pull out a bronze figure with four arms, and blow the dust from its shoulders. He's seated, bare-chested with a pitchfork in his upper left hand, a small drum clutched in the upper right. Around his neck, a snake is coiled, its thick diamond head poking out below the figure's left ear. The sticker on the bottom reads Tryambaka Deva, Three-Eyed God. Moon in his right eye; sun in his left; third alight with fire. I stare into that wide-open third eye, feeling pure light, only energy and awe.

A knife pain begins to skewer my right lung, a roaring heat rips through my veins, tears sinew from bone, each vertebrae unfastening.

I scream.

An old shopkeeper shuffles up behind me.

"Not long now," is all he says.

I stumble outdoors. The deserted streets are concave mirrors, sliding away from me. My body begins to pitch wildly in the dark. When my knees slam to the sidewalk, flames begin licking the back of my throat dry. I paw at my coat. My shoulders, elbows, wrists unfold like wooden yardsticks.

I look down, shocked to discover four extra limbs.

The change is transcendent. A revelation. Telling my friends proves more difficult.

...

Alicia R., ex-girlfriend and spoon-jewellery maker: no way! Gods have it way too rough these days. Look, I've got a whole book about body transmogrification in the thinning planetary atmosphere. We can abort the morph. Smudge stick, pink crystals, and a pinch of rosemary. You'll be godless by dinner.

Harlon B., college philosopher king turned indie-record-store lounger: you don't believe in God, so you invented one. Unseen forces? Nah. See this frosty craft brew I'm holding? That's invisible barley proteins, gas, and sweet mystery foam, my friend. In beer, I believe. But next time, go Greek, bro, not geek. Lose the vintage threads.

Werner M., best friend and roommate, sporting rockabilly lamb chops: Polymarpussle? That's an awesome name. Or you could call yourself Vikingman or Dragon Z, like in those post-punk Japanese cartoons. Name goes perfect with that crazy middle eye you have, and those extra gangly limbs. Chicks love the anime, dude.

The next day, I accompany Werner to the mega mall to survey my earthly dominion. With my extra limbs cloaked inside a large grey trench coat, I tuck a blue bandana under my ball cap to conceal my too-prominent third eye.

In the parking lot, we watch a woman torpedo her cart through sliding doors and load a nine hundred pack of toilet paper plus twelve identical pairs of sneakers into her car. When she backs out, two drivers screech to a halt, emerge from their cars bearing a squeegee and an ice scraper to fight over the recently vacated space.

"This is seriously messed up, Werner," I say, shaking my heavy head.

He's blue-lipped and shivering, but I'm teapot warm on this late-November afternoon.

"I've got to turn this planet upside down," I shout, drawing Werner closer.

He covers his head.

I lean forward and give the globe a wobbly spin.

From my third eye, I watch tectonic plates shift and shiver. Soon, great floods gulp up vast swaths of uninhabited desert. Tides begin reversing, pulling the waves apart, as if a massive hand had scraped the seabed and stirred up the oceanic trench, turning toxic, floating garbage patches into life-saving plankton.

Watching the 24/7 live satellite global news feeds later, we witness fully formed babies crawl out from the mouths of presidents, chancellors, princes, and prime ministers. Shedding their wrinkled adult skins, the snot-clotted, slightly purplish newborns emerge, shaking baby iron fists in the air. Me, me, mawrl, oop, garp, arlah, they say. Notice me! Feed me! Serve me! Someone spanks the US president and the Dow falls twelve hundred points that day.

The cradle of humanity is rocked! And it's nearly Werner's Saturday afternoon naptime, when my third eye gains a laser-like, microscopic focus.

Gazing into the corner office on the seventeenth floor of a big-tower metropolis in Chicago, I watch a third-year law associate reject her obligatory "living hell" years before

the founding partner. She promptly loses her job. Her
husband, who owns an international chain of organic Bun
'N Run Delis, famous for mindful multigrain and pre-loved
meats, tries to comfort his despondent wife by bringing
her to work. While he scans the daily wheat futures, she
punches out orders for double salami on their signature
whole wheat Kindness Kaiser. Crumb-filled faces smile
back at her from the deli, but she soon begins to dread
the long line-ups and leathery meats. One morning she
slides out the cash drawer and, stepping onto the sidewalk,
drops its entire contents into the lap of a homeless man.
With a quick about-face, she walks directly into the grill
of a speeding sausage delivery van. Her grieving husband
abandons his business, letting his extensive wheat stockpiles
fail, leading to the Great Kaiser Crisis.

Wheat harvesters, ever anxious to cash in on the global
grain frenzy, overwork their fields as cries of *cash for couscous*
and *save our semolina* resound across the planet. A global
run on wheat leads to violent military clashes across the
grain-producing subcontinent. One soldier abandons his
post, sporting a "No War for Wheat" button. He becomes a
media darling and motivational speaker. Wearing custom
camouflage fatigues, he strides onto the stage before sold-
out audiences and begins executing one-arm push-ups.
"Who's in charge, Sarge?" a stadium of devotees shout at
him in unison. "We are!" his acolytes reply. Growing weary
of the ravenous media attention, the man disappears,
later resurfacing behind a thatched-roof tiki kiosk on a
remote Polynesian island, selling penis-shaped black lava
rock sculptures. (The German tourists rave about their

ingenious sock holders.) Inspired combat fighters shed their battledress, trading in their jackboots to patrol the surf in flip-flops.

This leaves tiny but landlocked Liechtenstein, a principality founded by a family of gluten-free German yodelers to ascend as the last triumphant Old World superpower and active wheat producer. Before you can say "Yudl-ay-EEE-ooooo and pass the Käsknöfle," world power relations shift, reviving border wars between the famished and full. Drought and conflict-ravaged people awaken. Rejecting civil war clashes, despots and dysentery, they rise up, and they're super hungry. Pudgy leaders, recently having emerged from their awkward bottom-shuffling to crawl on all fours, can only bat at shiny things and hit round red buttons to make cute animal noises. When one overtired tot is struck with the business end of a shake rattle, all hell breaks loose.

"This is a total freaking disaster," I blurt out, lowering my multiple arms in the living room.

"Lost souls are pouring through my fingers like sand," I tell Werner, who is drifting in and out of a light slumber on the living-room couch.

When he doesn't reply, I decide to unroll my yoga mat and stand in downward dog until my calves seize. Shaking my legs out, I strike the half-moon pose for a full week, letting the blood rush to my swooning head so long that after a while, I feel a cry catch in my throat, a darkness only evil can answer. When I return upright, terror-stricken Werner is drooling all over the throw pillows, oblivious.

"Everything I touch collapses," I say, slumping next to Werner on a battered thrift-store armchair. My six limbs drape down to the floor. I rub my tired middle eye, feeling myself slipping into a tunnel dark. The sign at the end of the road reads "No Reason."

Werner begins licking crumbs from the inside of his spent dill pickle chip bag. "You need to eat," he says.

He coaxes me to the kitchen table, where he lays out two plates of plump grapes, butter crackers, the last of the sliced serenity salami, and fans of smoked gouda.

"Come on, Poly, you have to keep your energy up," he says, pushing a plate toward me.

I pop a grape that tastes like sour wine and pull my chair away.

"Come on," Werner implores. "Legends are born of great quests. Heroes are always on the road, like Siddhartha or Buddha or Jack Kerouac. Holy grounds need walking. Jesus had decent sandals, am I right?"

I bolt upright. "Yes, I'll walk!"

Along the darkest of pathways, along the most precarious of cliffs, I will walk. "But which direction?" I wonder.

Werner shrugs.

To the west, perhaps. Westward-ho, go west, young man! I think then slump back down on my chair. No. Maybe east. Where the sun rises, where humanity dawns, where Greek pantheons still flourish.

"What about the high Arctic?" Werner tosses out, slipping

his gouda wedge inside a roll of deli meat. "Calving glaciers. Ice barrens. Cute polar bears!"

"The last frontier!" I shout. "Yes. Yes. Just me, some fur-bound locals, and the giant-tusked narwhals spewing truth from the floe-edge of existence."

"You'll need a space blanket," Werner declares. "You know how much you hate the cold."

South then? I think, seeing myself as a human lightning rod now, an Aztec god leading fallen souls away from the underworld. I will scale the great wall of disillusion until the doves of peace flutter across my path.

But first I need comfortable shoes.

Barefoot, trench-coated, I hobble into a local shoe shop for a fitting. My tired and callused right foot sports a bunion protuberance. It's bloody embarrassing.

As I'm inspecting well-lit display shelves of wingtips and shiny black oxfords, a salesman in noisy green pleather pants approaches me.

"Those are some wretched-looking dogs, my friend," he says, patting the vinyl chair before him. "Sit down here and I'll fix you right up."

I scan his nametag. Lenny D.: Comfort Seeker.

Eyeballing my tired feet, Lenny pulls out his metal measuring device to deliver a professional fitting.

"What do you do, my friend?" he asks, sliding the moveable width bar against the ball joint of my right foot.

"I'm in sales," I reply, tapping the brim of my cap so it grazes the top of my nose, better concealing my third eye.

"And you're a perfect size 11½ E," he pronounces.

While Lenny is fitting me for a sturdy suede loafer, I notice his thick neck is a colourful canvas of fish-shaped tattoos.

"Why the flounder face?" I joke.

Rising to full height, Lenny smooths out his leatherette pants and inexplicably his eyes begin to well.

"Not long ago, I lost my wife," he says, brushing away a tear. "We were happy, you know? Well, at least I thought we were. Living the dream. A successful entrepreneur, a big-firm professional."

Lenny slumps down on the seat next to me. "She jumped in front of a delivery van."

"My God," I reply, resting my hand on his shoulder.

"This all happened before the Great Kaiser Crisis," he continues, "when people ordered meals from servers instead of barking into those damn boxes."

Lenny's face turns pensive. "What didn't I see? What didn't I do?" He pauses, and his eyes search the distant boot racks for answers. "When I finally pulled myself together, I asked the ancients why they had called me here. It was a quiet Saturday evening, around sunset. I remember a crescent moon like a Russian scythe swishing through a red Commie sky." Lenny dries his eyes with his shirt sleeve.

"On the day I was born, they answered, the constellations declared me a Piscean: selfless and strong, intuitive yet indecisive." He turns to me, imploring. "My destiny was already written for me in the stars." He looks down at his hands and starts picking at his cuticles. "At least, you know, I think it was, because I wavered a bit at first." Lenny suddenly claps. "Then a Tolstoy novel, the greatest book ever written, dropped from my bookshelf, splayed open to the page in *Anna Karenina* where Kitty's shoes 'delighted her feet.' Whammo! That's when I knew working with feet was my future."

Lenny slaps his knees and rises. "And so it will be with you, my friend."

My hidden palms are tacky inside the trench, after Lenny draws me into a bear hug.

"I'll take three pair," I blurt.

"You'll need suede protector in this climate. Only $7.99, friend." Lenny pops a breath mint, whips out his can of protector from behind the cash, and mists my toes liberally.

I arrive home with my new loafers and a reinvigorated spirit. Follow the planets as they dance through the cosmos, I hear Lenny whisper in my ear.

On the coffee table, I set out several library books about planetary alignments and read about each complex cycle: three degrees of Mercury. Uranus in the Fourth House. I plot and pace across the room, summoning the celestial bodies to me. With each breath, I gather more strength. My third eye is razor-sharp.

I hear Werner's key scratching at the front door. By now we've fallen into a comfortable routine. Werner, whistling off to work with his bagged lunch and a comic book. Me, reading scriptures, studying lunar cycles, keeping my heart line open to the next spiritual call.

"Werner," I say when he strolls in, "the ancients have spoken."

Home late from his gig at the electronic mart, I can tell he's in a food fog because he walks straight past me, opens the freezer, and stares inside longingly as cold vapours wash over him. He's having trouble deciding between chicken-stuffed tortellini and an all-dressed pizza topped with his favourite three-meat blend, he explains.

"There's a delicious tomato tang to each dish," he says, joyfully. "I love them both."

"Love!" I grab Werner around his torso and lift him from the floor.

"Rather than divine the truth in the governing celestial bodies," I pronounce excitedly, "I'll send the love planet hurling through the atmosphere! Forget the Moon square Jupiter. Forget forty days of retrograde. Forget fiery Mars. I'm going to spin Venus fast forward!"

When I carefully deposit Werner back on the ground, I plant my back heel, grab hold of Libra's ruling planet, and pitch reversing planet Venus fast forward.

The volcanic planet shudders in its orbit. My heart swells, glancing over at Werner, and a calm drapes over the room, soft as an oceanic mist.

Eager to witness this transformation close-up, I venture deep into the Venusian impact crater using my laser-sharp third eye.

Chemical collisions of oxytocin and serotonin swish inside hormonal bodies. Pulling back, I spot Yolanda, a nifty-fifty botanist with a line of cruelty-free cosmetics, swooning during a performance of Joseph Haydn's Paris symphonies in rondeau form. She falls back into the lap of

Gerome, a second-wave tech-boom titan just a shade over twenty-five, and their hypnotic attraction leads to a lustful, caffeine-buzzed affair as they criss-cross the continents. One heady morning after a dolphin-cove swim, Yolanda sees her future flash before her. Envisioning her sunset years crowned by inflamed joints and flatulence, she flees to Mexico on a Vespa bound for the capital. "Oh, the cruelty of age!" she shouts, her fortified hair flowing wildly behind her. Sputtering into Mexico City, Yolanda is seduced by Octavio, owner of *Zedillos café*, serving Oaxaca Pluma espresso and pesticide-free banana bread to the transnational "Hungry Generation" in the Zócalo district.

"Love is the only revolution," Yolanda sings, her youthful voice drowned out by revellers at nearby Ranchos Las Palmas Felices, where Misty Tableau, a Halifax-born busker and part-time party planner, is spinning her juggling wand before Max, a tennis star from a recently renamed eastern republic.

Enraptured by the heady mix of spinning fire and fast-flowing tequila, Max downs a top-shelf margarita and proposes marriage. *¡Híjole!* they are hot for one another! From the Baja Peninsula to *Isla Aguada* on the Yucatan, they explore the depths of sexual intimacy. Then, while Max is busy doing pool laps one day, he takes a near-fatal swallow of air after observing Misty juggling four wine goblets, three plates of *pollo ticuleño* tossed in garlic and oil, and Estaban, their chiselled towel boy. He promptly leaves her, proving that in romantic relationships, as in environmental disaster, oil and water don't mix. Bidding Misty a mournful farewell, Max sets off in search of a romantic afterglow he may never find in another's arms.

O sorrow's angry purge! Love is supposed to be a dish for gods, so how in heaven's name did this hot plate of hell happen? I glare into every loving soul, see the bitter glances, the trembling breakup talks. Anguish is spilling from every mortal pore. Then it's as if the stars were snuffed out. The sun has skipped its place in the cosmos.

Here I am, love's great fabricator, yet grief is ravaging the globe. And it's my own tormented, terrified fault, I think.

Returning home, I shake two months of dust and debris from my loafers. "Werner, I have to leave again."

"You've been gone forever."

"Permanently," I add.

"But I made chili!"

"I have no need for comfort."

"We'll get you a futon."

When I turn away from him to face the bay window, Werner approaches me and takes my multiple hands into his own. On tiptoe, he tries to stare into my cyclopean third eye, but I brush him away and hold out my arms, stripping down to my tube socks.

"What is known, I strip away. What is understood, I abandon. Only unconcealed may I venture into the merciless Unknown."

Werner grabs a wool throw from the couch to cover me up.

"What are you saying, Poly?"

I tilt my head back. My listless body is an empty urn. "I'm nothing but a muddled, prostrate mystic," I answer.

"You aren't nothing," Werner objects. "We need you. Alicia's worried sick."

I think about Alicia. How we had drifted so awkwardly from lovers to friends. I was a flack jacket of a man, always dodging low-velocity conflict. After the breakup, she stood her ground. We were friends first, she told me, that isn't changing. Even when my mother could no longer communicate, when the days and night slipped from her memory, Alicia brought in my mother's favourite music and kept me company in her room.

What can I offer her in return? My skin is too tight. My nails are too long. My third eye feels acid-stung and bloodshot. My thoughts keep wandering, never finding a quiet course.

My legs start to wobble and I collapse to the floor.

"Okay, that's it," Werner says, kneeling in front of me. He manages to hook his elbows under my armpits and lift me to my feet. I refuse to budge.

He finally resorts to calling Alicia, who orders us to pile in her car, and we drive to our favourite watering hole to find Harlon, bent over the pool table, poised for a tricky bank shot. Alicia marches over and plucks the cue ball off the table.

"Sit," she orders Harlon. "Poly's hurting, and no stupid beer metaphors, okay?"

I drag my chair to the darkest corner of the bar. I knot

my bandana, tighten my drawstring hood, and tuck my hands into my grey kangaroo-pouch pocket.

Harlon waves at me, raising his pitcher like an offering. "How are you doing, brother?" he says. "Vision quest becoming too much?"

I gesture at him to keep quiet.

"That third eye takes in millions of images per minute," he says, shaking his head. "Gotta remember to blink."

Angrily, Alicia pushes her chair back. "Really? Is that all you've got?"

Harlon fiddles with his coaster. "Well, okay, I guess Nietzsche would say to get moving. All truly great thoughts are conceived by walking."

"He's done the Messiah marathon," Alicia says, abruptly. "What else?"

Harlon tugs on his lower lip.

"Okay, okay, a good traveller has no fixed plans and is not intent on arrival."

"The Tao of jogging in place?" Alicia raps him lightly on the forehead. "Poly's stuck. Not still or at ease. Stranded."

I daub my aching third eye. It feels dense as a black marble.

"Okay, okay," Harlon says. He lets his forehead rest on the lacquered wood table. "Well," he says, lifting his head again, "Martha Nussbaum would say that it all comes down to community, the ability to bond with another human being."

Alicia and Werner exchange a telling look. I know what they're thinking. Is Poly even human anymore?

Werner walks over to me and pulls the hoodie off my head, causing my blue bandana to slip sideways.

He stumbles back, almost tripping over the barstool.

Alicia jumps up, startled. I can see it in her eyes.

In me, no regenerator of lost souls. I'm a fraud. A huckster.

My third eye is nothing but a bottomless black sea pooling sorrow.

Werner collects himself and gently guides me off the barstool.

"Forget this crap, Poly. Alicia and I are taking you home to rest. If a sign comes, we'll hail it down for you."

For days I sit on the edge of my bed, transfixed by the scuffed baseboards, the lint floating above the lamplight. I refuse to sleep.

When Alicia shows up again she marches straight into the room, and without a word, places a huge plate of sushi in my hands.

I look down at a firm mound of rice, the splay of pink fish sitting atop it.

"Can you bring that salmon back to life?" she asks, pointing down at the plate.

I look hard at the splay of exposed pink flesh and re-member Parson Lake. Ten years old, my back arched to the sun, diving into a lake so blue I remember white. Feel the tingling ends of my puckered fingertips, my tired, sunburnt arms, pink and lean, not the muscles I had hoped to form doing *Karate Kid* push-ups.

"Don't swim out so far," I can hear my mother shout from the shore, "not beyond the raft."

My head bobs as I wave back at her, my chin tapping water, paddling hard. I hoist myself up the raft ladder, keep glancing in the direction of the beach to make sure she's watching. She's got a book between her hands. Is she smiling? Can she see my cannonball leap? Then I am sinking, my eyes shut tight. When I open up, I see rippling coins shimmer across the water above me as I am swimming upward, breaking the surface. When I reach top, my mother's face is blurry; she keeps drifting away.

Alicia lowers my outstretched arms.

Werner throws a comforter around my shivering shoulders.

"Look, Poly," Alicia says, stretching to tap the top of my head. "You need to get rid of *this*." She pats my large head.

"What?"

"This anxious, truth-tuning radio frequency," she replies.

True. In my brain was an unruly buzzing. One minute I'd be with Harlon nailing kamikaze shots at a metal bar, the next humming game show tunes with Werner on the couch. No idea how I got here. Other nights I'd find myself listless, tortured by painful, plodding thoughts. And then the long, thin days. The times I'd remain expressionless, motionless. My life, sad, slow, and predictable. Like boy bands, or Macbeth, a crime that keeps returning to the scene.

"This has to stop," Alicia urges.

Werner puts his arm around my shoulder, and Alicia takes my arm.

I nod to them, walk unescorted into the living room, and stare out the bay window in silence. I cast my third eye beyond the row of bony poplars fringing the stream behind my mother's house.

"What can you see?" Alicia asks.

"It's raining purple asters."

My mother loved tea and burnt toast smeared with marmalade, I think. The bitter kind from Scotland in those tiny jars with the orange rinds that float in their strange, gelatinous spell. All those gold flecks in her hazel eyes. Marmalade. After breakfast, she wrestled weeds in the garden, wearing big yellow boots, while the sparrows chirped around the feeder she kept filled with millet. The males would perch next to her in the bushes, singing hopeful trills.

When the cherry blossoms begin to bloom in a few weeks, the sparrows will show up hungry.

My multiple knees buckle. Feeling light-headed, I let Werner and Alicia lead me back to bed.

When I awaken, I'm not sure what day it is.

Alicia pulls out a chair for me when I wander into the kitchen, dazed, holding my head. It's dark outside. Quiet.

My body feels weightless, sucked back into its mortal shrink wrap. There is no anxiety. Just a lingering sorrow. Werner jumps up from the table and promptly dresses up a plate of chicken wings with homemade coleslaw for us all. We devour three pounds between us. Later, we decide to stretch our legs in the living room, and from the bay window I can spot all of the planets, even Mars, a touch fainter than Jupiter, shining above Saturn in the southeast sky. Maybe life existed on Mars fifteen million years ago. There's no proof. No alien colony. No Martian signal beaming a lifeline from afar. What would it take for us to believe in it anyway?

Alicia and I decide to set up a folding card table in the middle of the living room, like it's one of our usual Friday night games. We invite Harlon over for a few rounds of poker. The four of us play Texas hold'em, Follow the Queen, and Five Card Draw. When it's Alicia's turn to deal, Werner passes. Instead, he jumps up to throw another load into the washing machine, adding my trench coat, sport socks, and sweaty blue bandana.

At the table, Harlon discards three cards and draws the same from Alicia.

"What do you need?" Alicia asks me, poised to deal.

I stare down at my gut roll, thinking I am six feet tall, soft in the middle, third-eye blind.

"I'll take four," I say.

My last hand isn't a good one, but I play it anyway.

Two Bucks from Brooklyn

Tu's thin and crooked, a dark, jagged line against the chalky white kitchen. Hearing the knock at the front door, he turns up the backbeat blues, the tight rhythm shuffling his brain, then bright orange cubes break the sample line, so close he has to blink them away.

Sliding the straps of a navy sports bag over his shoulder, he strides down the hall and pulls the double lock back.

"Where you been?" Tu asks, seeing Lewis sweaty and tired.

Lewis shakes his head. "Some fool comes running out at 110th Street station says he hears shots. People running. Bags flying. Police everywhere.

"Gun?"

"Fist fight," Lewis says, shaking his head. Took two hours to get back to the Bronx. He glances over at Tu's brother, who lies face up on the living-room couch, slipping in and out of an itchy haze. "Dar on the nod?"

"Stash got hit last night." The blue beats still bursting in his head, Tu pushes Lewis back toward the front door.

"Why you uptight?" Lewis says, removing his backpack and letting it drop to the floor.

"Got to meet Jello in Brooklyn."

"Fat man again? For real?" Lewis sighs. "I'm starving."

Tu puts a finger to his lips. Sliding the bag down his arm, he unzips and digs inside. With a glance over his shoulder to make sure his brother is dazed and dreaming, he pulls out a brick-shaped bundle.

"Dar's crew jumps the sidewalk in that rusty Impala and slams into the fence. Cops on foot after them. Dar gets out, springs across the empty lot, flinging his backpack behind him, and disappears. Cops catch up to the rest of the crew. I grab the backpack. No one saw a thing."

"Dar finds out, you gonna take a beating," Lewis warns, shaking his head.

"Came in so tweaked. Thinks the police got everything."

His heart motoring, Tu shoves the cellophane-wrapped brick deep inside the bag, below two pair of jeans and his three clean T-shirts. Into the large side pocket, he's tucked his books, a handful of CDs.

"We said no running," Lewis replies, in an angry hushed tone. "Ever."

"Don't turn down luck," Tu answers sharply. He can feel the beat in his throat like a hammer tap, then synth flying in shades of green.

Lewis yanks his backpack over his shoulder.

Tu can feel Lewis's anger simmering under his own skin so he grabs Lewis playfully around the neck. Turning his hip, Lewis sticks his leg out to pull Tu off balance, but he's going to need another twenty pounds on him, because Tu leans back and easily drops the boy on his back.

Helping Lewis back to his feet, Tu smiles and says, "I got you. We're getting out."

"Whatever," Lewis shrugs. "Better not take all night."

They step out into the hallway, fanning away the stench of garlic and burnt onion wafting down from 12C.

"Meet you out front. Got to leave Dar something," Tu says, and slips back inside the apartment, closing the door behind him.

Tu paces the kitchen linoleum, synth snare splashing green across his eyes. He punches out Jello's digits. "We're coming."

"I'm waiting," Jello says, and before hanging up, "You're on the rise, son."

Angelo Putello (a.k.a. Yo, Yo, turn it up, Jello) was going to be the next notorious Italian rapper. Any minute now. Any second. Jello was jumping the beats, working his heavy hip swagger scalping Yankees' tickets across from the House that Ruth Built. Business was popping, cops too busy cruising the stadium gates so they didn't call down much heat. All the heat was on the mound. Sticky, shimmering days when the Bronx was painted white and navy and the-Sox-suck-balls-red. Derek Jeter was off the hook, hitting eleven games straight, and Yankees-Sox matchups were setting the city on fire.

Game days, hardcore fans would join the regulars circling Jello, who was selling tickets and spitting his terrible rhymes.

Flash the cash, you got me running
Cuz Jeter's hitting like he's golden
Nomah and po-po gonna strike three all day
Batter out, beat down, like them Red Sox fans at Fenway

One Saturday, Jello had flashed his tight roll of twenties at Tu and Lewis, who were selling bootleg CDs just off the subway.

"Big leagues," he told the pair. "You wanna move up?"

Next Saturday, Tu and Lewis joined him across the street from the stadium. Jello taught them how to get triple face value. How to beat a loss. How to run scams on a nasty tourist waiting them out.

"Shake your head. Tell him all you got is premiums. Then switch them out at the last minute. Leave him shitting in the uppers with the pigeons."

After late games, Jello would drive Tu and Lewis over to Brooklyn to catch the million-dollar views at Sunset Park. They would slip in among the Puerto Rican gangs and Chinese grandmothers, draining Coors cans from Jello's trunk, watching Lady Liberty lord it over Manhattan.

Tu was smitten. No other way to describe it. Jello was twenty-six, a Brooklyn-born Italian son claiming roots that ran all the way to the old country.

"You got family up there in the projects?" Jello had asked Tu on the ride back.

"Dar. Like some bite that never heals," Tu replied and told him how his brother wound up selling drugs to make ends meet after their parents died. They were hit by a city bus, carrying groceries across East 147th. He struck a deal with his brother so he could finish school.

"Ask me anything," Tu would say, bouncing in the front seat of the ten-foot stretch of Mercury Zephyr.

"Booker T. Rosa Parks. Dr. King. M.L.K. saw the truth and set it free," Tu replied, defiantly.

"Makes you want to jump his ass," Lewis offered, smirking in the back seat.

"Destiny in your DNA," Jello agreed.

Jello traded stories about his great-grandfather, an Italian stonemason with callused hands who crossed the Atlantic to break brick in support of *la famiglia*. His *bisnonno* had boarded a steamship from Naples and two weeks later sailed into Ellis Island, crowding on deck alongside barefoot men in dusty derby hats to watch the Statue of Liberty rise up from the fog. All he had was a bag of tools, one creased hunk of bologna, and a striped shirt in his burlap bag. Sorted and inspected, he joined the other "guineas" who made their way to Brooklyn then crawled out of their East Side slums.

Jello described the stiff-backed Sicilian men bent over bricks—in Manhattan, East Harlem, and Brooklyn—right down to the cigarettes that had hung from their bragging mouths. How his *bisnonno* had carved out a piece of every building on their block in Bensonhurst.

Standing over his sleeping brother, Tu watches Dar blink yellow-tinged eyes, mumbling, tossing his head side to side.

He thinks of those Sicilian men. All the seasick bricklayers waiting in line while the doctors pulled down their eyelids to check for disease. And feels the familiar gut-punch-sick at the sight of his brother. Turf wars. Two crews beat down, five come back. Police chasing them at the park or on the way to school. Finding his brother slumped in dark corridors, getting beaten up over spillage, then dragging his ass back onto the streets.

One mistake was all it took after their parents died. They had nothing, and no one. Dar got drunk at a house party, copped keys and went on a joy ride, pissing off the wrong crew. For protection, Dar became a corner watcher, a dealer, a crook. Freedom, a threshold Dar could never cross.

Lime-tinged music filters in from the kitchen, then a whirlwind synth beat shaves spikes of soaring golden hues into Tu's brain, like a sound compass to his soul, sends his heart spinning free.

See it now. Into the wide open he would sail, and dig his heels in.

Since Tu belonged to a beaten corner of the South Bronx, but not to the project gangs, he knew he wanted an island to himself. After Jello, he was flooded with dreams of bricklayers, of immigrants writhing up from the mouth of the Hudson to dig ditches, lay down tracks, the tenement tramps who had built the city with their bare hands.

Tu unzips and handles the brick. Like a rapture humming hard in his head, he holds the blue beat in his throat, feels it expand, like a soft breath rising up from deep in his chest He shoves the brick inside the duffel's zippered pocket, thinking hard times are on their way out.

Looking through the window, he can see it all so clearly, beyond the drab walls, the grass-patched courtyard littered with broken bottles. He and Lewis will set up again in Brooklyn, take along hip hop, leave the conga-playing Puerto Ricans, cue the Bronx Remix, leave Dar's mad ghetto to hit bottom.

Tu stands and closes his eyes, picturing Dar's grey and dusty corners, the street a maze of gaping cement craters, sidewalks piled with dirt and garbage like they're living on Mars.

Leaving his drowsing brother, Tu heads out the front door to join Lewis. Turning to face the door, he grips the knob, pulls the door back so hard he can feel his own soul rock as he imagines his Lady Liberty reaching out to him over the harbour, whispering, The light is on and you're almost home.

Tu and Lewis skip the turnstile jump and pay the two-buck fare.

Packed tight, the D train is oily and hot. They watch strap-hangers file on and off along the fast track to Brooklyn. Tu presses his face to the glass to count sycamore maples. Fifteen. Lewis gestures for him to keep a sharper eye on the duffel. When the subway doors finally slide open at Bay Parkway, they climb down the stairs, wander past windows filled with creamy cassata, chocolate-covered marzipan, fresh-made *zeppoles* drizzled with honey. Lewis keeps rubbing his belly.

"Damn, I'm hungry."

Radiating out from 18th Avenue, they pass two Chinese takeout joints, a laundromat, and a bodega, then a long stretch of red-brick row houses.

Tu notices an old couple on their stoop, sipping espressos from gold-rimmed cups. An Italian flag sprouts from a potted fig at their feet.

"Look here," Tu points. "Owned their own stoops in less than fifty years."

"All I see are crackers and Jews, man." Lewis shrugs, still holding his belly.

Ducking inside a bodega, they buy sodas. Tu smiles, says the news is bigger than he knows.

"Jello's gonna hook us up East Side," he says, swallowing half the can in one gulp. "Set us up in some co-op his uncle owns."

"Why he do that? Fat man isn't about giving."

Tu pulls Lewis closer. "We bring in more cash for Jello than he could ever make on his own."

"Where is this place?" Lewis says, folding his arms.

"A studio in Sunset Park," Tu replies, pressing his sweating can against Lewis's flushed cheek.

"Free rent for three months," Tu says, laying out the images for Lewis in neat rows, tapping them down, the dream setting hard in his mortar mouth, until he builds a wall so high around Brooklyn neither of them can see past it. Soon they'll be living three stories up, like all those Brooklyn Italians, passing lawn Madonnas through the generations.

He can picture Lewis standing in the honeyed space of their walk-up, living on slices and red Italian sodas. Put away money, maybe get Lewis set up for college. See the truth and set them free.

"What do we got to do?" asks Lewis.

"Business as usual."

"He's not doing us favours."

"Got to think long term, man. We'll work with Jello. Year or two, make enough money to set up a place in Mott Haven."

"I don't know, man," Lewis says, shaking his head.

Tu pats the space between Lewis's shoulder blades.

Walking toward 21st Avenue, they find Jello leaning against his uncle's old Merc, putting the moves on some bored guidette. He's sagging in his Steelers shirt, his white belly fold rimmed by a thick band of underwear, a soft, ovoid shape against the gleaming grill of the ice-blue-and-grey Merc. Seeing Tu and Lewis approach, the guidette slips behind Jello.

"No time to hit that," Tu says, flashing the girl a toothy smile. She retreats inside the candy store, staring out at them from behind glass.

Tu crouches low and tries but fails to heave Jello off the sidewalk.

"Big man never budges," Lewis says, folding his arms.

Jello smirks when Tu makes a big show of opening the passenger door for him.

"Yeah, right. I'll drop you at Bay Ridge, let the white boys jump your ass," Jello says but climbs in on the passenger side anyway, three belly rolls from the glove compartment.

Tu takes the wheel and pushes the seat forward.

"How much you cop?" Jello asks.

Tu sees Lewis give him a surprised look then glare at him in the rear-view. Avoiding Lewis's gaze, Tu grabs the duffel from behind the driver's seat, dropping it in Jello's lap.

Removing the brick, Jello whistles. "How did you do it?"

"Can you move it?" Tu replies, looking into the rear-view as the Merc hums in heavy traffic.

"I can move Manhattan to Detroit and bring along the Hudson."

Tu slaps the steering wheel. With Jello along for the ride, they are on a speeding train. Two bucks and change your luck. Work on the straight with Jello scalping seats. Build up their stash in Brooklyn. One day, he and Lewis can make their way back to their corner of the South Bronx, set up someplace they should have been living all along.

Tu notices Lewis shoot him a pained look in the rear-view. His are sad, mortal eyes, but they can see a long way. He only wants Lewis to be safe. Boy is all chicken bones and asthma, lung-whipped on truck exhaust and soda. Just this one stake, he wants to say. Lewis keeps living every day like he's hungry. Tu only raises his eyebrow and nods into the rear-view, flashing a look that says, It's okay, Lewis. You've got to seed the sycamores to watch them grow.

Tu turns up the tunes, Grandmaster Flashing all the way down the boulevard. Fat blue-and-yellow cubes start to mount his syncopated skyline. He rubs his eyes. Rainbow colours twist and collide, stretch out across his mind. Tu has never told anyone he can see music. It's between him and Lady Liberty, who can see everything.

Jello gestures ahead to a crowd of students weighed down with books and backpacks. "Look at them. Too scared to get their hands on anything harder than their own dicks." He motions for Tu to turn right up ahead.

At the intersection, a young man approaches the Merc. Adrift in his hoodie and black Boston College ball cap, he stands awkwardly raising his shoulders. Jello rolls down the window partway.

"I'm looking," hoodie says, coolly, keeping his hands deep in his pockets.

"Best blow in Brooklyn, College Boy," Jello says with a nod. "Discounts for good Catholics."

Jello motions for the man to walk on. They pull up around the corner.

"We got a party going up in Jersey," he tells Jello. "Gonna wreck the place."

"Hang on," Jello says, rolling up the window.

Lewis leans forward. "Looks like some uptown junkie."

"Seen him around some," Jello replies. "He's Richie Rich. Heard he could take the rims off a Beemer on a red light. Now he's studying to be a fucking city planner," Jello laughs.

Tu is tapping the wheel, impatient. "How much?" he asks Jello.

Jello rolls the window back down. "What you need?"

"All you got," College Boy answers, hopping from one foot to the other. "Brothers got a McMansion up there."

"Nine large," Jello says, showing the brick portion with his hands, in a tone that suggests there's no room for negotiating.

"Gimme two hours," College Boy replies, pulling his black brim below his brow. "I'll get the cash together."

"No way," Jello says and gestures for Tu to drive on.

The man races ahead to meet the moving Merc, already rumbling halfway down the block. He knocks hard at the window that Jello reluctantly cracks open.

"Two large now," College Boy says. "Seven more this afternoon. Need time to collect," he insists, out of breath. "I'm fucking solid. Ask around."

Too many cars. Too many eyes. Neighbourhood's crawling with kids and cops. Jello has Tu pull up ahead and around the corner, suggests they meet College Boy in a low-rise they both know in Gravesend.

"We knock twice, do a count," Jello instructs, taking the young man's stack of bills and handing it over to Tu. "All good. Never heard of you."

With a few hours to kill before the meet, they drive on to Giovanni's and luck into three open stools. On fire with slices of spicy Italian sausage, Lewis drowns his throat in grape soda.

"You still seeing that pretty Sheyla?" Jello asks Lewis, throwing his shoulder into the younger man so he has to slide off his seat to avoid it. Lewis opens his mouth but says nothing.

"Academy girl. Works at the Walgreens on weekends," Tu pipes in, folding up his pepperoni slice. "Bossy, I hear," he jokes and flicks at Lewis's soda can, so the sticky grape spatters the teen's sneakers and jeans.

Tu presses his heel into Jello's Pumas. "Step off, man."

Laughing, the big man hip-checks Lewis again, staining the front of the teen's white T-shirt.

The owner orders them out.

On the sidewalk, Jello wipes his oily chin with the back of his hand. "We're just playing." He unfolds a crisp bill and slides it into Lewis's front T-shirt pocket. "Got you covered."

Same shit, different story is the look Lewis shoots Tu, who is watching Lewis blot the soda stain on his chest with napkins and spit.

Raise a hand to Lewis, Tu knew, and it was like beating clouds. He wasn't any kind of fighter. Never complained about anything but a missed meal. Lewis had a good mother holding up a good man who suffered a broken back and bad cataracts when he lost his job. His mother could stretch a meatloaf for days, filling it with oatmeal and ground beans. Lewis is scrawnier than shit and the strongest person he knows. Boy has learned to live on next to nothing, and that is his power.

Dance club trash explodes from Giovanni's house speakers; the sound pops and whines, shedding sound dust across Tu's feet.

"Chill out, Lewis," Jello says, still laughing. He offers to buy Lewis a fresh slice, keeping a grip on the boy's left shoulder.

"Get off me," Lewis says, knocking his arm away.

Bright and glittering, the music sprinkling between Tu's temples keeps crowding his courage. He isn't so sure. About Jello. About Lady Liberty's muffled voice in his ears.

Jello was rooted in Brooklyn. Tu and Lewis were mere shadows hanging over this stretch of the borough.

Jello looks up at the clock. "It's time."

Tense, bloated, and mean, they drive up to the building in Gravesend and park.

At two p.m., the back door to the low-rise is propped open, as agreed. Climbing the stairs to the second floor, they hear the roar of TV applause as they knock at 19B.

College Boy opens up. "It's all there," he says, handing Jello a Folgers coffee can stuffed with cash.

Jello passes it to Tu who counts the cash out then hands over the partial brick.

"Hold on," says College Boy. The door closes. After a minute, he opens up. "We're good."

Against a blast of TV cheers, they hear the bar latch and a chain slide across. More laughter.

The trio turn and walk back down the hall, Tu holding the coffee can tight to his chest. Lewis slaps the handrail, skipping two stairs when the bat strikes him behind the knees. Tu is struck, hits the carpet, inhaling ammonia and cat piss. He turns his head in time to see two men in balaclavas slam Jello against the wall.

"Be cool," one of the men orders, punching Jello in the chest, the other sends a knuckle swing skipping off his chin.

The taller of the two men retrieves the dropped Folgers can and collects the rolled bills, dropping them back inside the can. Another shoves an elbow against Jello's throat, pinning him against the wall.

"Nah, nah, nah." The man holding the pistol shakes his head when Jello tries to struggle free. He orders him to lie down by Tu and Lewis.

Tu tries to get up but feels a boot tip strike his rib. Someone clips Lewis behind the neck. While Tu and Lewis are on their bellies, the men rifle through their pockets, extracting coins, a wallet, a Yankees keychain. Then Tu throws himself over Lewis when they begin launching kicks, absorbing most of the blows. The keys to the Merc are deep inside Tu's front pocket. The men throw him off Lewis, roll him over, find the keys, and toss them out the metal door, sending the trio tumbling out after them. Tangled arms and legs unwinding, Jello finds his feet first. He rushes the door, but the men take aim.

"Be good," the tall man says, his arm level with Jello's throat.

They retreat while the metal door closes with a coarse, heavy clink.

"Never got rolled like this," Jello says, pressing his jersey sleeve to his bloody mouth.

Lewis is elevating his fat, throbbing wrist.

"College Boy was known," Jello keeps saying, shaking his head. "Fucking cokehead." He bashes the dash with his high tops.

Tu closes his eyes. His head falls heavy against the headrest in the idle Merc. He won't go back to Dar, stuck between East 134th and a twenty-four-hour watch.

Tu peels back out into traffic, his mind driving him around. Gripping the steering wheel tight, Tu feels the Merc front-end dip at the intersection, sending an electric shock through his fingertips.

"Give him a hit," Jello orders Lewis.

"No way," Lewis replies, refusing to hand over the small bag of what they've left behind under the seat.

Without another word, Tu wings the car around and points the chrome grill toward Gravesend.

Lewis leans forward, barking at Jello, "You led us right to them!"

With a sweep of his arm, Jello sends Lewis sideways across the back seat. Tu swerves across the line, corrects the Merc, then pulls in behind a parked van.

Throwing the Merc into park, he reaches over to grab a fist of Steelers jersey. "What are you doing?"

Jello has Tu's left arm behind his back while Lewis keeps yelling at him to stop.

They sit back in silence.

"We go back," Tu says, defiant.

Jello places his sweaty hand on Tu's shoulder, shaking his head. "Nah, nah. College Boy is probably reselling with his crew. They'll be hooked up with the pushers in Park Slope by now."

Tu turns the ignition over, pulling the Merc back into traffic.

"It's okay, man. I got big things coming down the line," Jello implores.

Only the thrum of the Merc in Tu's ears as they roar through Park Slope in heavy traffic, then south toward

Bensonhurst. He is staring over the dash, thinks he can see all the way across the bay to Lady Liberty, seven spikes in her thorny crown. Broken shackles at her feet. Into the wide open you can sail, she whispers to him.

Jello tells Tu that he needs to take a leak, so they pull over near a McDonald's not far from the 79th Street station.

When Jello's gone, Tu looks back at Lewis, who is folded up in the back seat.

"You a'right?"

Lewis shakes his head. "Think fat man gonna take us in now?"

"He made promises," Tu shouts, and turns back to spin the radio dial. A crackling buzz, then a jazz trio striking up a smooth rhythm, the sound full and ringing, a blues-infused "Sweet Georgia Brown," taking the long way home.

Closing his eyes, Tu digs his fists into his eye sockets, watching yellow swirls soar and drift away from him.

When Jello returns, Tu has questions.

"We'll get a little more cash together first," Jello tells him, and puts his arm around Tu's shoulder. "You know I got you, man."

"We got nothing," Lewis says and leans forward, his hand almost brushing the back of Tu's neck. "Let's go. Get the D. Go back."

Jello interrupts. "Got an inside track. We'll score five times, six times face for the playoffs. Split the profits three ways."

This time Tu can hear the strain in Jello's voice. The Merc has finally run out of road.

Tu sees steam rising from the hood of the Merc. He sits back, listens to the rhythmic *thump, thump, thump* of the train spiking the elevated rail above them. *Thump. Thump.* And the Dixie blues erupt in greys and greens. *Thump. Thump.* Sounds knocking in his ears.

"Come on, Tu," Jello repeats. "Whatchu think?"

"Think you've been doing us dirty all along," Tu replies.

Jello scoffs. He zips open his jacket, pulls out the handle of a pistol from his inside pocket.

"You think I don't know who's dealing?" he shouts, his belly jumping. "College Boy been running with me for five years."

Tu lunges.

They hear a *pop*.

Lewis slaps his neck like he's flicking a mosquito bite. Jello's whole arm is trembling.

"The fuck you do?" Tu screams.

Lewis is holding his wrist. He turns his arm over. The bullet hasn't even grazed his skin.

Jello drops his arm across the seat back, soaking sweat up with his sleeve. "Get out," he orders them, raising his arm toward Tu, then pointing back at Lewis.

While Tu is fumbling with the driver-side door handle, Lewis slides across the bench, managing to cuff Jello's neck while climbing out the passenger's side.

Fat man jerks. A *pop* like a dog's bark.

Tu feels a sudden wetness below his armpit.

Sweet Dixie sounds are a piano promenade in Tu's skull, a chain of blue cubes twisting up to the top of his hairline. He tries to count backward from zero, feeling the skin tighten around his skull. Heat begins shredding his veins, a liquid warmth slowly filling his torso.

"Fuck! Oh Fuck!" Lewis cries, and opens the passenger door Jello has left ajar.

He curses Jello who is lumbering hard down the street.

Tu is slumped down in his seat. Closing his eyes, he hears the orange sound, the street roaring in under them. He turns his head toward Lewis, tries to speak. Something in him, something private he can share with no one.

The way Lewis held him together when Dar drove him down. How they circled the stadium wearing identical number two jerseys, copping lower levels with their missing-brother routine. Chewing on the Boogie Down scratch and flow, bone-deep defiant as they strutted their way onto the D train. Holding the line on the single track while the loose-limbed b-boys danced windmill from the platform all the way home.

Lewis palms the horn twice.

In the honeyed light of the Merc, the warm yellow grooves swinging into his skull, Tu is drowning in love. Coney Island. Express line. Two of them, cruising the block on fat tires, bouncing around the park before everything fell apart.

An ambulance siren pulls a long, slow ache through Tu's chest. A bouncing red cube rises up and splashes red rain around his ears when the radio strikes up Duke's "C Jam Blues."

Lewis removes his hoodie and presses it against Tu's ribs.

Tu can hear muffled words, a sharp sting under his arm, but he needs to close his eyes for a while. The sound, a soothing percussive rhythm shimmering gold-green, is flooding his eyes.

He can feel his left hand being peeled open, another hand pressed inside his own.

"Hold on," he hears Lewis say, the voice rough and drawn, but Tu's slipping through sound.

The Merc door opens.

Tu's eyes flutter. Lewis is his beacon in the gathering darkness. Tu feels an arm braced behind his shoulder blades, hears Lewis saying something like please.

The piano notes strike up bright orange hues, are climbing a Technicolor pedestal in Tu's skull.

From her mount, the Lady descends, one arm draped around his waist, a warm blanket shrouding his body.

"It's all right, honey, we got you," a gloved woman says, reaching across Tu's lap. Tu feels a sharp prick on his left arm.

His eyelids heavy, Tu beams up at Lewis and feels the music drain from his face.

Ticker

You were weak when I brought you home from the hospital. Lying back, a hum ran the length of my breastbone and back. When I listened too closely, there was no beating. They told me to expect that.

This is the story I make of you. The way you made me with your cadaver's heart. After my long sleep, hitched to a ventilator, masked faces circling me like some cardiothoracic bedroom farce, you lingered in the room, whispered, You are not crazy, you are not alone. When they removed my tubes, you stayed, a muscle between my lungs, a yearning, a missing soul from some fugitive dream. Your ache in me was closer than a breath drawn.

How can I know how you lived? Who you loved? Your lost dreams? All those rhythms in between?

Did you fall apart when your girlfriend said she needed space, not more bullshit excuses? That you were the last person she wanted to see right now — ever? What made you turn on that deserted stretch of road where the semi-trailers cut across the No. 4 to make up time on the long haul? They might have found you out there, chest pinned to the wheel, wipers batting away rain, a surging pain growing in the back of your skull. Then that blinding stab before the final fade to black. But what they found out there wasn't you, was it?

I can't wash your metal taste from my mouth. Was there blood on the windshield? Or glass shards piercing skin? Before the final rupture, the great arterial brain bleed? When they laid you out on that stretcher, your head bleeding, your heart beating on (how the embattled heart beats on). Until the final sterile table where they cut you clean, disassembled you for parts. You: twenty-four-year-old male (name withheld), your whole life ahead of you.

In my mind, your mother breaks from the ER doctor's arms, unable to awaken from the news, from the flash so blinding it takes two orderlies to lift her from the polished floor. And your father kneels in the quiet room of the ICU, begs, bargains, asks, What did we ever do to deserve this? But does anyone ever get what they deserve? Do you ever wonder why some sorry fuck like me — Chris, thirty-six, hack sports writer, two subway stops from the hereafter — gets to live thanks to your bleeding heart? You weren't supposed to remain with me. Now yours is the first name on my lips. You, DG (Dead Guy), you hardly had the chance to fuck up. But you would have. Guaranteed.

Feeling light-headed again. Shaky hands, the same fat face in the mirror — can't even look. Just stare down at the bowl. Piss it away. Four weeks after the transplant, and every sound is sonar. A rush echoes in my ears as my veins carry oxygenated blood from my lungs to the left atrium. The right ventricle pumps and the left stages its return to the body. Red blood cells course through my chest like a longing. A beat, a breath, the sound that keeps you coming back, DG. Now I'm grateful for every goddamn day we don't drown in our own fluids.

Count 'em out: twenty-three pills rattling around in bottles like bone fragments. Like chattering teeth. Cyclosporin. Prednisone. Another autoimmunosuppressoespresso down the hatch. Close your eyes. Make a wish, DG. Doc says the best way to try to avoid acute rejection or coronary disease is to toughen up the immune system so my body doesn't mount a vicious counterattack. A few more pills, DG, and Sheryl might not have to bail on us before this body gets a chance to. So stick around, show's not over. As long as these valves keep clicking, we'll never run out of breath.

Not like the first time I saw Sheryl. Dry throat, weak in the knees on a half hop, half shuffle to the bus stop, trying to catch the express pulling away from the curb. Only a block sprint, but I came up short. Crazy head rush, a mouthful of vomit. Crouched over, panting. The bus roared away, abandoning Sheryl on the sidewalk. She tossed a lumpy backpack over her shoulder, stuffed with term papers or books, or lab mice or something smart, and ran over to me, placing her hand on my back. Are you okay? Can you breathe? She knelt in front of me while I swallowed puke, waving her way. She wouldn't budge. Not so fast, she warned, when I tried to stand up.

I was wheezing, all turned around. Which way to the university hospital, I managed, over the hammer pound at my temples. She said about twenty minutes, pointing the way, before escorting me over to the bus stop. We sat down on a steel bench that left a long drizzle of rust on my jeans.

Three buses rumbled past as she told me about the strange world of mitochondrial DNA mutations, her hand curled around my forearm. Eyes clear, pulse steady, she was checking my vitals. I couldn't believe it. I stared into those silver-green eyes (the colour of morning sun over a frozen pond, I swear it), felt a tingle where she held my arm firmly. So I didn't answer when she asked me, twice, Do you teach at the university? No, *Star*, I stammered. I write for the *Star*, a sports writer.

She looked me over a long time, probably wondering to herself, What's a hot science chick like me doing with a broken-down jock like him. But what she said was, Leafs look powerful on the foreplay this year. Forecheck, I corrected her, you mean forecheck. Yeah, she winked, that's what I meant.

We rode the express bus across the city together before signalling my stop. You would have done the same, DG. You would have grinned like a fucking idiot, felt your mouth stammer, when she hopped on the eastbound to ride the thirty-five blocks with you to the campus hospital.

Damn lungs. Can't shake this flu, I told her when we reached the cardiology care entrance. I was bent over again, nose to knees sucking wind, and she put her hand around my waist. It wasn't about getting laid, DG. Sheryl just held her ground, watching sweat drip from my hairline, her gaze strong and steady, until I finally came clean. Was still standing there beside me when my body did a long slide, when they eventually came for me three years later.

I'm telling you, DG. Getting laid isn't the goddamn miracle. Meeting someone like Sheryl was fucking unreal.

Three winters passed, Sheryl never once complaining, through all the revolving hospital doors, the late-night emergencies, the downward flail before I finally made The List. The waiting list for donor organs. To even make the ranks, the docs had to put me through an extensive evaluation. Scans, X-ray, echo, urine TP, PPD, RHC, EKG, cancer screening—the whole prick-and-poke workup for patients facing severe heart failure. You try to hide, but they see everything. Decades of shoving fast food in your face, years of stress and spiking blood pressure, or just a crappy myocardial genetics. It's all there in your blood, DG.

So, in comes the cardiac surgeon with my thick file tucked under his arm, raising eyebrows at me that look like fuzzy larvae inching across his intense face. He lays his stethoscope and icy paws on my chest. Asks me, Have you tried to keep in shape, Chris? Yeah, doc, I tell him, I like to walk, eat my leafy greens, then flash him a smirk, saying he would love my friend Kale.

Nothing. Guy doesn't even blink, DG. Instead he tells me, straight up, I've got less than a 30 per cent chance to live without a new pump. He leafs through some papers, slides his finger up and down indexes, rattles results while my throat gets dry and tight, and finally mumbles that I may be a good candidate. Sheryl gives my hand a squeeze, but I want to plow this guy when he looks like a criminal on the stand, says, Are you prepared, Chris? If we get a match, you know you'll be on medication for the rest of your life. You'll need to return for frequent hospital exams and monitoring. You may need more biopsies. The transplant is a lifelong commitment to health. No alcohol. No drugs. Not ever.

Sheryl stiffens, her lips part, but she doesn't say a thing, bless her soul.

Then he slides his stool in a little closer, asks me if I've ever abused drugs or alcohol. Ever? His voice drops and he clears his throat. For example, did I tend to knock back a few too many beers after a rough day? Nothing but rough days, Doc, I want to tell him, but keep it clamped.

He was looking straight at me, DG. So close I could sniff the stale coffee stench on his breath. Doc thought he had me on the ropes. So I feinted, did a jab, cross, hook. No, I told him flat out. A few beers here and there, sure. And by the way, Doc, save the baboon heart for the next guy because I've got Sheryl, a novel in the works (a drugstore thriller languishing in a bottom desk drawer), and I'm not going to mess this up. Good, he says. Because you might be in for a long wait, Chris, he tells me, tapping his pen on the file. It's a roller-coaster ride. And if we detect a health decline along the way, a serious infection or disease sets in, a disorder such as severe pulmonary hypertension arises, we may have to remove you from The List. *Temporarily*, he adds after a plummeting silence. Sheryl digs her nails in my hand. Is he kidding me? Then in a commanding tone, he explains, What I'm saying is, you'll need to find all the emotional stamina you can manage. We expect all transplant patients to talk to counsellors. He looks over at Sheryl, then back at me. You'll also need a strong network of psychosocial supports. Family. Friends. Sheryl nods agreement. We'll set up a meeting between you, Chris, the hospital social worker, and a team psychiatrist you'll see, both before and after the transplant.

How long? I interrupt. Doc gives me this haughty, impatient smile. For a few months, he answers. Counselling sessions last about an hour, but expect months of interaction. No, no, how long? What time is left for me without the spare part? I say, trying to look defiant. His eyes soften but he eventually shakes me off like a pitcher on the mound, instead reeling off my list status, averages, odds, complications.

Sheryl shoots me a keep-it-together look when she sees my face, all fired up and frantic. She's been through it all. The quick temper, the slim hope, the plummeting moods.

Let's not get ahead of ourselves, the doc continues. One step at a time. We'll give you a beeper, you'll get a call when there's a match. For ideal viability, we obviously want a match relatively close to you geographically. I know it's hard, Chris, but you've got to be patient now, work with us. He looks over at Sheryl. Her back straightens when she sees my face redden. I look over at her, lean forward in my chair, and I want to say to this man—hell, I want to scream it in his face—Give me something to fill this cavity soon because I've finally got something left to lose.

...

There were surprises, DG. No matter how much you try to avoid curveballs, life will throw tons of them. For instance, you could have knocked me flat when Aardvark showed up on my first day in the ICU with a hatful of daisies. Because end-stage at the ICU is definitely not for the faint-hearted. It's not just the tubes and wires and drips running everywhere. It's a weak, disorienting, oxygen-sucking state of grace, when time battles over your soul, and you're barely aware of anything but drawing your next breath. Because you're all waiting for a fresh pump, for a miracle match, for the fucking machines to stop their endless whirring and beeping so you might be cut free. Life or death, DG. You just want something to end.

Aardvark's unexpected arrival went something like this.

He walked in and immediately tried to make me laugh. He would have given me his own pickled heart if he hadn't lost it, to a woman, a scrappy German he loved for years, before she left on a trip to see her family in Berlin, and he spent two dirty weekends wandering away from his vows; the beginning of his nine-month single-malt-scotch slide, after which she finally left him for good. Aardvark: original earth pig. He walked in the room, stood next to the bed, smiled at me, and said, Chris, my dick has seen more sucking than a roll of Mentos. And he stuffed those daisies into a pitcher on my empty feed tray. Don't think we're getting serious, he said, you never once put out. Not even after I bought you that triple A porterhouse. Asshole, I replied, but started to laugh-cough so my nasogastric tube slipped out and I reached up, flailing. Ended up pulling out some important looping plastic tubes. Aardvark leapt off the bed. Nurse! We need a fucking nurse in here! he shouted down the hall.

Deep breaths, the nurse said. She plugged me in, pricked me again in the arm. I've got you, she kept repeating. I was so grateful not to have a breathing tube yet, I settled down in a hurry. Then she handed Aardvark a paper bag, because he was hyperventilating. I took a few slow steady breaths, while Aardvark sucked and wheezed in the corner.

When the nurse left, Aardvark pushed his fist against his throat. He's a major accounts guy. Spends his days babysitting the big clients, holding their hands through million-dollar shoots, the way he took and held mine then. When I started to wheeze, he looked away, finally said, Did I tell you I ended up getting that Benz? SL-class convertible, two-seater, charcoal with a silver interior. Sweeter than the Batmobile. Did you take over a lease? I kind of choke-gasped. No, he said, a look of dismay crossing his face. Never go for pre-owned, he told me, trying to pull a smile, you can smell desperation in the leather.

He was close enough to get a good whiff of me. He blinked, patted the sheets around my legs, tracing what was left. Then I could see that he really needed to go. Goddamn itchy lids, he said, scratching his eyes, claiming rain and allergies. He mentioned he was taking the red-eye to New York to catch a double header at Fenway. Jim from his office had scored tickets behind home plate. He was swinging his arms, elbow high, showing me how close they'd be to home plate, imitating a batter cutting through the zone. Gonna watch the Mets beat up on Detroit, he said, but don't worry, I'll be here for the big swap-out. He patted the place around my feet. He squeezed my bony fingers. My head sank back on the pillow. Jesus, he said. Chris, we've got to get you the fuck out of here. I'll slip into the Mets dugout, rip out one of those young player's hearts. Okay, I whispered, but no pitchers. Too flabby. Get me a lean rookie outfielder from Florida. And make sure it's a leftie, I said — or more likely drifted off in mid-sentence.

When I woke up, Aardvark was gone.

He didn't get it. In the ICU, you're special. One-on-one attention, fresh IV lines whenever you need them, and specially trained staff. Because you have to be desperate, DG. You have to be down on your luck. The gravedigger has got to be hanging around the room, oiling up his shovel, the six-foot plot marked out and ready. You have to drift in and out, forget your own name. The pinkish skin tone has to drain from your flesh. You have to be one of the Pole People.

Pole People wander the critical care floors strapped to IVs, their hearts withering, eyes sinking back into their hollow skulls. Our end-stage condition so dire we need a constant infusion of drugs to keep the old ticker beating. Death row for the truly diseased is life spent awaiting the next surgical stay of execution. We lie there. Hanging on. For the last bit of life-saving news. While the surgeons sharpen their scalpels behind some curtained room, or rush up and down the hall scanning their beepers, we sleep sitting up, our bodies bloated due to lack of blood circulation. Our hands and feet are forever cold. So fucking cold, DG.

Cold as this grey day in February. Cold as the dark side of Mars. Cold as a fist of raw hamburger in the freezer. Cold as dissected brain tissue on the coroner's table, DG.

After sixty-one days in the ICU without a match, my body was barely functioning, but the machines kept whirring, like in some twisted arcade game. It was as if I could smell everything. The faint perfumes coming from the death-march visitor parade. All the barf and piss from the other moaning rooms, their grief spilling out like the shit draining from our own wretched holes.

Once I caught Sheryl glancing down at the small dimple on my chin, lightly kissing it when she thought I was asleep. I was dopey, but I could tell what she was doing. Memorizing. Remembering. Tracing the future she'd soon be left to face alone. And maybe a heart comes along, or maybe you die waiting. Pole People are suspended in a holy state, a sublime sensation, hovering between infinite suffering and transcendent hope.

So the transplant patient waits, like some immortal spirit. While the living stand over us, looking like Macbeth's ghost, looking for signs, tracing our last breath. We wait. For months, for years. Never forever. Wait for the do-it-yourself painter to fall off his ladder as he touches up the gingerbread trim. For the investment manager rebalancing her stock portfolio to ignore the blunt pain in her head another week. For the marketing exec to hop on his home treadmill, feel his head go heavy after the first mile, hit the blue heart-pace button instead of the red panic. And as he lies there, in his twisted state, pupils fixed, we don't pray for his soul. No, not ever. We count the hours. How long will it take his wife to pick up the dry cleaning on her way home? How long until the 911 call comes in, for the paramedics to arrive, drowning the streets in a whir of red and blue strobe lights? Will they keep him alive long enough for harvest time?

Then beepers buzz against hips. You better hurry, because there's only four hours of viability after the call, DG. If you're not prepped, checked, and connected to the heart-lung bypass machine, you've lost your place in line. Relinquished your lifeline. Sheryl told me to keep a journal. Days would pass in the ICU, but the ink kept smearing the page. I wrote and the words came out crumbling, as if the pen itself was leaking time. Guess time is always running out on someone. Like you, DG? Did you hope it would stop? Aardvark was right about second-hand ownership. You can smell desperation in the sheets.

I waited three years for you.

Today your tremor climbs my gut wall like a warning. Why does it start here? Why so low? This sick, steady feeling. Was it pepperoni slices, DG? Sharing warm beers on the couch with your Friday night boys, glued to the TV, cheering the men on the blue line. The boys raging when the breakaway was whistled off-side again. You watched the puck glide through the five-hole, with your chicken-wing mouth tearing into the ref, late for your movie date, knowing full well she didn't care if your team won in overtime. She was growing tired of your excuses, your game boys, your half-hearted gestures. (Remember the promised takeout Chinese and back-rub fiasco? The missing birthday pendant, all those promises set in stone? Never diamond or ruby.) Later, you wolfed your way back to her door. All that flesh between your teeth, the waitress wooed after midnight, then the last-chance pity crawl to her room, begging to be taken back. She grew blind to your tears, heard the home-team fans still roaring in your ears. She saw the road ahead, took the first exit.

Two months after surgery, I look like a Gerber baby and smell even worse. Ass-dragging tired. My feet are cold. So cold. Sporting this ugly chin strap of acne from the prednisone. And I'm all over the place. Paralyzed at the bottom of the stairway. Sobbing when Sheryl asks me about dinner. Throwing tantrums over a missed phone message one day. Turning sullen and silent the next. Doc says it's all post-op anxiety, plus the med side effects. Says excessive or irrational fears are common. He doesn't know, does he, DG? About you and me, living on the far side of fear. Because some days we wake up believing we can conquer the world, have all the powers in the universe. See this warrior stripe on our chest?

Sheryl gently kisses my knees, works her way up my hips, then along the length of my scar, a rubbery ten-inch exclamation point blemishing my breastbone. Her soft tongue tickles the scar's raised edge, running all the way up my throat. Then her wet mouth circles the small round point at the top of my scar. And I close my eyes, remembering our first time, how her tongue tested the tip of my penis in her bedroom. That slow, delirious ache when her lips slipped over my hard bone, taking me in. How I moaned, as her mouth quivered above my chest.

It's the drugs, Sheryl says, when I go limp right away. You're not in control of yourself right now. How can I tell her that I'm afraid the rush will leave me slumped like some dead seal. She looks me in the eyes. Gently, she presses her hands on either side of my rib cage, tries to hold the world together for me. She wants to close what's been open too long. How can I tell her? That our heart isn't two clenched fists, but a tunnel. There are no sealed chambers. Only exits.

You're a drowning man, I tell Aardvark when he shows up at my house with a six-pack and a wry smile. He says, Enough is enough, that Sheryl says I'm recovering very well. Well enough to hit the pubs with him while she is at her conference, and he throws his arm over my shoulder in the Benz. We pick a dark booth and watch Detroit choke on a three to one series lead. Aardvark orders a third round of his favourite single malt and it lands next to my fizzy drink. He grimaces then slides his tumbler across the table. Alcohol and recovery don't mix, I say, pushing the glass back at him. Look, it's been four months, he insists, you deserve to loosen up. Christ, I almost lost you. And this

I don't expect, DG. Because Aardvark looks away, doesn't even pretend that he's busted up over Detroit. He wipes his eyes with a napkin and covers it with a bad joke.

But it's not long before he's glancing over my shoulder at two young women laughing in another booth. You take the brunette, he winks at me. Isn't Sheryl at her conference for a few more days? Sheryl's been through the worst with me, I tell him, frowning. Aardvark lifts his glass to the ladies, who glance over at him, a look of pity and boredom crossing their faces. Aardvark leans forward, whispers, Just tell them that you've got a new ticker, they'll be fighting over who gets to bang you first. I watch him a long time while he glances up at the TV, thinking I can't help you conquer Germany. She's gone. We're gone, Aardvark. Neither one of us is coming back. But his gaze is restless, his eye on the sure thing.

When the waitress returns to ask us how we're all doing, she doesn't ask how you're doing, DG, but I know.

I know the girl who first took your breath away. Feel the flutter in my chest, that delicious twinge the moment you wrapped your arms around her. You thought she could save you. You felt her rapture in your dreams. And then the moment your life fell apart, sent you tumbling in the wrong direction, the young man's free fall into the inscrutable darkness. No one ever told you that the end of the world comes many times in one life. And that knowing it doesn't make things any easier. Your cry catches in my throat at night, keeps haunting my dreams. Teamed on this inexplicable ride, who would have guessed we were the perfect match?

...

Two more flights of stairs without a weak-knee dive, and I'm
ready to lay back and take it like a man. When Sheryl is on
top and we are going at it—I mean in a sticky trance, hot
and heavy—right in the middle of things, she rolls off and
falls onto her side. Her worried eyes scan my chest. What if
you're not quite ready? she says, patting my breastbone. In
my fantasy, I flip her over, show her what it's like to cheat
death from behind. In reality, her mouth moves, my cock
aches, but I can't feel a thing. Like there's a numb barrier
between us. How can I tell her what you've become? That
there's a space between her lust and mine. How could she
possibly know? That she's sharing her love with a wreck of
a man who couldn't see straight when his life hit a curve.

Am I running out of time to ask? What comes after death?
Resurrection? The old-fashioned Jesus walk? Don't rise too
high, you'll fall too hard. Life is all tiptoe and timing. It's
like you're the runner on first base, trying to get a jump on
the pitch, DG. Poised for the windup on his mound, the
pitcher glances over, keeps you in his sight. He stops, fakes
a toss to first, driving you back to the bag. You shake your
arms out, step off first again, do a little sideways dance on
the balls of your feet. Cheat a bit when you see the pitcher's
foot slip from the rubber again, keen eye, delicate, delicate.
Go—before the pitch even reaches home plate. The
catcher throws off his mask, launches a laser to second.

You do a bent-leg slide, try to clip the base with your heel, but the catcher's tag is clean. You're caught stealing.

I should have known there would be trouble. Me wheezing my way through the past decade, knowing last call was going off in my ears. Then a long, floating slide in the ICU, before the brilliant resurrection. Now this constant *frrrrip, frrrip, frrrriip* in my ear. Your mitral valve when it closes at night. And all the closings and contractions and endings, DG. The surgeons think they fucking saved me. You're the only one who knows we both made it out alive.

No one asks anymore. But if they did I'd tell them. Imagine lying in a room so bright you have to shield your eyes as an orb grows broad against your chest. Feel a prick at your neck, the fluids floating through machines that bleep and whir, pump and click. As you lie there, spread open, a nurse asks you your name, while a masked man snuffs out light. They're all preparing to stop your heart. So don't move. Don't blink. Don't sway left or right as the steel clamp splits you open, tearing your breastbone apart. The machines are vampires draining you of fluids, while your life hangs between scalpel, steel, and wire.

And as you rise, hover halfway between life and death, the blood pumping so fast to your cavern core, it's a rush so sweet, so warm, at first you fail to notice the figure. His face floats before you. He's the man who went away, who left without saying goodbye. He rises with me off the table, his sweat clings to my cheeks. No one else is coming, he says. Whatever happens now, it happens to us.

...

The play-by-play commentary on my first night back in the arena might go something like this: sick man collapses forward in his hockey-arena seat, his lap stained with beer. The painted-face patrons drop their signs. A nearby security guard radios for help, thinking the fan may have scarfed back a few too many cold ones. The man collapses on his side, making a mad clutch for his chest. His eyes are dilated. Fans howl into their cellphones. Punch out 911. The security radio crackles. Row forty-two, seat five, section F. Yes, it's an emergency, the hapless security guard screams into his walkie-talkie. Don't move him, the voice crackles back. Better meet the ambulance at the gate.

A woman, let's call her Sheryl, stands over the prostrate man, screaming at the pressing crowds, Don't touch him, give him room, he's got a heart condition. Two more security guards try to settle startled fans back into their seats, but no one is moving. Help is on the way, one of them says to Sheryl, reassuringly. A few minutes later, in section F, the stands fall silent. Hands over mouths, no one following the score anymore. The paramedics arrive, say, Stand back, we'll take it from here. The man's vitals are checked. He is loaded onto a stretcher, carted away with haste.

Outside, the paramedics do not hit the siren in the ambulance cab, do not flood the street with blue strobes, scattering traffic. Do not sprint through sliding doors, past the monitors, the crash carts, behind curtained rooms. Sheryl does not see my hand reaching out for hers, my fingers twitch for the last time under the stretcher sheets.

...

Or maybe the incident is four years from today.

DG, can you see all that's crowding in my head? The fool who breaks down at parties. The prick sports writer so busy covering all the angles he doesn't even understand his own story. Our lungs puff and screech, DG, still the heart calls all the shots. Fills with red courage, swells with false pride. Our vessels are open wide. Can't keep this beat much longer.

Your pain flutters in my breastbone tonight, a fast beat, then a murmur rises from the back of my throat, the sound of a man slipping away.

Please. Tell me.

Did you feel your heart pound like a rocket ride on that sharp highway curve? Did you hear death knocking hard against your steel chamber, envision an end more divine than dawn? Did you hear a sound like a shot when the impact came? Did you crawl out from that crumpled cave, or sail through broken shards, your shattered face turning stone to blood?

Where is our road show now?

Let's go back to the Pole People. To wander with them through the halls, in search of the last gasp of life we know, not to cry with the living. Maybe you and I, we can take it on the road. Map out some new destiny, piss our dreams to the wind. Like in those showdown at sundown road movies with hard shadows and dark, poetic twists. We'll crank up the brooding mood music. Someone will quote Shakespeare or Kerouac or Mad Max. Something about love's impediments, about blindness, about pain. We'll travel all the way to the end of the earth on just one last breath.

So, where do we go from here?

Acknowledgements

My enduring and heartfelt thanks to the following people:

Zsuzsi Gartner's remarkable devotion to these stories as an editor and early reader is a gift for which no words of gratitude here can equal. She is the greatest champion of storytelling and authors I know. Thank you, ZZ.

My agent, Samantha Haywood, has been a fierce, funny, and indomitable literary champion throughout this process. I want to thank her, as well as the wonderful Stephanie Sinclair of Transatlantic Agency.

Thank you to the superb team at Goose Lane Editions: Susanne Alexander, publisher; Julie Scriver, creative director; Martin Ainsley, production editor. Your commitment to this book, and to independent publishing, makes me proud to be part of the GLE family.

Embarking on this adventure without the piercing intelligence and deliciously dark humour of my editor, Bethany Gibson, seems unimaginable. She helped me steer a ship with a crooked mast through a choppy sea and find its true course. B-Town, thank you.

Paula Sarson brought to this collection an open heart and critical eye that enabled me to enter the work with fresh insight. Working with such a perceptive and precise copyeditor has been a pure delight.

My friends and family have been kind and enthusiastic cheerleaders. For their support and strength over the years, many thanks to Lisa McNulty, Maureen, Kelsie, and Sam Phelan and to George, Pat, and Christina Larsen. The wisdom and experience of Rupi Sidhu also pervades these pages. Many of these stories were first published in Canadian literary magazines. "Monsoon Season" appeared in *Descant*; "WOOF" in the *New Quarterly*; "Fingernecklace" in *PRISM*; "Ticker" in the *Fiddlehead*; and "Battle of the Bow" in the *Dalhousie Review*.

Thanks also to the judges of the Writers' Trust/McClelland & Stewart Journey Prize for including "Monsoon Season" and "Fingernecklace" in that esteemed anthology. "If on a Winter's Night a Badger" pays homage to the inspired wit and boldness of Italo Calvino and to his great novel *If on a Winter's Night a Traveler*.

Finally, Kim Larsen was the first to read and edit these pages, often enduring the angst and uneven temperament of the author. Her brilliant ability to find the still and silent in life and language continues to astonish me. She lends grace to wisdom and is the reason I write.

Lori McNulty was born in Ottawa, Ontario. Her work has appeared in the *Fiddlehead*, the *New Quarterly*, *PRISM international*, the *Dalhousie Review*, *Descant*, and the *Globe and Mail*, as well as a number of anthologies. She has twice been nominated for the Journey Prize, making the shortlist in 2014 for her story "Monsoon Season." She has also been a finalist for the CBC Short Story Prize, the CBC Creative Nonfiction Prize, and the Edna Staebler Personal Essay Contest. A global traveller and digital storyteller, she now resides in Vancouver.